# A Novel HOLIDAY

By

## L.L. Diamond

A Novel Holiday

By L.L. Diamond

Published by L.L. Diamond

Copyright ©2024 L.L. Diamond

Cover and internal design © 2024  L.L. Diamond
Cover design by L.L. Diamond/Diamondback Covers
Cover art: Young Woman Illustration by Volha Hlinskay Courtesy of Shutterstock, Snow frame.Frozen by Brovko Sherhii Courtesy of Shutterstock, Christmas Cake by Olga Selyutina Courtesy of Shutterstock, Christmas Lights by Tally18 Courtesy of Shutterstock.

ISBN: 978-1-960057-13-6

Facebook: https://www.facebook.com/LLDiamond
Instagram: @l.l.diamond
Bluesky: https://bsky.app/profile/lldiamond.bsky.social
Blog: http://lldiamondwrites.com/
Austen Variations: https://austenvariations.com/

For my friends and family who are always there
to listen and to support me.
Thank you!

# Prologue

The bell on the elevator chimed, the doors opened, and I stepped out and into my uncle's foyer. A sizeable room with a curved staircase wrapping around one wall. "Zio?" My voice echoed through the marble-floored room as I stilled so I could hear his response.

"In here, Betta."

I smiled. Although my name had been Elizabeth since birth, my uncle had been the only one to call me Betta, a throwback to his Italian heritage.

By the volume of his voice and the direction, he could only be in the library, so I headed for the door that was nestled under the staircase. I should've known he would be holed up in his favorite room. When he wasn't sleeping or working, my uncle spent most of his time reading in the brown leather armchair by the windows. He had a view of the courtyard below and the rooftops of the Upper West Side, the part of New York City he loved.

As I entered, I tossed my gown, stole, and mortarboard onto the sofa, then plopped into the chair across from him. It had been an interminable day.

Zio, otherwise known as my uncle Luca Philips, marked his place in the large book he was reading and let it rest in his lap. The son of an Italian mother and an English father, he had been raised near Venice, yet still retained his Italian accent after living in America for close to sixty years. In fact, Zio meant uncle in Italian and had been what I'd always called him.

His blue eyes peered over his glasses at me. "Your father insisted you take a place at the company with him, didn't he?"

I grimaced. "Of course, he did. He wouldn't take no for an answer." My father had spoken of nothing else but me joining Longbourn Investments since I first showed an aptitude for numbers. Only, eventually running a company that traded stocks and set up mutual funds was the last thing I wanted. The very idea sounded like the acutest form of torture. Even imagining it made my legs twitch in an effort to escape the noose slowly coiling around my neck.

My uncle's olive-toned hands rested atop his book. More weathered than when I was a little girl, those strong hands had held mine many times over the years, particularly when my parents had disappointed me, which was often. "I've always known business was not what you held dear, but I've seen you adore many things since you were little: reading, cooking, playing the piano. You've finished a graduate degree you pursued more out of obligation than passion. But, what is your passion? I had hoped you would tell me in your own time, but you've never said a word. So, now I want to know. What is it you dream of doing?"

I gave a laugh that was odd, even to my own ears, and shook my head. "My father would never speak to me again. It's impossible anyway."

Zio leaned forward, his beloved hands grasping my own. "You haven't lived with your parents since you began Columbia, and you truly only keep in contact with Mary. She won't abandon you now—after all, she'll soon be in a similar situation. Your father and mother will expect her to be what they wish, and she'll need to decide whether she desires to pursue her own happiness or whether she'll play the part of the dutiful daughter."

That was true. Zio had offered me an apartment in one of the buildings he owned when I was accepted into Columbia— under the guise of being close to campus, of course. My uncle owned an enormous bookstore on the Upper West Side. He'd started small when he was younger, eventually purchasing a building that had once been a mansion. The house had been split into smaller homes over the years, but Zio gutted it and revamped it. He renovated the top two floors into a penthouse of sorts for himself. Over time, he'd acquired other adjoining buildings and had expanded the store. The year I'd graduated high school, he'd bought a smaller building next door. I don't know what he'd planned for the property since other than offering me the apartment on the third floor, he'd left the bottom floors empty. His health had taken a turn, and I suppose he'd put the project on the backburner.

His hands squeezed mine. "What is it, cara? You followed the path your father wanted. You attended Columbia and received your MBA from NYU, but what do *you* want?"

I bit my cheek and exhaled heavily. "Do you remember that baking class you and Zia enrolled me in as a Christmas present one year?" I'd spent an evening twice a week baking and decorating cakes. I'd enjoyed it so much; they'd given me one on pastries for my birthday.

He lifted back. "You want to bake?" The pitch of his voice was high. I'd surprised him.

I began tapping my foot. "More than that really. I'd bake cakes and pastries. I could take orders for weddings and birthdays, but I could also have a small café where I serve them as well as coffee and tea, maybe sandwiches one day..."

With a lift to one side of his lips, he rested back into his chair. "Do you know what I'd once planned for the building you live in?"

I shook my head.

"Some of those big chain bookstores have a coffee shop inside. I'd thought to expand with one on the bottom floor. There's even the courtyard that wraps around that building where outdoor seating could be offered. When I had the heart attack, I put the plans on hold. Perhaps now would be a good chance to revisit them."

My heart leapt into my throat, and I rocketed straight up in my seat. "Are you serious?"

He chuckled. "Don't look so surprised. You've learned to run a business, haven't you?"

"Well yes," I said with a one shouldered shrug. "But entrusting me to start a business you're funding would be considered a huge risk to most. I've never put what I've learned into practice—not yet."

One of his fingers rose. "I do have one stipulation."

I nodded. "Of course, anything." He'd be giving me what I wanted most. How could I say no?

"It'll take time to renovate the building and prepare it for business. While that's being accomplished, I'd like you to take pâtisserie courses at Le Cordon Bleu in London. I own a flat in

Notting Hill where my father once lived. You may stay there while you go to school." With the last, he pointed a knobby finger at me with a nod.

I made to speak, but he again held up a hand.

"While you're in London, we'll speak often to discuss the kitchen design as well as the aesthetic of the café, though we'll want it to be a pleasing transition from the bookstore." He set his book on the table and pushed up from the chair. "Come, let's see about this course."

"How do you know about culinary school?" My uncle owned a bookstore. I would've never expected him to suddenly be a fount of knowledge concerning baked goods.

"I ask questions, cara. Whenever we've hired chefs for certain events, your Zia and I always asked about where they learned their art. I remember the best desserts I'd ever tasted were from a young man who'd studied in London."

Despite the knobbiness of his fingers, they flew over the keys of the laptop in his study with an agility that was unexpected. I pulled a chair around, and no more than an hour later, he had me enrolled in the first course, a seven-week intensive study during the summer. I'd take the intermediate course in the autumn—three months, then the study for the superior certificate starting in January. If all went according to plan, I'd return in late March or early April of next year. Yes, it would be almost a year before the business was up and running, but so many wait for decades to open their own bakery or restaurant. My uncle was offering me the opportunity of a lifetime. I'd also not be here for the fallout when my father was forced to accept that I was truly defying him. My heart beat so fast and so hard, it seemed like it would burst from my chest.

"Now, do understand that the bakery and café will be a part of the bookstore business, but you will run it, and the financials will be separate. For some of the marketing and other aspects, we will need to cooperate. If you need advice or have questions, I'll always be available."

I shoved my thumbnail in my mouth and bounced my knee.

He stopped my leg with a steady hand. "What's running through that brain of yours?"

I sat back up with a jolt. "Forgive me, Zio. I feel terrible asking, but what if something happens to you? I mean, it was just six years ago you had that heart attack, and you've had a couple of scares since. I wouldn't want—"

"You'll keep your business, cara. I promise you that. Okay? I'd never have you lose your dream because I died." He dipped his chin, lifting his bushy eyebrows as he leveled those shrewd eyes upon me. "You must know that I don't intend to give in anytime soon. I miss your Zia, but she wouldn't want me to hurry to my grave. She told me that often enough after the cancer spread. So, I honor her wish. Death is going to have to chase this old man down and take him by force."

I often caught Zio talking to pictures of my aunt. He had them scattered all over the two-story home—on his desk, on his bedside table, in the library as well as in the living room and the parlor. He kept her near to him, always. I wanted that kind of love one day—not that I was ready for it now.

"Come, I have tiramisu in the refrigerator."

I gasped. "Zio, you aren't supposed to eat that!"

He waved off my chastisement. "Let an old man have his vices, especially before Mrs. Hill finds it and throws it in the trash. I've been fortunate to keep it in there for most of the day."

Before we reached the kitchen, he stopped and faced me. "If you don't know where your passport is, you'll need to find it now. I'd rather have you fly to London sooner rather than later. My assistant will book the tickets, and he'll need your passport number. You'll want to get settled in before your classes start. It'll also give you time to explore the local pâtisseries. I'm sure you won't mind sampling their confections."

I laughed. "No, not at all." I rubbed my forehead. "I'll need to figure out what to tell my father." He'd be pissed!

Zio shrugged. "How difficult is it to say 'no?' Besides, your MBA will help with running the café. It's not as though you won't be using it."

"He'll rant and rave about the cost of school."

A bark flew from Zia's chest. "You mean the education I paid for? Not that I'd bring that up. Let him rant for a time and hang up. It'll be better that way. Let your parents continue to fawn over Jane."

I rolled my eyes. Jane had always been the perfect child. *"Jane was valedictorian, Jane was accepted to Harvard law. . .Jane, Jane, Jane."* My older sister and I had once been close. That had deteriorated over the years, no thanks to my parents. Jane could do no wrong in their eyes as well as her own.

My uncle pulled the dish of tiramisu from the fridge and set it on the island. Soon, we each had a substantial serving and a glass of red Moscato.

My uncle held his glass in the air between us. "To celebrate your accomplishment. It's not every day you graduate NYUs MBA program summa cum laude. Cheers, cara." We tapped our glasses together. "And I heard what your mother said today at the ceremony. You are to ignore her. Do you understand?"

"My GPA is better than Jane's was in law school." I'd almost informed my mother of that fact—almost.

"Exactly. Your Zia never understood your mother, even though they were sisters. When you were born and as you grew, we suddenly understood why God never gave us our own children. You needed us to be the parents your own were not. We always hoped we fulfilled that duty."

My eyes burned as I blinked back tears. "You did, Zio. You both did." My aunt and uncle were present for every milestone from elementary school through college and graduate school. They were truly more my parents than my own had ever been.

I took a bite of my tiramisu, the creamy blend of mascarpone, sugar, vanilla, and coffee exploded on my tongue. A moan escaped before I could hold it in. Zio chuckled. As I took another bite, movement in the corner of my eye made me turn to where Mrs. Hill, my uncle's housekeeper, stood ramrod straight with her hands on her hips.

"Luca Tommaso Philips! Where did you get that?"

"*Merda*," he muttered.

All I could do was smile.

**Five years later**

I stepped off the elevator and into the foyer of my uncle's home as I had so many times since I was a little girl. Only this time, how was I to keep from dissolving into a puddle of tears and sobbing upon the marble floor? My beloved Zio would never again answer my call from his library, he would never wrap me in his arms and comfort me, he would never make me laugh with his wicked sense of humor. He was gone. It didn't seem real. I blinked hard. I would not cry—not again.

From the moment Mrs. Hill had called me this morning, I hadn't stopped moving. I'd been here when the ambulance came, and when they'd pronounced him dead. Before I'd even had a chance to breathe, his assistant, Mr. Stone had brought me to the funeral home. Of course, Zio had arranged everything.

His obituary had been written, his urn selected, and his place in the mausoleum next to my aunt awaited his internment, but nothing could've prepared me for what came next. Weren't wills usually read after the funeral or memorial service? In movies, it always seemed like days or weeks before people knew of their inheritance, but no, my uncle had apparently insisted it be done without delay.

"Oh, Lizzy, Mr. Stone texted to say the car service had dropped you off." She came up and put her hands on my shoulders. "How are you, my dear?"

"He left me everything," I said in almost a whisper.

"Well, of course he did." Why was her voice so matter-of-fact? Was I the only one who didn't see this coming?

My vision blurred through the tears stinging my eyes. "But I don't want it. I want him back. How am I supposed to run everything without him? I need him." With a sob, I collapsed into Mrs. Hill's arms.

"Oh, dearest, you were the closest thing he had to a child. He loved you and your aunt more than anything and anyone. You also proved yourself with the Buttercream Beanery. You were the vision and the talent behind that endeavor, and you were the one who made it a huge success. He was so proud of you. You know that, don't you?"

I nodded against her shoulder. He'd told me more than once that what he'd planned would've never been as successful as what I'd created. I never had room to doubt myself when Zio was there to provide encouragement and praise.

"Your uncle was a brilliant man. He recognized you had the acumen to run his bookstore and keep it earning a profit. How often did the two of you discuss books? The two of you also looked at the release lists on the publisher's websites and predicted which would be successful. No, he knew exactly what he was doing."

She drew me back with her palms on my cheeks. "Now, we'll need to move your belongings from your apartment here. If you'd like to stay in your room here tonight, I can help you gather an overnight bag."

The grandmotherly woman regarded me with raised eyebrows. She expected me to move in now? I hadn't even had time to even consider the idea. Between the funeral home, the lawyer's office, and Mr. Stone telling me what would need to be done in the next couple of weeks in the car on the drive home, my brain was fried. It was all too much! Couldn't I just crawl into bed, cover my head, and cry?

"Can I stay in my apartment for the night?" Why did I sound like a child asking for permission?

Mrs. Hill smoothed the hair back from my face. "Of course you can, dear."

I glanced around the white foyer. "I need to go."

The older lady did no more than watch me as I pressed the button for the elevator and stepped inside after the doors opened. When the construction had been done to connect the bakery to the bookstore, they'd also renovated the buildings in such a way that I could get from my uncle's house to my apartment without going through the store or going outside.

It didn't take long for me to navigate the offices on the fifth floor, unlock the adjoining door, then my apartment. As I stumbled inside my living room, my shoes were kicked from my feet on the way to the bedroom, and I fell on the bed in a heap with another sob. A nudge to my head made me look up at the black and white tuxedo cat I'd adopted last year.

"I've had the worst day, Atticus. Zio is gone."

He gave a loud *"merow"* and nudged me again before plopping down beside me, purring loudly.

I wasn't fooled. The walking stomach, disguised as a rather large housecat, wanted food. He always wanted food and was willing to do anything to get it.

After cuddling with him for a while, I dragged myself out of bed, put some kibble in his bowl, then climbed under the comforter, pulling it over my head. I'm sure there was work to be done in the bakery, but I'd get up early and take care of it in the morning.

## WILL

"Darcy! I found it!"

I looked up from the paperwork in front of me. One of Pemberley's corporate attorneys Charles Bingley, stood just inside my office door, a wide grin covering his face.

"What did you find?" I had him working on many things. How was I to know which he'd finally figured out?

"Luca Philips didn't have a will; he had a trust. That's why it was never filed and will never go through probate."

I sat back and crossed my arms over my chest. Pemberley Books had been trying to acquire Novel Books, an enormous bookstore on the Upper West Side for years. The owner refused to sell, and his store was popular enough with the locals that no chain retailer tried to compete, particularly once he added a café and bakery. It seemed like everyone in Manhattan ordered their cakes from that shop—heck, even Georgiana studied there with her friends at least once a week!

"That does explain a lot. Is that all you've discovered?" I'd have expected Charles to have more than that if he was coming to me.

"No, his niece, Elizabeth Bennet inherited the entire estate—the bookstore and the café, which she masterminded from what I understand."

My eyebrows lifted. "So, do you know if she'd be interested in selling? We wouldn't be interested in the café or bakery. We'd just ask that she coordinate with us for certain events or sales." The coffee shops in our stores were an agreement with a chain coffee shop, so that wouldn't be a problem.

Charles sat across from me. "I actually spoke with her sister Jane. We met earlier this year while filing papers at the courthouse. I thought the connection might pay off one day, and I was right. She informed me of the particulars and that Elizabeth Bennet's parents are suing for a portion of the company. Jane, who went to Harvard Law, is representing them. She'd been required to learn the particulars for the case."

I narrowed my eyes. "You asked this Jane out, didn't you?"

He grinned. "She's an angel, Darce! I'm telling you. You should see her. Blonde hair, blue eyes, and a body—well, you get what I mean."

I struggled not to roll my eyes. Charles liked the ladies, and the descriptions he offered of them were often very similar: hair color, eyes, and body. He definitely had a type!

My knee bounced under my desk. We could offer to buy the business and offer to take on the lawsuit for Elizabeth Bennet, but perhaps it'd be easier to wait until she could sell—.

"By the way, from what Jane, Elizabeth's sister, understands, she won't sell. Miss Bennet's already been approached by two book chains about purchasing the store and its contents. Her parents want to sell and pocket the proceeds, which is why they're suing. They were also expressly left nothing. Luca Philips stated it outright in the document."

"Ouch."

"I know, right?"

I flipped my pen, pushed it on the desk until my fingers had slipped to the end, then flipped it again. "Don't approach Elizabeth Bennet."

"What?" Charles had leaned forward a bit, his ear tilted in my direction.

"You heard me. Yes, I want that store, but if she's been made two offers and her parents are suing, she'll dig in her heels and refuse before she even hears a dollar amount. We're going to wait."

"I don't think that's a good idea. What if her parents win the lawsuit?"

I shook my head. "I think it's doubtful. If Luca Philips wrote them out and went so far as to say it in the trust, then I doubt any judge will ever award them so much as one percent of the company. No, let's see what this Elizabeth Bennet makes of it. If she runs the bookstore into the ground, we'll get it for less than what we'd be willing to offer her now."

Charles blinked—appearing like a lost puppy. "But I've been working on this for years."

"Yes, you made multiple offers to Philips, who rejected every single one. If he and this niece were close, she surely knows about them. When combined with the other offers and the lawsuit. . .No, we need to back off. We'll revisit Novel Books in six months and ascertain whether they're worth pursuing. Until then, keep an eye on how business is faring, but stay away. Is that clear?"

"Crystal."

# Chapter 1

*October 11th (present day)-six months later*

I stepped into the glittering ballroom and scanned those dressed in their finest tuxes and gowns while they milled around the room and gathered in small groups to chat about this or that. Waiters dressed in solid black wove through the guests with sparkling crystal glasses of champagne while a long oak bar along the right side of the enormous room beckoned to those who craved something stronger.

God, I missed Zio! While I held onto his arm, he would walk me through the room, whispering his scathing criticisms of those he disliked and ensuring I was introduced to those he tolerated. My uncle could navigate a room and avoid every pitfall and snake in the grass with an ease and grace I'd always envied.

Now, as I watched the crowd, my stomach was tight, and my fingers gripped my clutch so that the beading dug into my flesh without mercy. It wasn't that I disliked parties, per se, but a charity gala with the supposed social "elite" wasn't something I'd become accustomed to. Would I ever get used to this?

"Lizzy!" Marianne King, heiress to a magazine conglomerate, waved me to join her. We'd both gone to NYU; although, Marianne was a few years older than me and had gotten her degree in journalism. Her father had made her work for one of his magazines while in college, and as soon as she'd graduated, she was brought on staff. However, she'd busted her ass to make her way to editor-in-chief. While her father gave her the start, he wasn't one to promote his own daughter over someone more qualified and had left it to the head of that magazine label to choose the new editor based on merit. Marianne had still earned the promotion. Her work over the years had spoken for itself.

I met her halfway, and she gave me a one-armed hug. "How are you doing? I've called, but I haven't heard from you since the memorial service. I'm sorry for not making more of an effort."

"I'm the one who should be sorry, Marianne. I've been so overwhelmed learning about the company and keeping up with the café that I've neglected everything but business. Until recently, it's been all I can do to get into the bakery kitchen a couple of times a week. Thank heavens for Charlotte, my assistant—she's been a godsend. She can bake everything we offer and direct the staff with no help from me, so she's been running the bakery." I'd met Charlotte Liu at Cordon Bleu in London, and we'd hit it off like we'd been friends for decades rather than a few months. She'd moved to New York after we'd both received our certificates. Zio hadn't blinked at me hiring who I felt was the best person to be my right hand. In fact, after a ten-minute video call, he hadn't hesitated to approve my choice.

"But you won't be running both businesses day to day, will you? After all, the Buttercream Beanery was your brainchild, not your uncle's."

"The bookstore has a management staff. We're in the process of mapping what will happen in the future. I will likely spend my mornings running the bakery and café, then spend an hour or two in the afternoon tending to some of the business of the bookstore. Zio didn't spend much more than that. He'd delegated most of his responsibilities during the past ten or so years of his life. He just liked hearing the latest and being a part of the ordering decisions. He'd stayed on top of what was up and coming."

"Just like you."

I shrugged. "I do try, but I have to give my management team a ton of credit. We all keep our ears and noses to the ground for any rumor of something amazing coming down the pipeline."

"I'm sure your uncle would've understood if you kept to the café and bakery side of the business."

With a sigh, I shook my head. "I don't know about that. After I had the café up and running, Zio brought me to these charity functions and insisted I meet everyone. He'd call me to the meetings where they discussed book orders and new releases. He's been preparing me for this since he brought me into the business. I was just too blind to see his intentions for what they were.

"Did you know he bought a smaller building in the East Village and intended to open another store?"

Marianne's forehead creased. "Are you going to carry through with his plans?"

"I don't know," I said and bit my bottom lip for a moment. "I feel like we're sandwiched in by Pemberley Books. They own most of the big bookstores when you leave Manhattan. I don't even know if I should make an attempt. I found out a month ago that they've been watching and waiting for me to fail so they can buy Novel Books for a song."

"You're kidding," said Marianne. "How'd you even find that out?"

"My sister Jane of all people. When the lawsuit she'd filed in an attempt to gain part of Zio's estate failed, she was furious and told me. I think it was for shock value, but you'd be proud of me. I didn't so much as flinch."

My long-time friend put a hand on my shoulder. "But you haven't failed. From what I can tell, business is better than ever. I absolutely love the Halloween story time event you've started—and promoting it through the local schools was brilliant. My sister took my niece on Saturday, and she raved about it." I'd mentioned the idea during one of our management meetings, and the idea had flourished from there. On weekends in the month of October, we had employees, children's authors, and even actors who would dress to the theme of whatever book they were meant to read and set up in a corner of the children's department. The turnout had been amazing. Every few hours, we had dozens of kids who would appear dressed as everything from a cat to a Marvel character to a terrifying witch.

"It's been a lot of fun. I'm reading one of the weekends before Halloween. I can't wait."

Marianne glanced over my shoulder. "Oh, my father is giving me the 'help' signal. He's been caught by Cruella de Bourgh."

I laughed, and not so softly, at her name for Catherine de Bourgh. My uncle had mentioned Mrs. de Bourgh here and there. As anyone could imagine by the nickname, she was not known for her kindness.

"I haven't met her yet."

"Do yourself a favor," said Marianne. "Make an effort not to."

I held my breath so I wouldn't snort in response as she kissed my cheek and rushed off. I pivoted on my heel glancing around the room. Marianne had stepped next to her father and was smiling and nodding to an imperious-looking woman with grey hair that was pulled back in a severe bun. She held a cane with one knobby hand while she dipped her chin with the air of a queen. Poor Marianne.

As I pivoted to take in the room, I sighed. This was the first event without Zio. Hopefully, I didn't look as lost as I felt. I could do this!

I drew myself up and began walking toward the bar. I would pretend I owned the place—I would act as though I was in the café, except I'd never wear a couture evening gown in the café. My usual attire was leggings or jeans and a t-shirt when I was baking. If I worked the front, I usually wore jeans and a bakery polo. Now, standing here in a floor-length, fitted silver sheath gown with a halter neck and gunmetal beading, I was out of my depth. The vintage store down the street had called me the moment they'd gotten this piece, and I couldn't argue with the price—not when I could never bring myself to buy a similar dress brand new. Nothing was out of place with the gown. It was me who was convinced I shouldn't be here.

After speaking briefly with two friends of my uncle, I searched for the ladies' room. Maybe a moment with fewer people around would allow me to gather myself. I used the facilities and washed my hands before stepping in front of one of the large mirrors to ensure I had no toilet paper stuck to my heel, or my seam wasn't hopelessly twisted around my body.

I took one more deep breath, exhaled, and opened the door to step into the large corridor. I'd taken no more than a couple of steps when I was bumped into from behind. My foot slipped to the side on my strappy heels, and my hands shot out to brace myself as I fell. However, the blow never came. Instead, strong arms wrapped around me, and the next thing I knew, I was hauled back to my feet.

"I'm sorry. I should've been looking where I was going."

A pain shot through my ankle, and I winced. "It was an accident. No harm, no foul, you know."

The man straightened from picking his phone and my clutch up from the carpet, and my entire body froze at the first glimpse of his crystal blue eyes. Holy hotness, Batman! No sooner had he handed me the clutch than I clenched it to keep from fanning myself.

"Are you hurt?" His watered-down English accent washed over me. I could've melted at the mellow baritone he possessed, but instead, I cleared my throat and glanced down to my feet.

"I don't think so." I took a step back and almost lost my balance when my foot slid from the sole of my shoe. My arms nearly burst into flames when he steadied me.

I lifted my foot. "One of the straps on my heel broke. I can't wear them like this." I started to hobble over to a chair, and he wrapped an arm around me to steady me.

When I sat and began to remove both shoes, he backed up a little. "You mean don't mean to walk around the gala with bare feet, do you?"

"You act like the floors are filthy. Besides," I cupped my hand like I was going to tell him a secret, "they'll be hidden by my dress. No one will know." I'd stage whispered in a tone that would've made my mother proud.

His eyebrows lifted while I unbuckled the straps on the good shoe. I'd had these heels for a few years and had used them often since silver matched just about everything. I suppose they were doomed to fail at some point. The timing was unfortunate, but what could I do? It wasn't like I had a spare pair of shoes in my tiny clutch. I'd also break my ankle if I tried to wear them around the gala.

"Why even carry one of those? They seem rather useless?"

When I looked up, he was pointing to my bag that sat next to me on a side table. Although, it was more of a case since it had a clasp and wasn't soft. "I have an ID, a little cash, a credit card, and some lip gloss in case of emergency."

"Lip gloss," he said dryly.

"No self-respecting girl would leave home without it."

I stood once I'd taken off my heels and grabbed my clutch. As soon as I'd tossed the shoes in a gold trash can near the ladies' room door, I ensured my feet were hidden by the hem of my gown. "See, no one will know."

He stared down at where my bare feet were concealed. "This is all my fault. I know it won't make up for the shoes, but can I buy you a drink?"

I squashed my inner teenager who was jumping up and down at the hot guy offering her a drink. She would ruin everything. "That would be lovely, thank you."

When he held out his arm for me to take, I bit my cheek. A gentleman? How many men offered their arm these days? My uncle would've, but like I said, these days.

I slipped my hand into the crook, the expensive fabric of his coat tickling my palm. When we reached the bar, he waved down a bartender and leaned over to me. "What would you like?"

My eyes wandered over the selections. Zio and I always ordered Scotch at these functions, and it seemed appropriate to continue the tradition, particularly when my scan stopped on a familiar dark brown label. "The Balvenie seventeen-year double wood, please."

Again, the man's eyebrows shot up on his forehead. "You drink Scotch?"

"Mostly when I come to events like this," I said, arching my brow to meet his look.

His lips quirked up on one side. "I'm Will." He held out his hand.

"Just Will?"

One of his shoulders lifted. "For tonight, yes. If you don't mind." He leaned over the bar and ordered.

When he straightened, I tilted my head. "Then I'm Liz." I couldn't explain why I'd given him that nickname. No one called me Liz. My family had always called me Elizabeth, except for Zio, of course, and in England, everyone had called me Lizzy. I hadn't minded. That was the beginning of a new life, so the change seemed appropriate. Now my friends and employees all called me Lizzy.

"So, how often do you come to these things?" asked Will.

A laugh spluttered from my chest. "I'm sorry, but was that meant to be a pick-up line?"

He frowned for a moment, then his expression lightened a little. "Not exactly. Call it genuine curiosity."

"This is the first I've attended by myself. If I'm being honest, I miss the company and feel kind of lost on my own."

The bartender put my drink beside me, and I curled my fingers around the glass, the familiar weight of it as I lifted soothing some of that unease in my chest.

"I suppose your excuse is better than mine."

"What's that?" Now *my* curiosity was piqued.

"I despise galas and balls and having to put on a polite face. I'd rather write a check and be done with it." Will held his glass out, and I met it with mine. "To new acquaintances."

"Not quite acquaintances you could say. It's not like we're giving each other much about ourselves."

He lifted a shoulder. "I suppose if you consider identity, you're correct. That doesn't mean we aren't sharing our true feelings on other matters."

We both sipped our drinks, and I closed my eyes for a moment to savor the warm vanilla notes that lingered on my tongue. When my eyes opened, Will watched me with a strange look in his eyes.

"What is it?" I asked.

He shook his head. "Nothing. Forgive me. I know very few women who drink Scotch much less seem to enjoy it as you just did."

"Perhaps I have a more refined palate than most women you know." I allowed a small smile. Yes, I was flirting just a bit. I couldn't deny this man looked like he'd just stepped from the pages of a GQ tuxedo spread. The designer tux he was wearing fit him to perfection, and his mahogany curls were a little long but were swept back some, allowing a view of his handsome face. I could stare at him for hours—if I wouldn't make an idiot of myself.

He glanced around the room. "The ballroom is becoming crowded. Would you like to go to the balcony?"

I tore my gaze from him to where people were beginning to gather around the bar. "Yes, I think I'd like that."

He offered his hand to help me weave out of the crowd and held the glass door open for me when we exited the room. The cool air of the evening hit me, and I let it wash over my skin. The ballroom had become warmer since I'd arrived, which wasn't surprising with the number of people who'd entered since I'd left for the ladies'.

"Are you cold?" He set down his drink on the stone balustrade and reached for the button on his coat.

"No." I held out my hand for him to stop. "It's nice out tonight. I promise I'm not cold."

He nodded and picked up his drink. "You'll tell me if that changes?"

"But if you give me your jacket, you'll be cold."

"I'd still be wearing a long-sleeved shirt. Your shoulders are bare. What kind of a gentleman would I be if I let them become goosebumped?"

I laughed. "Goosebumped? Is that a word?"

"I don't know, but it is now." He gave a full smile this time. He was attractive before, but with those dimples peeking from his cheeks, he was every woman's book fantasy—the image in their mind of the handsome leading man. He'd be my perfect adult version of Gilbert Blythe—like after Gilbert and Anne married in *Anne's House of Dreams*. God, I loved Gilbert!

# Chapter 2

## WILL

It'd been a long time since I'd met anyone at one of these over-stuffed and supposedly full of social importance events that intrigued me, but this woman did. From the moment I'd bumped into her outside the bathrooms, she'd held herself with the poise of someone who was comfortable wherever, disguising well the unease she'd hinted at earlier.

Her almost ebony curls were pulled up, with one here and there draping in a way that framed her face. My eyes were continuously drawn to her full lips, even though her dark eyes sparkled and beckoned me to stare into their depths. I'd never found a woman so intriguing so quickly, yet the moment she tossed her shoes into the trash, I'd been fascinated. No one I'd ever met would traipse around a charity gala barefoot—even if you couldn't see her feet.

My foot tapped as I took a sip of my Scotch. Another aspect that made me long to know her better. She drank Scotch, and not just any Scotch, but one of my favorites.

What had made me insist upon first names and first names only? Not only that, but no one ever called me "Will," yet I'd introduced myself to her with the shortened version of my name without so much as a stutter. She'd called herself "Liz." Had she done something similar? God, how I wanted to find out!

"Are you okay?"

Her head tilted a little to one side, highlighting the curve of her creamy neck, and I gripped my glass a little tighter. She had no idea how lovely she was. The silver gown she wore highlighted every curve of her fit body. Did she work out or was her figure one that was effortless?

"Yes," I said nodding. What the—? Why had my voice cracked? She was turning me into an adolescent boy. This was mortifying! A question! I needed to ask her something to divert the attention from my voice. "Have you ever traveled?" There! That was a good question, wasn't it?

"I have. I lived in London for almost a year and a half, which made Europe very accessible. My friends and I would go online when the airlines offered reduced fares and take a bank holiday weekend in Italy or spend a day in Prague, sometimes leaving early in the morning and flying back late at night."

"What holiday did you like the most?" She ran her teeth over her lower lip while she looked up at the sky, obviously thinking, the plumpness of her lip bouncing back as the pressure was released. I could've groaned.

"I had favorite bits of most of my trips: the Louvre and eating pastries in Paris, walking through the carriage ruts in Herculaneum, wandering Rome and finding hidden treasure around an unexpected corner, the charm of the Christmas market in Heidelberg with the castle visible and lit up on the hill above, or the size and fun of the one in Cologne."

"You don't seek the usual though," I said. "Most look at the overall picture and not the individual parts as much as you seem to do." I certainly never had. Her perspective was unique.

"I believe people would appreciate more if they turned their attention to what is beautiful and concentrated on that versus what isn't appealing. We should remember as much as we can with pleasure, shouldn't we? Why mire ourselves down in the negative?"

She boldly held my gaze, and I couldn't look away. A throat clearing made me jump. Had I been leaning in to kiss her? Her cheeks became pink, and she turned to face the view of the city.

"Mr—?"

"Yes?" I replied before my aunt's assistant could say my surname. The anonymity I'd enjoyed while speaking with Liz had been freeing. I wasn't William Darcy of Pemberley Books; I was just Will. I could be me and know that if she responded, it wasn't because of the company or my bank account. If only that freedom could last longer!

"Your aunt is demanding your presence. She's cornered—?"

"I'll be there in a moment." I didn't need him to tell me who my aunt wanted me to speak with. She'd harped on it incessantly in the limo on the way to the gala. How was it I was the CEO of Pemberley Books, and my aunt still seemed to believe she could lord herself over me? It was as though I was still a young man spending my summers interning in every department, a requirement my father insisted upon every summer before I received my undergraduate from Harvard and my MBA from Wharton.

Collins, my aunt's lackey, just stood there. Good Lord, he was the biggest kiss-ass of this century, and my aunt savored every bit of his flattery and subservience as though it was a gourmet meal.

"I said I'll come in a moment."

"Your aunt said now." Collins's eyes bulged. "She'll be displeased if I return without you."

"And you can tell her that *I* said I'll be there when I get there. I'd like to say goodbye to my friend first, and you don't need to be here for that." The little rat-faced fink would tell every last detail to my aunt. She'd tried to run my love life since my father died, but I'd be damned if I actually let her do so!

I leveled my fiercest glare on Collins, who scurried, like the little rodent he was, back into the ballroom. "I apologize for that. My aunt seems to believe I'm a child who still requires parenting. Not even my own parents tried to control me as she does."

Liz glanced toward the doors then back at me. "My parents tried, but I was fortunate enough to have family members who loved me for me and not what they wanted me to be."

"That must have been difficult," I said, my voice soft.

"In the beginning, when I wanted desperately to break free but was terrified of what that would mean, yes, it was, but once I made my choice and lived my life for me, it was easier. My parents were irate, of course, and don't speak to me now, but their love had conditions attached. Love should be without conditions; we shouldn't have to buy it, if you know what I mean."

I cleared the fog from my throat. "I do."

At a knock on the door, I startled and turned. Collins's beady face was almost pressed flush to the glass. A laugh bubbled from Liz that made me smile.

"He's persistent. I'll give him that."

"Too persistent," I growled. "Let me see what my aunt wants. Are you leaving soon?"

She shook her head. "No, why?"

"Would it be okay to find you after? I'd like to talk more."

Her smile widened some. "I'd enjoy that."

I opened the door for her and let my hand rest on the small of her back as I led her through the throng. When we reached the bar, I helped her into a chair. "Don't go anywhere. I'll do my best to hurry." The floral notes of her perfume tickled my nostrils while I spoke close to her ear. The natural scent of her combined with the fragrance made drawing back nearly impossible. I swallowed hard as my gaze met hers once more. She nodded, and I forced myself to walk away—to stride to where my aunt sat like a queen with her subjects crowded around her. Collins now stood to her right and leaned down to whisper in her ear as I approached.

"Nephew! It's about time you showed up!"

## LIZ

My heart beat like it was running a race as Will walked away. At some point, he disappeared behind the other guests, and I relaxed, rubbing a palm over my stomach. It was tumbling as if I had a team of gymnasts in there. Had it been my imagination, or had Will just begun to lean in when that Collins guy had interrupted? A part of me had wanted me to shove that weaselly little man from the balcony then invite Will to continue what it seemed like he was going to do. I'd never been much on kissing a virtual stranger, much less telling them about my parents, so what was it about Will that had me throwing caution to the wind? I didn't even know his last name!

Marianne appeared in front of me and crossed her arms over her chest. "Okay, Lizzy, spill! What were you doing with William Darcy?"

"William Darcy?" The name was familiar, but for the life of me, I couldn't figure out why.

"Yes, William Darcy, the CEO and owner of Pemberley Books?"

I was mid-sip of Balvenie when Marianne delivered that nugget. Scotch burned at my nostrils as I almost shot it out of my nose. I coughed. "Pemberley Books!" I stage-whispered. What was it about tonight that was making me behave like my mother?

Marianne sat in the chair beside me. "You didn't know?"

"No, he bumped into me outside the ladies'—literally bumped, mind you. The strap on my heel broke, so he bought me a drink to make up for it. He simply introduced himself as 'Will.' I wonder if he knew who I was, and that's why he insisted upon not using last names."

"Maybe." Marianne frowned and crossed her legs. "But I've never known him to go by Will. Everyone—*and I mean everyone*—calls him William. His actual name is Fitzwilliam for his mother's family, so it's already shortened. It's also strange for him to dissemble the way he did with you. My family has known his for years, and I've known William to insult people with his honesty rather than lie outright. His bluntness has never bothered me, but most people speak of him like he's an old curmudgeonly man in a young body."

"A young, hot body," I said low. The last thing I needed was for him to return and overhear what I'd said.

"Tell me about it. He dated a good bit when he was younger, but after a particularly bad break-up with the sister of one of his friends, he's never seen with women. I've heard a rumor he doesn't date at all. Makes him a bit perfect for you, though, doesn't it?"

"When do I have time to date?" I'd barely had time to do much but sleep since Zio died.

"You need to fix that. Your uncle wouldn't want you eating, breathing, and sleeping Novel Books."

"I know. When I was living in London, I dated Denny, but he had no intention of leaving England, and I was returning to New York. It didn't make sense to stay together. Neither of us would ever consider moving to be with the other. We were more friends with benefits than lovers. I've dated since, of course, but nothing that ever stuck. No one lit a fire under my skin; you know?"

"Yeah, I do."

The crowd parted for a moment, and my entire body jolted at the sight of Will striding back in my direction. My insides warmed at the sight of him.

"What am I going to do? He obviously didn't want me to know who he is." I turned to Marianne who shrugged.

"I don't know."

When I turned, Will was only about five yards away but had been approached by a man with blond hair and a wide grin.

"Charles, you didn't mention you were coming." They were close enough that if I concentrated, I could hear every word.

"My fiancée found my tickets on my dresser and was adamant we come. She'd heard about the gala but had never been able to come."

My stomach clenched when a tall blonde I recognized easily slithered up and looped her arm through Charles's. Since when was Jane engaged? Not that I talked to Jane or my parents, especially after the lawsuit trying to steal part of Zio's bookstore—and the bakery as well for that matter—but Mary, who I still spoke to, hadn't even mentioned it.

"Isn't that—?" asked Marianne.

"Yes." I took a sip of my Scotch.

"What were you doing with my sister?" Jane's voice carried well through the ballroom. Even though her back was to me, she could've been standing beside me the voice was so clear.

"Your sister?" asked Will.

"Yes, the owner of Novel Books; the bookstore you wanted to take over."

As I lowered my glass, my eyes met Will's over the rim.

"I had no idea who she was. She introduced herself as Liz."

"Liz? What a joke. No one calls her that. The only nickname she's ever had was Betta, and only our uncle called her that."

Will glanced at Charles, who only looked back and forth between Jane and Will as though it were a show, and he had a front row seat. "It doesn't matter. I was only being friendly after almost knocking her over when I came out of the men's room. It's not like I'd ever consider dating her. She's not my type—not my type at all. It's not like she's beautiful—she's tolerable I suppose." His eyes met hers for a moment before he averted his gaze to the floor then back to Jane.

"As my friend Char would say, 'What a wanker,'" I said to Marianne. I downed the last of the Scotch Will had bought—no, that William Darcy had bought—and stood. "Maybe it's time to go home."

"You're not leaving because of what William said, are you?" Marianne took my hand as I turned to face the bar. "In my experience, he's reserved, but never outright rude, so I can't explain what just happened."

"Maybe he's just full of himself and thinks he's so important he can't be bothered with someone who only has one bookstore. Oh, and who he supposes is tolerable."

Marianne squeezed my hand. "One huge bookstore and a successful bakery. Seriously, Lizzy, I keep hoping you'll open another site of the Buttercream Beanery, preferably somewhere near my office. Do you know how often I crave one of those sinful chocolate turtle cupcakes? They're so moist. I don't know how you do it. My assistant is Celiac, and she raves over your gluten-free cakes and pastries. Thankfully, she lives on the Upper West Side, so she brings them into work on occasion."

I shook my head. "I don't know how I'd ever manage two locations. Char would need to run one, and how am I supposed to make it without her?"

"Hon, you'd have her train a new Char before she moved to the new shop."

My chin dipped as I adopted as serious an expression as I could. "No one could replace Char."

Marianne glanced over her shoulder and sighed. "William's still talking to your sister and Charles Bingley. He hasn't moved."

"Will can do whatever he wants, Marianne. I'm not going to waste my time on him. He's not worth it."

"That's the attitude," said Marianne.

"Now, if you want a cupcake, let's go to the shop. We'll have a cupcake and some amaretto and catch up. Zio and I would always do that, and I was kind of not looking forward to going home to an empty house and carrying on the tradition alone."

Marianne's face brightened. "You don't need to ask me twice. Just let me tell my father I'm leaving. I don't want to disappear on him."

I followed my friend around the edge of the ballroom while I trained my eyes everywhere but in the direction of William Darcy, Jane, and whoever that Charles guy was. What did I have to gain by letting William Darcy know that his words stung? How my insides flinched when he dismissed me like I'd been an obligation, a duty, that he'd discharged.

No, I was going to go home, eat a cupcake, drink some amaretto with Marianne, and cuddle my cat, the only dependable male in my life. I didn't need William Darcy. I didn't need any man to validate my success or validate my worth. William Darcy could kiss my ass!

# Chapter 3

*October 20*

I stood on the sidewalk while I stared at the façade of the Buttercream Beanery and sighed. Of course, Georgiana would want her birthday cake from this particular bakery—of course, she had no idea what I'd said when Jane told me who I'd been talking to at the charity gala either. I'd be fortunate if Liz—Elizabeth Bennet—hadn't put laxatives in any food she served me. I hadn't missed the narrowing of her eyes when she'd heard my comment, and no one in eyeshot would've missed the roll of her eyes as she'd laughed and turned toward the bar to face away from me.

My behavior was abominable. I could admit it. Yes, I was shocked to know "Liz" was in fact Elizabeth Bennet, but I could've handled it better; not that I'd say as much to her! If I'd insulted my housekeeper, Mrs. Reynolds, that way, she would've baked my favorite brownies and put as much chocolate-flavored laxative in them as possible. and I have no doubt I'd be stuck on the toilet for days while I cried like a toddler. Mrs. Reynolds was like a second mother to me and had witnessed on occasion my less-than-sociable side, which she despised. As a teenager, she'd once hauled me out of a party at our home by my ear to read me the riot act over my haughty behavior. She'd have done it at the gala too if she'd been there to witness it.

Enough with the stalling! I sucked in a breath in case Liz was in the shop. Maybe she wasn't and I'd get in and out without her ever knowing. My palms were coated in a sheen of sweat. Why was I so nervous? Yes, my aim was to avoid her. The problem remained: how do you avoid someone in their own place of business?

After I climbed the steps, I waited for a mother and daughter to exit before I stepped inside. The rich aroma of fresh espresso and decadent pastries hit me in a wave and beckoned me to take in a huge breath while I glanced around the interior.

The space was large and bright and likely took up the entire first floor of the building. Pristine white walls gave the shop a clean aesthetic with pale slate-blue accents and several windows that provided a view into a courtyard set up with brick pavers and large urns filled to the brim with autumn-colored mums, decorative brown grasses, and a colorful pumpkin here and there.

To the left was the entrance to Novel Books, the bookstore, while a large counter ran across the back wall and curved around the right corner of the shop. To the left, a display case filled with pastries, cupcakes, cookies, and cakes invited customers to indulge in every decadent chocolate and sugary morsel followed by the coffee bar and the registers before the counter where drinks were picked up near the door to the courtyard. Tables filled the rest of the interior but weren't so packed people couldn't walk through. To bring a touch of the season to the space, an orange pumpkin decorated with flowers adorned a place near the registers as well as smaller pumpkins, autumn flowers, and other décor that were sprinkled throughout.

My eyebrows were surely high on my forehead. I was impressed. When I'd heard Philips had given the go-ahead for a bakery and café, this hadn't been what I'd envisioned. Liz had done exceptionally well. Even during the middle of the workday, people sat and drank coffee not only inside but also in the courtyard, men and women in business attire hurried in to grab coffee before rushing off to who knows where, and a few mothers allowed their young children to select sweets from the array of cupcakes and cookies on display. Liz had created a thriving business, but why had she stopped at one location? With the success she had here, why not market the same business plan in another part of the city? She was missing a golden opportunity!

As I stood, no doubt gaping at the sight in front of me, my gaze came to an abrupt halt at a familiar ebony-haired beauty, who wore an elaborate black witch costume, a tall hat perched on her head. Liz stood about ten feet away, one eyebrow arched just so, and her arms crossed over her chest. Shit! I was busted.

"Is there something you needed, Mr. Darcy?" My spine stiffened like someone had scraped her pointed green fingernails down a chalkboard. I much preferred when she called me "Will." I also preferred a more friendly tone, but what could I expect after the gala?

I shifted on my feet. "My sister has raved about the cakes from here since not long after she started Julliard. Her birthday is next month, and I wanted to order a custom cake."

This time, her eyebrows shot up. "From *my* bakery? Notwithstanding your sister's praises, I would've thought you'd rather purchase from anywhere else in New York. Once, you were hoping our business would fail, weren't you? Or maybe you still are. You also seem to know *my* sister—which is not an item in your favor."

With a sigh, I prayed for patience. "Yes, Pemberley Books has hoped to acquire Novel Books. Your uncle's bookstore is large enough to make it difficult to open our own location on the Upper West Side much less Manhattan. We did our research, and your uncle cornered the market here decades ago. Novel Books is big enough that we would be in direct competition. Buying this store out and converting it would've been much simpler; however, with your uncle's death, we shelved the idea to see what happened with the lawsuit brought by your parents—"

"Who were represented by my sister Jane."

"Yes, Charles Bingley, Pemberley's legal counsel and a long-time friend, had the information on the trust and your inheritance of it from your sister. He has since become engaged to her."

Liz shook her head with what had to be a snort. "Good luck to him. He's going to need it. My sister cares about no one but herself."

Although I'd met Jane only a handful of times, I'd guessed as much. Bingley was entirely too cheerful, but he did have an impressive demeanor in court. He could argue his way out of most situations—and had never paid for a speeding ticket despite his perpetually heavy foot.

"I'm not friends with your sister if that helps."

"One mark in your favor." She pursed her lips to one side for a moment. "Fine, have a seat." She pulled out a chair at a nearby table before saying a few words to the girl behind the counter. A binder was handed to her, and she made her way back, sitting in the chair beside me.

"Before we get started, would you like a cup of coffee? I had come to grab one before helping to set up for the event."

I glanced at the extensive chalkboard menu that covered the back wall. "You have peaberry coffee?"

"Yes, it's imported from Costa Rica."

I loved peaberry but most of the larger chain coffee shops didn't carry it. "I'd like a cup of that." I started to stand. "Here, I'll come up so I can pay."

She held up a hand. "I offered, Mr. Darcy. We'll consider ourselves even after the Scotch you purchased at the gala."

I frowned. "That was to make up for breaking your shoe."

"I'd had those heels for a couple of years, and they weren't expensive. No need to make up for what I probably should've replaced long ago."

Before I could respond, she whirled around in a swish of black satin and some frilly fabric I didn't know the name of. What was it about Liz that made my tongue thicken in my mouth and my brain muddle? I didn't have this problem at the gala—not this bad anyway.

She spoke to one of the girls behind the register then returned. "We have a full staff behind the counter, and it gets crowded, even without this dress I'm wearing, so Mia will brew our drinks and bring them over.

"That's an interesting outfit. Is that your normal work attire?"

She sat stiff and didn't even crack the tiniest of smiles. "I'm reading for one of the Halloween story events at two." She flipped open the book. "Do you want a fall-themed or a traditional birthday cake?"

"My sister is gluten-free."

"That's not a problem. Eight months ago, our renovations on the third floor of this building were completed, and we've now a dedicated gluten-free space as well as a peanut-free space, and every order is boxed or wrapped before being brought down for sale."

My eyebrows lifted. "That's an expensive endeavor."

"Word of our gluten-free cakes spread, and the pantry-sized space we were using hadn't been adequate for some time." She pushed the binder in front of me. "These are the birthday designs we currently offer."

I turned from page to page, finally stopping on a cake where the icing at the bottom was piped on to look resemble a beehive, the cake showing through for contrast. The pattern gave way to the icing at the top where a pair of bees decorated the confection. White flowers gave an extra touch and a nice decorative element. "Georgiana would adore this. She loves bees."

Liz frowned. "Georgiana? Do you mean Gigi; a tall, thin girl who talks about almost nothing but the piano?"

I opened up my phone and showed Liz a picture from her last performance.

"*Your* sister is Gigi. She's so sweet and kind. What happened?" The slight curve to one side of Liz's lips gave away her tease. "Never mind, I shouldn't have said that anyway. Forgive me. So, if this is for Gigi, you'll need a vanilla sponge with hazelnut buttercream. I'll add a little Frangelico to the buttercream for the center filling as long as that's okay with you."

"It sounds amazing, but you're going to make her cake?" It was a legitimate question. How often did the owner get down and dirty in the trenches?

"My uncle made me attend the Cordon Bleu in London for over a year to learn the nuances of baking and pastries, and I absolutely loved every moment. When I started Buttercream Beanery, it was just me and Char, my assistant, in the kitchen.

We have more employees now, of course, or we'd never keep up with the demands of the café or custom orders, but I still bake every morning. Most of the bookstore business is tended to later in the afternoon. Char and I both collaborate on the menus and specials for the coffee shop business—the sandwiches and salads served at lunch, as well as the cakes and pastries we offer in the shop.

"We have extensive kitchens between the baking and kitchen space on the first and second floor to the dedicated allergy kitchen and baking spaces on the third floor. I've never handed over the management of the Buttercream Beanery to another. I have a manager who makes the schedules for the front of the house. Char is my back-up in the kitchens."

"Which is why you haven't opened another location yet. Right?"

She clamped her lips shut and pulled a tablet from under the binder. "You need one Bees Knees cake, vanilla with hazelnut buttercream and a Frangelico filling. When did you need it?" I sat back. Was she always so defensive with everyone or just me? Her tone was more relaxed and open with Marianne King, at least the little I'd overheard.

"October 31st."

She winced. "Oh, that must suck having your birthday on Halloween."

"My parents always put my sister's birthday first. She never had to share anything with the holiday like those who have their birthdays close to Christmas."

Liz's shoulders relaxed a little. "I love that they put her first. Your sister's a sweet girl. She deserves to be made a fuss over."

"I have to ask; how do you know one customer among so many?" I couldn't name a customer, not that I spent much time in our stores.

"That's easy. She came in all upset one day. I served her some coffee and a piece of cake, and she told me about a boy who'd made fun of her. I played the part of big sister and told her he wasn't worth her time, and that one day, he'd no doubt live to regret his words. I believe it was her first week at Julliard. The next day, she came in as she did the day after. By the end of the week, she'd brought in a friend she'd made. Since then, she comes in frequently, and almost always with others from her classes. They study, have coffee and talk, and sometimes have lunch."

"She'd mentioned what happened the first day," I said, "but never about you. I remember being surprised she'd come to such a mature outlook without talking to me or our housekeeper, who's like a second mother to us both."

The sparkle in Liz's eyes dimmed some. "Gigi told me about your parents. I'm sorry."

My insides gave a jump at the mention of my mother and father. Georgiana rarely mentioned them to anyone unless she trusted that person completely. How'd I never known of her friendship with Elizabeth Bennet?

"Thank you."

She cleared her throat. "Anyway, what time do you want to pick this up?"

"It's a Saturday evening party. Why don't you come? You can bring the cake with you, and I'm sure Georgiana would love to have you there." I gave a start. Had I just invited Liz to the party? Where had that come from?

Liz's chin hitched back. "Okay, first, I'm not a delivery service; however, if that's requested, I can accommodate you. We have a company we hire out to at an extra charge. And second, Gigi hasn't invited me."

"So, it'll be a surprise."

She shook her head. "I don't want to crash a party."

"You won't be." I leaned forward and set my arms on the table. "Look, Georgiana never speaks of our parents to anyone—except maybe me and Mrs. Reynolds. The fact that she talked to you about them says loads about her trust in you." Which was true.

"I caught her at a particularly vulnerable moment."

"And have you talked to her since?"

Her eyebrows drew down a little in the middle. "What do you mean?"

"I mean does Georgiana seek you out or speak to you when she comes into the shop?"

One shoulder lifted. "Well, yes."

"How often?"

She blew out a breath and sat back. "I see her a few times a week."

"Then I think you should come." I was going to be extraordinarily uncomfortable, but I'd already issued the invitation. I wasn't going to take it back. Besides, inviting Liz wasn't about me. Georgiana had never had an easy time making friends. Even if Liz was somewhat older, I'd move heaven and earth to ensure my little sister was happy at her party. What doting big brother wouldn't?

# Chapter 4

"I have no idea what I was thinking, Char. How am I supposed to attend Gigi's birthday party and behave as though I belong there? It's not like I can pretend the gala never happened."

Char, or Charlotte as she was known to everyone else, stepped from the massive walk-in refrigerator where she'd just stored some cookie dough for the next day. "I can't believe the wanker never apologized. I also can't believe you agreed to bring the cake. Why not have the delivery service drop it off and show up dressed to kill later? Make him eat his words from the gala. I still can't believe dear, sweet little Gigi is related to the tosser."

I straightened with a piping bag of chocolate in my hand. "Hey, I did charge him for delivery. I don't care if he invited me. He's not getting off if I'm bringing the cake." I bent over and continued piping out bat wings on parchment paper.

My best friend laughed and turned on the mixer. "Well done, you. I would've made him pay for the coffee too."

With a shake of my head, I bit my lip while I concentrated on keeping my lines steady. "No, I don't want to be indebted to him in any way, nor do I want him indebted to me. After the party, all will go back to what it was. Gigi will come into the shop as she always has, and with any luck, I'll never see William Darcy again." I stood. "There, that's the last one."

Char's eyes narrowed, and I stiffened so I didn't take a step backward. "Oh, my God. You like him!"

I startled. "No! No, I don't."

My best friend guffawed, a boisterous laugh for someone who stood about five foot two. Charlotte grew up in London, the daughter of Chinese immigrants. She spoke fluent Mandarin, which did come in handy in one of the most culturally diverse cities in the world. The woman could also bake anything, and I mean anything.

She propped a hand on her hip. "I know that look, and I've heard that denial before. You can't hide shit from me, Lizzy."

I dropped the bag on the counter and threw up my hands. "Fine! When he first bumped into me, he was kind and asked if he could buy me a drink. We went out on the balcony, and I suffered from just enough verbal diarrhea to embarrass myself—"

"You talked about your family," she said matter-of-factly. What could I say? Char knew me better than I knew myself sometimes.

"Yes," I said in a groan. "I wasn't going to turn down a drink. Despite the pinched, judgmental expression he sometimes wears, he's hot. I doubt he'd ever give me a second glance otherwise."

"Stop!" Char pointed at me with a hard glare and her lips pressed into a fine line. "You always do that. Stop letting what your parents said in the past color how you see yourself. You had more than one guy at culinary school wanting to ask you out before you started seeing Denny. Get your head out of your ass and realize that you're gorgeous and have a figure that would make most men drool." She glanced down at herself. "At least you don't have the curves of a ten-year-old boy."

I almost spit out the sip of water I'd just drank. "You've never mentioned having an issue with your body."

"I don't have a problem with it. I'm a lesbian. I like curves, but I don't care if I have them." Her relaxed posture and slight shrug reinforced the truth in her words.

"Then why mention it?" Seriously!

"Because if I was straight, I *would* think it was a problem and would envy you. How many men check out a woman with no tits and a flat ass?" She pointed at me again. "Don't laugh. You know it's true."

I covered my face with my hands. My water had almost ended up all over those chocolate bat wings I'd just finished. After I shook my head, I let my hands fall. "Well, you never had to grow up with the epitome of beauty. Jane attracted the attention of every boy in high school, and my parents never let me forget how perfect she is."

Char lifted a hand, palm out. "I get that, and it's a fucking shame. She may have a more classic look with her blonde hair and willowy figure, but you're more of an exotic beauty with your black curls and dark eyes. Don't discount yourself. As women, we have enough people who try to bring us down, the last thing we need to do is diminish our own value. Men may have ideals of a woman who looks like Jane as their wife, but you're the one they fantasize about at night."

My cheeks burned so bright; the glow could surely be seen in New Jersey. "I can't believe you just said that."

"Why? That's not a bad thing—as long as they don't treat you like a one-night stand, that is."

I waved my hands in front of me. "Okay, no more. I have a serious question, and I need a serious answer."

Char leaned against the stainless counter. "Why? Being serious isn't fun."

"After the Halloween reading I did, Mr. Goulding, Zio's attorney called. That space my uncle bought to open a smaller location of Novel Books has another building next door for sale. He wanted to know if I was interested."

Char crossed her arms over her chest. "What are you thinking?"

I exhaled to relieve the tightness in my shoulders. "Well, I've been asked more than once in the past month or so why I've never opened another location of the Buttercream Beanery. I could say a bunch of reasons: the one location keeps me busy, what if it doesn't work out, and lastly, you're the only person I'd trust to run it and I don't want to lose you."

She gasped at the last. "You'd expect me to run it?"

I tilted my head back and forth. "Who else would I hire for the job? You know this store backwards and forwards as well as all of the recipes and can do my job as well. If I ever expand, you're the only person I can envision in my place there."

"Where's the building again?"

"The building Zio bought is in the East Village. The building next to it and on the corner has a restaurant or coffee shop front with a lot of glass and there's room on the sidewalk for outdoor seating. As people have moved out of the apartments on the second and third floors since its purchase, the spaces haven't been let out again. At this point, we have enough room to gut those floors and have a decent-sized bookstore—not as big as this location—but it was never meant to be as large. The other building would be attached to the bookstore, like here, but it would carry a smaller menu. You'd still have special orders and the pastries. What do you think?"

Char gave me a side-long look. "I'd get a raise?"

I rolled my eyes. "Of course you would. We'd have to renovate first, so dates and such will be set in stone as soon as the building is purchased and we have a contractor hired. You'll need to be involved. These are going to be your kitchens, and they should be set up to your specifications."

"We collaborated on the ones here. I'd rather keep to what's familiar."

"That's easy enough. The lawyers are finding out how much of the second building is let before we make an offer. I'd like to have a large shop on the first floor and the kitchens on the floors above. If there's an empty flat, you could move in as part of the agreement. That way, you can live on site." Char currently lived in an apartment on the other side of Zio's—well, now my house. He'd kept the apartments to rent out on the top floor, and when one tenant moved out, he'd offered it to Char. From the moment she came with me from England, he'd treated her as though she was another niece. We'd shared my tiny apartment for over a year before he'd been able to offer her one of her own.

She rocked on her feet, then covered her mouth with her hands and shook her head. "I can't believe you're giving me this opportunity."

"Hey, we need to buy the building first. If we can manage that, I think we're home free. Zio was saving and preparing to expand the business for a while. I've just decided that maybe those who've been asking me about it were doing so for a good reason."

"Who was the last person who mentioned it?"

"Would you believe William Darcy?"

Char paused her movement and leveled a heavy gaze on me. "Are you sure this isn't some tactic to cause the business financial difficulties? Everyone knows he wants Novel Books. I doubt he'd pass up Buttercream Beanery. We've built up a steady business and clientele. He'd be a fool to sell us off or underestimate us."

I shook my head. "No, I don't think so. Something in the way he said it... I don't think he was scheming." I picked up the piping bag to put it away. "Do you want to go with me tomorrow afternoon? The realtor is supposed to give us a showing."

"I'm in," said Char without hesitation. "Lizzy?"

I'd turned to put the chocolate away but looked back at her.

"Thank you. I'm perfectly happy to work with you here, but that you'd offer me this opportunity means everything." Before I could react, she lunged forward and hugged me. I froze for a moment. Char never hugged anyone.

"Hey, you've been my best friend since we met that first awkward day of classes. You taught me how to live in London. I love you."

"I love you too."

"Are you crying?

When Char drew back, she wiped her eyes. "No! And don't you dare tell anyone otherwise! Oh, and before I forget, Annie wanted me to invite you to Thanksgiving dinner. Her mother is going to France for two weeks, so she's decided to entertain her friends." Char had started dating Annie eight months ago. They were taking things slow, especially since Anne had yet to come out to her mother.

"How's that going?"

"About the same," said Char with a sigh. "Nothing will change until she comes out, but I can't and won't force her. The situation has to be right for her. I'm just tired of sneaking around and pretending we're nothing more than friends."

"Have you thought about how long you're willing to wait?"

She shrugged. "I'll give it another couple of months, at least I think I will. If nothing changes, I'll have to move on."

Her tone was a bit tight, but only someone who knew her well would hear the subtlety. It was obvious Char had developed feelings for Annie quickly. The last thing I wanted was to scrape my best friend's heart up off the floor.

"Enough of the serious talk," said Char. "What do you have in your closet that will knock William Darcy on his arse? After all, if he last saw you in that witch costume, we need to remind him of how badly he screwed up at the gala."

"You've seen everything in my closet." Char dug through it often enough, usually bemoaning that she couldn't borrow my clothes. Our figures were drastically different.

"That's true. We should go shopping."

"No," I whined. I hated trying on clothes! For my gala gowns, I had Vera's Vintage down the street who called me when they had something I could wear. It was so much easier than searching through racks of dresses at one of the department stores.

Char held up a finger. "You also need to replace that pair of silver strappy heels the wanker broke when he ran into you. Not a cheap pair this time either. You need to dress as the owner of two successful businesses—two successful and expanding businesses. Maybe we need to look at some Jimmy Choos or Louboutin's."

"You're living vicariously through me. Don't think that I don't know—"

"Yes, I am, my lovely. Come on. Let's get changed. We can't go out covered in flour and powdered sugar."

I suppose I couldn't argue. Char would never let me.

# Chapter 5

*Halloween*

"Lizzy?" Gigi's eyes were wide as soon as she opened the door. "What are you doing here?"

I did my best to quash the twisting of my stomach and held up the cake box. "I'm delivering your birthday cake, and your brother invited me to the party. If it's for your Julliard friends only, just say the word. I don't have to stay."

"No!" Gigi stepped aside and waved me into the large penthouse apartment. "I considered inviting you, but I didn't know how to ask. We talk a lot when I come into the café, but I wasn't sure if we were friends or not. Does that make sense?"

I couldn't help but chuckle. "Yes, because I felt the same."

She glanced at the box in my arms. "Now, I know you never do deliveries. Please don't tell me my brother insisted you bring the cake."

"I wouldn't say insisted. There's no point in paying someone else to deliver when I'm coming anyway. I did charge your brother for my time though."

"As you should," said Gigi in almost an indignant tone. She waved a hand for me to follow. "Come, let's give that to Mrs. Reynolds. She'll know where to put it. Did you pick the flavors or did my brother?" She nudged my shoulder with her own. "Please say it was you."

I grinned. "I didn't give him a choice; vanilla cake with hazelnut buttercream and a Frangelico filling."

"I should pledge my undying love for you. You combined all of my favorites."

"You've also given me your opinions on samples and the cakes that I make, so I should know well, by now, what you like. I even baked it myself."

"Then I know it'll be amazing."

My eyes widened when we stepped inside a chef's dream kitchen where an older woman was arranging hors d'oeuvres on a serving tray: cherry tomatoes with a basil leaf and tiny mozzarella ball, mini quiches, and antipasto skewers that looked good enough to die for. My mouth began to water.

"Mrs. Reynolds," said Gigi. "This is Lizzy. She owns the Buttercream Beanery."

The older lady wiped her hands on a towel. "I'm pleased to finally meet you. Gigi has brought home some of your desserts. I'm going to gain entirely too much weight if she keeps it up."

My heart swelled just as it always did when someone gave me such a great compliment. "Thank you so much. My friend Char is as much responsible for what we serve as I am. I couldn't do it without her."

Mrs. Reynolds reached out to take the box. "I assume this is our dear girl's birthday cake."

"It is. Do you need some help getting it onto the cake stand?" A wood and marble cake stand was ready and waiting on the corner of the granite island.

The older lady pulled out a pair of scissors and cut through the seal. "Let's see."

"There's a cake board underneath." I couldn't help but fidget. This is why I preferred not being at people's homes when they unboxed my cakes. However, it was clear this was not Mrs. Reynolds' first time. She unhooked the corners of the box and with careful hands exposed the entire cake.

"Oh, this is beautiful."

Gigi gasped. "I love the design."

"That was all your brother," I said. "I had to give him something to take credit for."

"He's too good to me." Gigi had her hands clasped in front of her.

I set down my purse. "Do you have an offset spatula?"

Mrs. Reynolds rummaged through a drawer. "Do you mean one of these?"

"That's it." I took the instrument and ran it under hot water at the sink. "I chilled the cake before I left so it would be easy to move. The ride here wasn't long, so we should still be good." I ran the warm spatula around the bottom edge just in case some of the buttercream had stuck to the box. Once I was sure it was clear, I lifted the edge, slipped my hand beneath the cardboard round, and shifted the cake, just as I'd done so many times at the bakery.

Once I had it situated on the cake stand, Mrs. Reynolds took the spatula. "You did that without marring the frosting. I don't think I've ever managed that."

"That's why you chill the cake and heat the spatula."

She shook her head. "I love to cook but I've never been much of a baker. Gigi brings home desserts from your bakery when we need them."

"That's usually when I come first thing in the morning," said Gigi. "I don't usually get to talk to you on those days."

"Because I'm in the kitchen. We start at about four in the morning. I have three employees who get right to work on bagels so they're warm and fresh from the oven when the first customers walk in at six. Char starts on the croissants, and I get the muffins in the oven. After, my morning is spent baking whatever else is needed, as well as icing cakes to be picked up that day and replenishing any we have stocked in the displays. Char joins me when she has time, as do the others. We have two more employees who come in at five to prep and wrap the breakfast sandwiches. It's a system that's slowly evolved since the doors opened and we've been able to acquire more kitchen staff."

"It sounds brutal," said a male voice from the door.

"William," Gigi gushed. "I adore this cake. Thank you!"

My body was still stiff while Gigi hugged her brother with a wide grin. He appeared so different than usual. He embraced his sister fully and closed his eyes for a moment while he accepted her open affection. He seemed more relaxed than at the gala, but this was his home. I'd hope he was more comfortable here than anywhere else.

"Miss Bennet," he said when Gigi released him. "I'm glad you could make it. Let me take your coat. Georgiana seems to have forgotten."

"I couldn't very well take her coat while she was holding the cake, now, could I?"

With a start, I unbuttoned the front. I'd forgotten completely that I was wearing it. My breath caught when his fingers grazed my shoulders as he pulled the deep wine peacoat from them. It wasn't a typical style with its flared hem, but I loved the color and the unusual cut. Underneath, I wore a dress in a similar shade. Char had insisted the fitted top with the ribbed almost sweater-like fabric would show off my breasts and the tie at the waist would accent that as well as the flare of my hips. The short length was to show off that I had the legs to go with the rest of the package. At the glance my legs received as Will passed me, Char's assessment of the dress was correct.

"You should join us in the living room," he said over his shoulder.

Gigi looped her arm through mine. "Come on; it's this way."

When I stepped through the door, I came to an abrupt halt, and Gigi almost pulled my shoulder from its socket. What the heck? None of Gigi's friends from Julliard milled around, chatting while enjoying snacks. No, instead, the blond-haired man from the gala stood in the middle of the living room with Jane beside him. What was his name again?

"Elizabeth Bennet," said Will as I approached the group like I was nearing a rabid dog, "this is Charles Bingley, my friend and the lawyer for Pemberley Books. Of course, you know Jane."

Every muscle, tendon, and ligament in my entire body was tighter than a bowstring. "We may have met."

Jane let one side of her lips curve into a smile that I knew from experience wasn't friendly.

"And this is Richard Fitzwilliam, our cousin and head of marketing at Pemberley Books."

My insides twisted my stomach so badly, it had to have been tied into a knot. Why did this feel like an ambush?

"It's nice to meet you all, but please call me Lizzy." What else was I supposed to say?

"My aunt was supposed to come," said Gigi. "But, thank heavens, she decided she was too tired."

"Georgiana." Will's tone was low. He may not have scolded her outright, but his reprimand couldn't be missed.

Gigi gave a labored sigh. "Sorry, but you would've suffered through her presence too. She makes everything a misery."

Her cousin Richard gave a slight chuckle. "I agree, Gi, but you shouldn't say it aloud."

"How's business?" asked Jane. She was looking at me with that false serene expression she used most of the time.

"Better than ever." I tried like hell to smile as though I wasn't bothered whatsoever by her. The question was a dig, but I wouldn't react.

Gigi grabbed my arm again. "Lizzy, you should come see my birthday present from William."

I didn't fight her as she tugged me from the room. Without warning, I was yanked to the side and a door was closed, shutting me into the powder room with Gigi.

I glanced around. "Somehow, I don't think this is your brother's birthday gift."

Gigi crossed her arms over her chest. "What in the crap is going on? There's an undercurrent that's almost hostile out there."

Lord, give me patience! "Gigi, you do know your brother wants to acquire Novel Books, don't you?"

She leaned back against the vanity. "I don't keep track of Pemberley Books business. I mean; I own shares of the company. I inherited them when our parents died, but I leave them for William to manage, and he's my proxy for board meetings. It's part of why I'm thrilled my aunt isn't here. She's never hidden the fact that I'm a disappointment to the family for studying music instead of getting my degree in business or law."

My heart split and bled. "You don't believe you're a disappointment, do you?"

"No! William has made it clear that I'm free to do whatever I want. My parents made him promise I could pursue music if that was my choice. If William had chosen a different career path, they would've been supportive then too. He would've still been part of the board of directors, but he could be whatever he wanted."

She shook her head. "Enough of that; who is Jane to you?"

"Gigi, do you know her last name?"

Her chin hitched back. "No, Charles has never said, at least I don't remember him ever telling me."

"Try Bennet."

Gigi's eyes became the size of silver dollars. "No!"

"Yes, my sister, the lawyer who sucks the souls of small children for a living."

Gigi covered her mouth as she gave a slight guffaw. "I'd thought you were joking, but from the little I've been around her, she's truly awful."

"Yes, well, she does try." I waved my hands in front of me. "Now, for one of my questions, why are your guests your cousin and your brother's work associates? Where are your friends from school?"

She bit her lip, and one shoulder lifted. "William said I should invite them, but my brother is so overprotective and Richard's not much better. Could you imagine their expressions when Lydia walks in with her piercings and short skirt? My brother would have an aneurysm."

I pressed my lips together for a moment, trying not to laugh. "I think it could be free entertainment. He turns a million shades of crimson while trying not to stare. Where's your sense of adventure?"

After laughing, she leaned against the vanity. "So, you don't like my brother much do you?"

"That's a complicated situation," I said without a pause.

"Why? I've kind of always wondered if the two of you would get along." She almost mumbled the words while she shifted on her feet.

"You wanted to set us up?"

"I didn't know he wanted to take over Novel Books. That alone is enough to kill any sort of relationship before it started. I just wish he'd find someone. He's such a good brother, and I know he's lonely. And you're amazing. You'd be perfect for him."

I relaxed some for the first time since walking into Gigi's living room. "You've spoken of him in such glowing descriptions that I believe that's your reality. I don't know him well enough— not really." It was true. He'd been so back and forth since I'd first met him, he was more of a Dr. Jekyll and Mr. Hyde, and I never knew which I would get. Right now, I was more inclined to think he had a split personality rather than being just an all-out wanker as Char called him.

"You better show me this gift," I said. "They'll be expecting us to return soon."

When Gigi opened the door, my insides jumped into my throat, and we both gave a cry.

"You went to the bathroom together?" asked Richard with a lop-sided grin.

"I needed to ask Lizzy some questions." Gigi lifted both eyebrows and shoved her cousin aside. "Girls' stuff."

Richard fell into step with her. "Okay, but you didn't need to take her into the bathroom for that. Have you shown her your brother's present yet? Mrs. Reynolds has brought in the food, and Darce won't let anyone eat until you come back."

I lifted my single eyebrow at her.

"Yeah, I know. You told me as much."

Gigi led me into a tall room with floor to ceiling windows on two walls—clearly the corner of the building. The view of the city was stunning, but what was even more stunning was the grand piano in the center of the room. As I approached, the Steinway & Sons stamp could be easily seen on the front, over the keys. The shiny black finish glowed in the setting sun and gave no doubt that the instrument was brand new.

"It's beautiful." I stood in front of the keys, my hands clasped in front of me.

"Do you want to try it? You mentioned once that you took lessons."

I almost snorted. "Gigi, I hardly ever practice. I just don't have the time between running Novel Books and the bakery."

"But you did when your uncle was alive. You told me."

"Squirt, if she doesn't want to play. . ." said Richard.

Gigi huffed. "Her uncle once claimed she had a talent for expression—or so Char told me."

"He exaggerated," I said. "He was like a proud grandfather the way he'd compliment my efforts."

"So, prove it." The tilt of Gigi's head and her stance with the challenge was more confidence than I'd ever seen from her. She wouldn't give up.

Those butterflies that used to appear whenever I was forced to perform began flying in high circles in my stomach. I despised performing.

I glared at Gigi as I slid onto the bench. My hands had a slight tremor as I set them over the keys. After a deep inhale and an extended exhale, I played the first chords of Debussy's *Clair de Lune*. My uncle always asked me to play the piece, and it was one I could manage from memory. After a moment or two, the melody absorbed me, and I welcomed its embrace.

When I played the last notes, applause snapped me back to the room. Gigi wore a wide grin and Richard nodded and smiled as I rose from the bench and turned. Will stood in the open doorway with Charles and Jane behind him. Will clapped politely as did Charles while Jane looked as though she'd sucked on the sourest lemon imaginable.

"That was lovely," gushed Gigi.

I did my best not to squirm now that I was aware everyone had watched me. "I'm sure compared to yours, it's barely passable."

"Have you ever heard Gi play?" asked Richard. "Technically, she's brilliant, but her professors want her to have more expression—they want her to lose herself as completely you just did. Thank you for giving her such a brilliant example."

Will nodded. "I agree."

The doorbell rang, and Jane perked up. "That must be Caroline." She hurried off.

"Caroline?" I said out of the corner of my mouth to Gigi.

"Charles's sister."

Will, Richard, and Charles turned to leave as I leaned a little closer to her. "Do we like Caroline?"

Gigi grimaced. "She's as bad if not worse than your sister."

"Oh, yay! I'm definitely going to need to thank your brother for inviting me." I kept my volume low, even if I exaggerated my enthusiasm.

Gigi burst out laughing. "I'm thrilled you're here, but if it gets too bad, we'll come up with some excuse to leave—but not without stealing the cake first."

# Chapter 6

I squeezed the bridge of my nose and did my best to disguise a heavy sigh. I didn't mind Charles so much, but now that any invitation to Charles included Jane, I'd be happy to never see the man outside of working hours again. And we'd been friends since primary school!

Then, there was Caroline. Had Charles mentioned the party or had Jane invited her? That was one question I hadn't quite figured out, not that I needed to. She was here whether I liked it or not. For the record, the answer was "not."

Georgiana, at least, seemed happy. She'd plastered herself to Liz's side from the moment her friend had walked into the penthouse and hadn't moved. My sister's ease with her was noticeable to everyone and had earned more than one sneer from Jane and Caroline. Georgiana was happy to have a friend there, but I *had* offered for her to invite her friends from Julliard. Liz had commented at the bakery that my sister often came in with a regular group, so why would Georgiana refuse to invite them?

Ugh! How I wanted to drop my head to rest against the back of the plush sofa. The light in the room had dimmed since the sun had set, and I hadn't mentioned turning the lights in the room brighter in an effort to save myself from my current torment; a feeble attempt to ward off the pounding now rattling my brain.

"Here's the cake!" Mrs. Reynolds placed the creation on the table with the candles lit. Caroline, with a grin that made my muscles load as though readying for escape, began singing *Happy Birthday*. I moved my mouth along while I tried to fake that I wasn't dying a slow and painful death. Hadn't anyone ever told Caroline she was tone-deaf?

I took a large sip of my Scotch as Georgiana blew out the candles.

Mrs. Reynolds held out a knife to Liz. "Miss Bennet, if you'd cut it since you're the artist who created it?"

"Artist?" Caroline gave one of her tittering laughs. "It's a cake. No one will be putting it in a museum."

"It takes time, a careful hand, and talent, Miss Bingley," said Mrs. Reynolds. "Whether or not you believe it to be art or not is irrelevant, since beauty and art are in the eye of the beholder." That voice was all too familiar. I'd heard it anytime I'd spoken out of turn as a boy. Mrs. Reynolds was also right.

Caroline may have considered herself an artist, but as far as I was concerned, the jury was still out on that label. She made sculptures out of found objects, more specifically dismembered baby dolls. Charles had once begged to stop by Caroline's during a ride back from lunch, and as much as I'd tried to refuse, he'd insisted I come up to say "Hi." I swear I walked inside as though walking into a minefield. Caroline's studio was boxes and crates and tables full of baby doll hands, baby doll feet, baby doll eyes. I shuddered. Between those and her sinking those pointed blood-red fingernails into my arm, I'd had nightmares for a few weeks where I was being dragged by blood-red talons and drowned in a huge vat of baby doll hands. A shiver went down my spine.

"I'll fetch the plates," said Mrs. Reynolds. Without another word, she hurried from the room.

"Richard," said Liz, "I'll take that Scotch now if you don't mind. I believe I saw a bottle of Aberlour over there; two fingers, neat, please."

My cousin stood. "I like your style, Lizzy." He'd offered her a drink an hour ago. I wasn't shocked she'd suddenly decided to take him up on it now. Anyone with a sane mind would've sought oblivion once they understood how trying tonight would be.

Liz plated slices of cake, which were accepted by everyone but Caroline and Jane, who declined due to watching their figures. Both could be mistaken for toothpicks and had no need to restrict their diets, but it wasn't worth it to argue. Instead, I let my plate rest in my lap while Liz took a bite of the confection, her plump lips wrapping around the fork in a way that made my pants tighten. When her tongue peeked out to lick a bit of the frosting from the corner of her mouth, I had to grip the handle of my fork not to jump over the coffee table and lick it off for her.

Good Lord! Where had my self-control gone? I'd never experienced such a reaction to a woman. I cleared my throat and took another larger drink from my glass.

Georgiana glanced at me and narrowed her eyes. "What's wrong with you?" she mouthed.

I gave a curt shake of my head and took another sip.

A low laugh I knew well came from beside me. When had Richard sat there? Last I'd looked, he was following Liz around like a lost puppy.

"A little hot under the collar, cuz?" he asked me by my ear.

"Shut your gob."

He laughed harder. "I haven't heard you say that since you first returned from Eton. She's really got you bothered."

Thankfully, Charles was recounting some ridiculous story or another. I couldn't tell which one. He had a million or so of them, all designed to make himself look good in some way. In other words, no one had heard Richard's comment.

Another torturous hour later, Liz stood. "I should be getting home. I need to be up early in the morning for work."

Tomorrow was Sunday. Didn't she take a morning off?

I stood, as did Georgiana, who hugged Liz and whispered something I couldn't hear into her friend's ear.

"Let me grab your coat, then I'll show you out." I was going to take the reprieve from the room and run with it! After grabbing Liz's coat from the closet, I walked with her to the door and held it out to help her put it on. My finger brushed the soft flesh at the neckline of her dress and goosebumps shot up my arm. I needed to learn to control this response—not that I ever expected to see her again.

"Thank you," she said.

"Did you have a purse?"

"No, my keys and phone are in my pocket." She patted the bottom left buttoned flap on her coat.

"Ah, well, thanks for coming. . .and the cake. Both made Georgiana's night."

She tilted her head. "Can I ask you a question?"

I gave a small jolt. "I suppose."

"Why do you call your sister Georgiana?"

My hands shoved their way into my trouser pockets. "Because that's her name. It's what I've always called her. Why do you ask?"

"Well, she introduced herself to me as Gigi. Even Richard calls her "Gi," but you don't use that name. I was just wondering why. Have you ever asked her what she wants to be called?"

My back stiffened. I'd been my sister's guardian since my parents' deaths. I'd always ensured she had everything she needed. How dare Elizabeth Bennet come in here and—?

"Feel free to ignore me; I was just asking. If it was someone I cared about, I'd seek their opinion. It would matter to me. Anyway. . ." She held up a hand. "Good night."

Without waiting for me to open the door, she left.

"Before you get all hot and bothered, she has a point."

When I turned, Richard stood leaning against the wall, holding a fresh drink in one hand.

"Just because Georgiana has her friends call her Gigi, doesn't mean she wants or needs me to do it."

"No," said Richard, "but as Lizzy just pointed out, have you ever thought to ask?"

"Did you?"

He nodded. "Yes, and she told me she'd understand if I didn't, but she'd prefer to be called Gigi. I get her name has meaning to you because it was an ancestor's name as well as a mix of your mom's and dad's names, but she thinks it's old-fashioned and would like something more modern."

I rubbed my temples. Was Gigi truly more modern? To me, it sounded like a bad name in an old French film.

"Ah, the Caroline headache rears its ugly head," said my cousin with a chuckle. "I bet it's twice as bad with Caro's little protégé out there. I can't believe Jane and Lizzy are sisters. They don't look much alike, and their personalities couldn't be more different. That said, I've always thought your type was more along the lines of Jane Bennet's figure and looks, but low and behold, who knew you had a bent toward curly black hair and a siren's figure?"

"Shut up, Richard."

He sipped his drink while he regarded me so intently, I had to walk past him. His free arm across my chest prevented my escape. "If you're that attracted to her, why aren't you acting on it? She's the real deal: gorgeous, talented, has a good sense of humor, and your sister loves her. Moreover, Lizzy seems to genuinely care for Gi, which makes her even better."

"And she owns Novel Books and the attached café, the Buttercream Beanery."

His eyes widened. "Novel Books—as in the bookstore on the Upper West Side you've been salivating over for the past five years?"

"Yep, that's the one."

"How's that acquisition look for you?"

"Well, her business is thriving, especially the café and bakery."

He kind of tilted his head back and forth. "If that cake she made for Gigi is anything to go by, I can see why. I've never had a better gluten-free cake. Gi has been raving about the food from there for the past year."

"She and her friends from school go there regularly to study and have coffee."

"Elizabeth's businesses have an amazing social media presence. Whoever does their Instagram and TikTok is a genius. I'd love to steal them from her." If Richard was complimenting her online marketing expert, they had to be incredible. I avoided anything related to social media. That was why I needed Richard. He oversaw all our online marketing and had hired those who headed up the different platforms.

Once again, I tried to escape while I had the chance, but Richard grabbed my shoulder and stopped me. "Hey, so what if she owns Novel Books. Pemberley doesn't have to take over the world. You could ask her out, and if the two of you hit it off, then you never discuss your business plans unless you can separate your own interests from hers and give her your impartial opinion."

"How am I supposed to do that?" He couldn't be serious, could he?

"Easy—you stop living Pemberley Books. You run it, but you don't eat, breathe, and sleep it every single day. Eventually, at the rate you're going, you will burn out, and that won't be a pretty sight."

"My father ran Pemberley Books for thirty years. He never burned out."

"Your father prioritized your mother, you, and Gi. From what my parents have said, the moment he set eyes on Aunt Anne, she was his world. Yes, some days, when it was necessary, he worked late, but you work in some capacity every evening and every weekend, even if it's from your study here. You take time for little but Gi, and I'm glad you do that or you'd have already run yourself into the ground. You don't date—"

"I've dated."

Richard dipped his chin. "Not really. You've taken women with no substance to events if you had to, and I know you've had a few friends with benefits arrangements."

I flinched. I tried like hell to keep those under wraps. Not only did I not want Georgiana to ever know of them, but they were usually women I met through work—publishing reps, an agent or two. No one I had any power over and never to close a deal. Just two people who hooked up from time to time for sex.

"Richard—"

"As I recall, you had a year-long arrangement with that woman from Calvert Publishing."

"That was five years ago," I said in a low tone. "I don't want to talk about this."

"Darce, you're thirty-two. You started college at seventeen and completed your business degree in three years and were almost twenty-three by the time you started working with your dad at Pemberley. When your father died and you took over the company, you were twenty-seven. You've never stopped pushing yourself."

"That's not true."

"When was the last time you took a vacation—even took a day off? I'm not kidding, Darce. Gi's friends want her to move into an apartment closer to school, but she's terrified to leave you. She knows that if she didn't ask you to watch a movie with her or have her here to eat dinner most nights, you'd never stop working."

"That's not fair, Richard."

"No, it's not fair to her at all." We stood, gazes locked for a moment, before I stepped back.

His hand fell to his side. "Think about it. It's all I'm asking."

I exhaled, nodded, and returned to the living room. As I entered, Caroline's high-pitched titter sent a jolt of pain down my spine.

The most pressing issue at the moment wasn't Georgiana or Elizabeth Bennet. I needed to get Caroline, Jane, and Charles out of my house, or I wouldn't be responsible for the carnage I'd inflict. A jail cell was looking better by the moment!

# Chapter 7

Sundays were my favorite days of the week. Without the early morning business rush, we didn't need the staff we did on weekdays, so it was usually my day off. Char's was Saturday, and the rest of the staff traded out weekends so the scheduling was fair. I did have one or two who preferred to work weekends, which made it easy as well. They were the ones who filled in for me and Char so we could take a much-needed break. As much as I loved to bake, I needed days to clear my head and get out of the kitchen. The reprieve kept us both from burnout.

Most Sundays, I would find something to do outside of Novel Books or the café, but while the bookstore staff knew well how to change over the décor from Halloween to Thanksgiving, Char and I had a tradition of holiday decorating the café ourselves.

The urns in the courtyard would remain as would the floral decorated pumpkin by the register, but the orange, purple, and green twinkle lights would need to come out of the trees in the courtyard and the windows of the store. We also had cornucopias and colorful gourds that we would place on shelves around the shop along with the display books.

"I talked to Declan and Michelle about the changes to the menu. I'm prepping the crescent roll dough the day before, and they'll bake them before lunch." Char's turkey salad crescent rolls were a hit every Thanksgiving season. The rolls were shaped like cornucopias and baked, then stuffed with Char's recipe for a turkey salad that contained dried cranberries. The only sandwich that was as popular was one she'd stolen from home in England, and that was her Holiday Feast sandwich which contained all the traditional components of a British Christmas dinner. It was rich but so good!

"I saw Mia adding it to the chalkboard. She's also putting up the apple cider cake as our 'Cake of the Month.'"

Char stood at the base of the ladder coiling the lights. "We need to talk about December's cake. Have you had any ideas?"

"I've narrowed it down to a spice cake with eggnog buttercream and an orange cranberry that's topped with a white chocolate ganache."

"Ooh," said Char. I knew she'd love that one. She adored Jaffa cakes and chocolate oranges. It made sense that would be the one she'd gravitate toward. "Maybe we should declare it a tie and offer both. Is it the same orange sponge recipe you had for the creamsicle cake two summers ago?"

"Yes, but with a cranberry filling instead of vanilla. I've also added the Christmas designs we worked on to the binder, so we can take preorders now. I'd rather be able to stay on top of those rather than having everyone putting in their orders at the last minute."

"Agreed." She continued to loop the lights over her wrist while I removed them from the tree. Thankfully, it wasn't supposed to rain until tomorrow and the day wasn't freezing, but cool with a nice breeze.

"Elizabeth!" I pivoted on the ladder.

"Mary? I didn't know you were going to be in town today."

"Dad had a client he met early for golf, then Mom's joining them at the club for lunch. I told them I was going to the library to study. It's not like they track my whereabouts anyway."

I stepped down and hugged my little sister. "I'm glad you're here. I hope you don't mind helping us change over decorations. Then, we can hang out—watch a movie or whatever you want to do."

Char hugged Mary as well. Then flashed me a wicked grin. "Lizzy, you never told me what happened at Gigi's birthday party. She was in the shop Friday and told me to tell you 'Thank you for being a lifesaver.'"

"Gigi? The girl you introduced me to?" asked Mary.

"That's her." Char practically sang the words. She was totally throwing me under the bus.

I leveled what I considered my shut-the-eff-up glare at Char. "Gigi's brother came in before Halloween to order her a birthday cake. He also invited me to the party. Anyway," I climbed back up the ladder, "It was a clusterfuck." Thankfully, no one was nearby to hear me swear. "She hadn't invited her friends for fear of her brother's reaction to some of them, so it was just me, one of Will's friends, his sister, their cousin, and Jane."

Char's eyes widened and her eyebrows drew down. "What was Poison Ivy doing there?"

"Jane? As in our sister-from-hell Jane?" Mary leaned against the tree so she could see my face.

74

"Yes, that Jane exactly. She's dating or is engaged to Will's friend Charles Bingley, who's also the counsel for Pemberley Books. At least, he mentioned she was his fiancée at the gala."

"So, you had a *lovely* time," Char said drawing out lovely so it was sarcastic. We'd joked often when I'd moved to London how Americans rarely said lovely in a manner that wasn't full of sarcasm where the English used it frequently and with its true meaning. By the time I'd moved back to the States, I'd been indoctrinated and used lovely often and not sarcastically.

I shook my head. "It was one of the most awkward evenings of my life. Will stared at me most of the time. I swear, Char, he was judging everything I said, everything I did, what I was wearing. He must despise me for maintaining Novel Books' success."

Mary frowned. "Why would he have a problem with that?"

After quickly explaining the connection, I handed Char the last of the lights in my hand and stepped down from the ladder to work on the trunk.

Char shifted closer. "Lizzy, what if that isn't it at all?"

"What do you mean?" asked Mary. "If he wants Novel Books, why would it be anything else?"

"Well, before he found out who Lizzy was at the gala, he'd bought her a drink—an expensive one—and invited her to talk on the balcony. He was supposed to return after seeing to whatever his aunt wanted, wasn't he?" She turned to me at the last.

I lifted one shoulder. "Yeah, so?" While I folded the ladder and moved to the next tree, Char hurried to my side.

"So, what if he stares at you because he's intrigued? What if he was interested from the moment he met you, but Poison Ivy shocked him with who you are?"

I stopped two steps up the ladder and surely gaped at her. "No way."

"I'm serious. Gigi has said her brother can be awkward and stuck up his own ass, but what if he's never liked someone or been attracted to them the way he is you?"

"He's got to be in his thirties—"

"Thirty-two," said Char without missing a beat.

"How do you know that?"

She gave a one-shouldered shrug. "I Googled him."

"Are you kidding me?"

She lifted her hands. "Why haven't *you*? Aren't you the least bit curious?"

Mary, whose head had whipped back and forth as we talked, held up her hand. "I am."

"Well, I'm not," I said, starting to unwind the lights from the branches of the next tree. "I see no point in looking him up on the Internet. What do I need to know about how much money he makes, or if he was Forbes magazine's Man of the Year."

"Whatever you think of him, I'm willing to bet he likes you."

Mary nodded. "I agree."

I scoffed and handed Mary the lights. "If that's true, he can like all he wants. I'm not interested."

"I call bullshit." My insides jumped at Char's decisive declaration.

When I stepped back down to the ground, I propped my hands on my hips. "What makes you say that?"

"Because you've never cared what someone has thought of you until him. Someone could say your ass is as big as a barge, and you'd roll your eyes and laugh. This time, you've developed a loathing for the bloke unlike any I've ever known."

Mary laughed. "She has a point."

"No, she doesn't. But since you're speculating, I'll put a few things to rest. Yes, I find him hot, but no, I'm not into him. I'm also not going to date him. His friends would bore me to tears. His cousin is friendly and more my type, but that would mean I'd be forced to see Will at every holiday. No, thank you! No matter how much I like Gigi, I won't put myself through that."

Char leaned against the brick wall. "Might be different if you were part of the family. I doubt he'd tolerate Jane and how she treats you."

I shook my head. "I think you're reading more into it than what's there." Way more!

"Maybe, but I doubt it. You've never been good at noticing when someone's into you."

Since I'd just unwrapped the last of the trees, I glared at Char and Mary before I strode inside. I loved Char, but she was completely and totally wrong about William Darcy. He didn't like me, he wasn't attracted to me, and I had no interest in him! But Mary taking Char's side was completely out of the blue. She was supposed to be loyal to me. She was *my* sister.

I walked inside the door, and my world went black as I ran into a dark wall of cotton and wool. "Watch out." Strong hands took my shoulders and shifted me back. "You okay?" I blinked. Richard Fitzwilliam stood in front of me, his lips curved into an amused smile.

"I'm so sorry. You didn't have a coffee or anything that I spilled." I started scanning his clothes and the floor. "I'll replace it—get you something better. I'm so sorry. I'm never this clumsy."

"No, I was waiting to collect my drink. I have to admit I was hoping to run into you, though not literally."

I stepped back. "You were?"

"Yes, I wanted to thank you for Gi's cake. Darce commented that you made it yourself, and I'm sure you have employees who could've done it for you. I know it meant the world to Gi since she thinks so highly of you."

"It was no biggie," I said with a wave of my hand. "I still work in the kitchens most days, and I love making cakes. I'm glad I could bake it for her."

"Richard!" called Mia at the counter.

"Can we sit down and talk for a moment?"

I nodded as he stepped over to pick up his to-go cup, his head turned to see my answer. "Yes, that's not a problem."

Char lifted her eyebrows from where she waited near the door with Mary.

"Give me five minutes," I mouthed with my hand up and all five fingers displayed.

After a nod, she and my sister disappeared into Novel Books. We had a storage closet for decorations in the bookstore's huge stockrooms.

I accompanied Richard to a table. "Hey, do you want to be a guinea pig?"

He laughed. "Is that a trick question?"

"Are you allergic to anything?"

"No."

"Hold on." I rushed into the kitchens and cut a slice of the cake I'd baked this morning. When I returned, I grabbed a fork and a napkin from the buffet that held sugar, cream, napkins, and utensils for the patrons and placed them in front of him.

"What's this?"

"It's a prosecco cake with prosecco buttercream. I've been working on it for a while now but haven't ever gotten it quite right. I could use an impartial opinion on it."

"What's the filling?"

"A blackberry and prosecco jam." I bit my lip as he put the fork into the cake and a fluffy piece clung to the tines.

As soon as he began to chew, he moaned. "Wow, Elizabeth, this is incredible. Will it be a regular offering on the menu?"

"No, I come up with different holiday specials during the year. This one's for New Years."

"Ah, which explains the prosecco."

I nodded. "The trick was the fresh fruit on top. I'd had a champagne and strawberry cake last year, which was difficult as well. I prefer to use local produce and farms if I can. Do you know how hard it is to find a local greenhouse that produces berries in the winter?"

He chuckled. "I'd have no idea. I'm a marketing guy, remember."

"So, nothing you'd change or nothing that sticks out that I'd need to know about?"

"Honestly, it's probably the most amazing cake I've ever eaten—aside from Gi's birthday cake."

The restlessness in me calmed. I'd been playing with the recipe, perfecting it, for months. I'd had the idea during the summer when we'd had a huge shipment of blackberries. I'd made the jam and it'd been stored in the freezer since. I'd just needed the cake and some fresh blackberries for the garnish."

He straightened in his chair and ran his hand through his hair. "So about why I wanted to talk to you."

"Oh, I'd almost forgotten. Is something wrong?"

He frowned. "Nothing's wrong per se. I just wanted to ask you to be kind to my cousin."

I straightened. What was he talking about? "Why would I be unkind to Gigi? She's amazing and kind of like a little sister."

He gave a shake of his head. "I didn't mean Gi."

This time it was my turn to frown.

"I mean Darce. I know how he may seem, but he's not as confident as you might think. There's little he shares with anyone besides me and Gi, and he doesn't even share everything with us. I know Gi is always worried about him because he spends so much time alone. He hasn't had a serious relationship with a woman since college. He was eighteen at the time, and it didn't take long to find out she was using him for his name and the family money."

I couldn't help but cringe. "I'm sorry that happened, but I don't understand what that has to do with me."

Richard exhaled. "Look. I'm convinced he likes you, but by the way you behave around him, I'm also convinced he's put one or both of his ginormous feet in his mouth. When and if he approaches you to go out or whatever, I'm just asking you to be kind."

"You expect me to accept?" Did I have a stamp across my forehead that said, "William Darcy likes me?" Not that I believed it one bit, but why else would Char and Will's cousin both believe the same thing?

"Not unless you want to," he said. "I'd just prefer he not get his heart stomped to death."

"You might not be able to prevent it. He could like someone else entirely."

Richard gave a tight curve of his lips. "I doubt it. If Caroline or Jane had been leaving the other night, he wouldn't have helped them with their coat. He would've had Mrs. R. walk with him to the door and *she* would've helped them with their coats. If you haven't noticed, he didn't have Mrs. R. accompany you, and he held *your* coat for you."

"Maybe he doesn't feel threatened by me. Jane would toss that Charles guy in a heartbeat if she thought she could date your cousin, and I imagine Caroline isn't much different. She clung to his arm for the entire night, and frankly, she may as well have been Freddy Kreuger with the way he looked at her. If you ask me, he appeared terrified."

Richard grinned. "It's hysterical, isn't it? I shouldn't be amused by his pain, but I can't help it. If he'd just tell her to remove her spiky claws from his arm and to get out of his house, he'd be free of her—for a few weeks at least. I will say that he's never given her any kind of encouragement. Whatever she thinks she sees is all in her head."

I laughed. "I can believe that."

When Mary returned with the leaf garlands, I bit my cheek.

"I understand if you have work to do," said Richard. "I've said what I came to say, but I'm going to finish this cake if you don't mind."

I started. "Of course, I don't mind." I waved Mary over. "Richard Fitzwilliam, this is my little sister Mary. Richard is Gigi's cousin." I said the last while leaning in toward Mary.

He nodded. "It's nice to meet you."

Mary smiled. "It's nice to meet you too."

With a wave, we went to the window and began hanging the garlands around the edge.

"You haven't mentioned your birthday in a while." Mary's eighteenth birthday was at the beginning of December, and I fully expected her to show up on my doorstep with all of her belongings. "What's the plan?"

"I'm going to be staying at home for a while."

I paused and frowned. "What do you mean you're staying?"

"Something is going on, and I want to know what it is."

My hand went to Mary's arm, to turn her a little more in my direction. "What's that mean?"

"I don't know yet, but when I do, you'll be the first person I tell."

I frowned as I returned to the garland. "I better be." I didn't like Mary waiting. Yes, she was still in high school, but at eighteen, she could get away from my parents and their toxicity. What could possibly induce her to wait?

I'd have to keep asking. The sooner Mary got out of that house, the better.

# Chapter 8

It was eleven a.m. on a Wednesday, and I stood outside the Buttercream Beanery, staring at the door as though I had nothing else in the world I should be doing. A wreath resembling a ring of leaf-shaped cookies in fall colors was poised to draw inside the hungry and those in need of caffeine and a sugar fix. Garlands of maple leaves in different hues of reds, oranges, and yellows trimmed the windows, which framed the customers inside while they either sat at tables or waited for their coffees and pastries.

This was the second time I'd found myself here. The first time, I'd dreaded going inside and now. . .well, what was that slight buzz that shook every muscle? I'd never experienced anything like it, which was disconcerting in and of itself.

I sucked in a deep breath and steeled myself before I strode up the steps and into the shop, the mouth-watering scent of sugar and rich coffee overwhelming my senses as I closed the door behind me. A couple of people stood in line to order, and I made my way to the end while I glanced around the busy café. Liz wasn't in the front today, but it was earlier than the last time I'd come in.

I'd never before told my assistant I'd fetch my own coffee, so why had I done it today? Gavin appeared as though he'd faint at the idea of me taking on such a menial job. When I grabbed my coat, he gawked at me while I asked if he wanted anything. All he did was shake his head.

Yes, I'd lost my freaking mind. Since Gigi's birthday, I'd been thinking about Liz more often than I'd like. At the most inopportune moments, I'd wonder what she'd say about something in particular or what she was doing. I was losing my mind. What was it about her that had turned me into a man obsessed? I won't even mention the dream I had last night!

The woman in front of me shifted down to the order pick-up, and I stepped forward.

"Good morning, sir. What can I get you?"

"I'd like a twelve-ounce cup of peaberry, please."

The girl touched the screen in front of her. "Anything else?"

"What would you recommend?"

She gave a slight smile and leaned against the counter in front of her. "Well, are you wanting savory or sweet?"

"Let me hear both, and I'll go from there." I was never this flexible.

"So, I adore the turkey salad cornucopia." She pointed to it on the chalkboard menu. "Then Lizzy made apple pie doughnuts for the special this morning. That one in the display is the last one. They're amazing."

"They've sold out before noon?" It was only eleven.

"This is only the second time she's made them so far this year. By the end of the month last year, they were sold out before eight. People were buying six or a dozen at a time."

"Then I'll have to have one. Can I get the turkey salad thing you mentioned to go?"

"Of course, but don't leave it too long. The crescent roll will get a bit mushy. They're better fresh."

I nodded. "I understand. Thank you for the suggestion."

After giving her my name and swiping my card, I tipped the girl well before moving to the end of the counter.

"Peaberry and apple pie doughnut for Will!" called a twenty-something guy with a septum piercing.

I stepped forward and collected my drink and the doughnut.

"The sandwich will take a moment. We'll call your name when it's ready."

A table was free by the window, so I brought my order over and collected a fork and napkins from the buffet against the wall. The doughnut was covered in cinnamon and sugar and would likely be a mess to eat, so I'd need to be prepared.

The doughnut cut easily, and the apple pie filling oozed out as I picked it up with my fork. The second it hit my tongue, the bright cooked apple combined with cinnamon, sugar, and another spice I couldn't identify exploded on my tongue. I paused while I chewed. Liz's cake had been amazing, especially for gluten-free, but this was. . .I was at risk of sounding like a pre-menstrual woman devouring chocolate if I wasn't careful. Apple pie was my favorite, and this was even better!

After my second decadent bite, I was sipping my coffee when Liz entered through the customer entrance with a woman that I'd only ever seen a picture of. She was Asian with short-cropped black hair, and her hands waved around when she spoke. Her eyes met mine, and she set a hand on Liz's arm before nodding in my direction.

Liz turned, and I lifted a hand. Geez! That came off more Tom Hanks in *Forest Gump* than his character in *You've Got Mail*. I winced. If Gigi hadn't made me watch that movie with her, I'd have never known it at all. Now I was making comparisons with the characters. Note to self: Next time my little sister wants to watch a rom-com with me, I'm making her watch *Die Hard* or *Pulp Fiction* instead.

"I'm surprised to see you here," said Liz when she approached.

"The cake you made for Gigi was delicious. I wanted to see what else you could do."

She pulled her scarf from her neck. The weather wasn't cold, by any means, but the breeze held a chill. Liz wore a light jacket, and the scarf had looked nice with it.

"From what you said at the party, I thought you'd be in the kitchen."

"I had a meeting this morning. Char, my best friend and assistant, came with me."

"Lizzy?" The young lady from behind the counter stood by Liz's side with a steaming mug. "Char thought you might want this. She said to take your time. And sir, here's your turkey salad order."

"Thank you." I took the handled paper bag with the shop logo emblazoned on it.

As soon as the girl hurried off, I held out my hand toward the empty seat across from me. "You're welcome to join me."

Liz glanced around then pulled out the chair and sat. "By the name you used, I take it you talked to your sister."

"I did. She prefers Gigi, so I'm endeavoring to remember that. Her name holds sentimental value to me and our family. It's hard to let that go."

Once she'd swallowed her sip, she set her cup on the table. "I can understand that, but it's not letting go of the name completely. She's not legally changing it, and you never know, one day, she may embrace the sentimentality and want to use it

86

again. Don't forget that she's young, and at that age are social pressures that don't always exist when you leave college and start working."

What she'd said was true, of course, although I'd never found the pressures of college to be as strenuous as those in high school. "With so many people on a college campus, I never had the same issues fitting in as I did when I was in boarding school."

She smiled. "You do know the enrollment at Julliard is less than a thousand. I don't know about the high school you attended, but where I went was only about a hundred or so less."

"Where'd you go?"

"Chapin," she said, her finger fidgeting with her cup. "I then attended Columbia and NYU."

"I thought your sister went somewhere else." Jane had mentioned it a couple of times. I'd probably tuned her out when she said where.

"She went to a private school in Queens. My parents wanted to put me in public school, so my uncle paid my tuition and had a car pick me up every day and bring me to Manhattan." She cleared her throat. "You went to boarding school?"

"Yes, Eton College in England."

"What made you go there?" A voice inside me nagged that she was changing the subject. Whatever the reason for her parents' decision, she didn't want to tell me.

"My mother was English. The men in her family all went to Eton, so she wanted to continue the tradition. My father agreed for the first part of their marriage to live in the UK with her. They stayed until I went to Eton, then moved back to New York. Pemberley was simply too big to manage from abroad and my father didn't like traveling and being away from her so often." Instead, I'd flown back and forth for summers and holidays. I hadn't minded. That was how I became close to

87

Richard. My uncle had dismissed the tradition and sent Richard to a private school in Manhattan, on the opposite side from Liz actually.

"How many students do you think attended Eton?"

"Probably not much more than Julliard, so point taken. But I had my undergrad at Harvard and my MBA at Wharton. You attended both Columbia and NYU?" I winced at my tone. Why had I sounded so surprised?

"Yes," she said slowly. "I earned my undergrad in business at Columbia and my MBA at NYU. I wanted to bake and not work for my father, so Zio and I worked out an arrangement so I could start the bakery. That was when I attended the Cordon Bleu in London."

"So you had the business background as well as the culinary training to pull it off."

She shrugged. "I had a lot of help since the bookstore was attached. A lot of credit goes to shoppers with a fresh book in their hands and the tantalizing smell of good coffee. My uncle also ensured the bakery and café were promoted well."

I pointed my fork at the doughnut. "I think this is my new favorite dessert."

Her smile grew a little but wasn't quite right. "I'm glad. If you like apple pie, I have several desserts that are exclusive to the holidays with that flavor profile."

"I can't wait to try them. You'll have to let me know when each goes on special."

An incredulous laugh burst from her. "I don't keep a set plan for specials. Most of what goes on that board is dependent upon what's in-season and what my suppliers have in large quantities."

After wiping my mouth, I drank the last of my coffee. "I think I shocked my assistant when I left to get coffee, so I should get back. Thanks for the company."

She gave a stiff nod. "Your assistant might stroke out if he knew you'd come here."

I barked out a guffaw. "Very likely." I put on my suit coat. "Maybe I'll see you again."

Once I'd buttoned the front, she handed me the to-go bag. "You ordered Char's turkey salad cornucopia?"

"It came highly recommended by the girl at the counter."

"I hope you enjoy."

I took the bag and peered back through the window when I'd stepped down to the sidewalk. Liz had picked up her scarf while she watched me leave, her coffee cup in her other hand. With a smile, I continued to walk.

"Maybe I'll see you again?" I muttered. Where'd that come from? It was bad enough that I'd let impulse bring me to her bakery—and sheer insanity that had me sit there to eat. Some part of me had longed to see her—to make her smile. I'd thought about nothing else all morning. Somehow, I needed to learn to rid myself of this compulsion. I had no other choice.

LIZ

"You should've heard the surprise in his voice, Char." I pushed the dough with the heel of my hand before folding it and shoving it together. I never made yeast breads—not because I couldn't, but because I preferred to make cakes and other pastries. As soon as Will had gone, I'd mixed up a batch of cinnamon roll dough as soon as I'd stepped into the kitchen. Now, I was venting my frustration on the dough before setting it to rise.

"Lizzy," said Char. "Give me the dough." She looked at me as though I had a bomb strapped to me that was about to detonate.

With a roll of my eyes, I put it in an oiled bowl before covering it with a towel. I set it near the ovens where it'd be warm but not so hot it'd kill the yeast. I then took the next part and started treating it with the same venom.

"I doubt he meant it the way you took it."

I lifted my eyebrows. "Then what do you think he meant by it? Lizzy, who was only smart enough to learn to bake."

"At one of the most prestigious programs in the world. Not everyone chooses uni, and it doesn't mean they're not as smart as someone who does. I just think he didn't realize you'd ever studied anything but baking. Have you ever really watched him?"

"What's that supposed to mean?" I kept punishing the dough in my grip.

"Only that he looked extremely awkward while the two of you spoke, like he was nervous."

I scoffed. "What could William Darcy have to be nervous about?"

Char crossed her arms over her chest. "Maybe he gets tongue-tied talking to women he likes, or maybe he's just socially awkward anyway."

"Maybe he's just a dickhead." Why was Char taking his side?

"It's possible," she said. "I've never had a conversation with him, but he helped raise Gigi and she's one of the sweetest girls

I've ever met. I have a hard time believing he's as bad as you think he is."

"He hangs out with Jane."

Char held up a finger. "Yes, but that isn't a point in his favor."

I threw up my hands. "Why's he gaining points all of a sudden? I'm never going to consider dating William Darcy! I can't stand the guy."

"Then why does he aggravate you this much? You've known assholes before and never been this riled up by them. You usually laugh off whatever they've said. You'd think William Darcy committed mass murder by the way you talk about him."

"I don't do that."

"You most certainly do, and maybe you need to consider why he makes you this angry."

I laughed. "That's easy. It's because he's an asshole."

"Okay, Lizzy. Whatever you say."

# Chapter 9

"Lizzy!" Gigi waved at me when I glanced up from putting a tray of maple pecan puff pastries in the display.

As soon as I slid the panel closed, I straightened and paused. Who was she with? He was older, more her brother's age, and had his hand on her lower back while they waited in line—the placement a bit overly familiar for an acquaintance.

I stepped around the counter and walked over. "How are classes going?"

The man was attractive with dark eyes and longer dark hair that fell around his face in waves. He could model if he had the inclination.

"Classes are good," said Gigi. "Lizzy, this is Greg. Once upon a time, his dad was an executive at Pemberley Books, and my dad was his godfather." Okay, that could've explained the hand if the pinky side hadn't been riding and even dipping a little below that line where Gigi's ass began.

He removed his hand from Gigi's back and extended it. "It's nice to meet you, Lizzy. Gigi's mentioned you and your bakery often enough that I decided I had to come give it a try."

I smiled. "Gigi's one of my best customers. She's become a friend too." Something about this guy made the hair on the back of my neck stand on end. His handshake gave me the urge to run and sanitize my palm before I so much as went to the bathroom. "Do you live in New York?" He had an accent similar to Will's, or was that my imagination?

"I just moved back. I've been modeling in London for a while now. My agent got me a few jobs in New York that I couldn't pass up."

"No, I imagine not."

They stepped up and ordered. Greg ordered the peaberry Will preferred, one of the most expensive drinks we offer, while Georgie ordered a latte and a slice of one of her favorite cakes. When Mia told them the total, Greg reached for his wallet, but Gigi set the chip of her card on the machine.

"Not on your life," she said. "This is to welcome you back."

Greg gave a lop-sided smirk until Gigi turned, then he grinned widely. "Thanks, love. I'm glad to be here."

"I need to go to the ladies' room. Greg, would you watch out for our drinks?"

"Of course."

Before I could return to the kitchen, a hand on my arm made me turn to face Greg. "Can I help you with something? I do need to get back to work."

"Oh, I don't want to hold you up."

"It's fine. Like I said, Gigi has become a friend. I'll always take a moment or two to say 'hi' when she comes in."

His hands clenched and released. "It's just Gigi mentioned that you know William."

"Her brother? Yes, I do, but we're not close. Why?"

"Well, he and I had a falling out when we were younger. It was so bad that William refused to honor his father's wish for me to work for Pemberley and didn't even give me the money set aside in my godfather's will."

I frowned. "His father ran Pemberley Books when he was alive. Why wouldn't he have given you the job himself?"

"It was a letter included with Mr. Darcy's will. I received one that was sent after his death, and when I came to ask for the job, William refused to honor his father's last wishes. Mr. Darcy paid for my education at Eton with William and after at Harvard, although I didn't finish my degree."

Which was probably why Will wouldn't hire him. How many jobs at Pemberley Books didn't require a degree? "I don't understand why you're telling me any of this."

"Because I'd rather you not tell William that Gigi and I are hanging out. Gigi has been like a little sister to me for as long as I can remember, and I don't want to lose that again."

Huh? An older brother that lets part of his hand slip to Gigi's ass? I don't think so. "I hardly speak to William, so I don't think you need to worry." There, not a promise of silence, but not a lie either.

Greg's expression immediately brightened. "Brilliant! I knew you'd understand. After all, if you've met William, you know what a daft prick he is."

"Yes. Yes, I do." I couldn't argue with the man there!

"Gigi!"

The man in front of me startled. "Ah, there's our coffees. I better grab those."

I pointed over my shoulder with my thumb. "And I should get back to the kitchen."

"See ya," said Greg.

"Hopefully not," I retorted once the door swung closed behind me. Gigi could do better. Way better than Greg whatever his last name was!

A timer went off, and Char hurried in front of me to the ovens. "That's another batch of pumpkin muffins. Last I looked, we were getting low in the front."

Char placed them on the work surface, and we set to work removing them from the pan. I got one of the serving trays we used in the display and set to work ensuring the front was stocked while Char and our crew continued baking.

Every time I brought out more stock, my gaze landed on Gigi, who was laughing or talking to Greg at the table near the window—the one where Will and I sat two days ago. It was all I could do not to heave when Gigi fed Greg a piece of her cake from her fork. He grinned at her after and nodded, but that same heebie-jeebies sensation rocketed through me at the sight.

I shoved the door back into the kitchen harder than I'd intended, making it slam against the wall, and picked up a tray.

"Lizzy, wait!" Char rushed over and swapped the tin in my hand. I'd grabbed the cranberry spice muffins to replenish the plate, but not the cooked ones. "What's wrong?"

"Gigi brought a guy into the shop."

"Okay, yay, Gigi," said Char with a shrug. "She comes in with her male friends all the time. What's the big deal?"

"This one isn't one of her friends from school. He's a model—"

"Still not seeing the problem."

"Let me finish then!" I huffed. "He's a model, he's also her brother's age—"

"Ew," said Char, her nose scrunched.

"Yeah, and he had his hand on her lower back when they walked in. At one point, she angled herself to the side some, and I could make out where his pinkie and ring fingers were both on the top of her ass. I'm telling you, Char, he makes the hair on the back of my neck prickle—and not in a good way."

Char took the tray from my hands. "Give me this. I want to see." She disappeared into the front. A few minutes later, she returned with the muffins gone from the tin and shaking her head.

"He's good looking, but too old for her. Gigi's mature in some ways and still very young in others." Char shook her head. "I don't like it either. What are you going to do?"

"What can I do? She's an adult."

"With a trust fund," said Char. "What if he's trying to get access to her money?"

I groaned. "He acted like he was going to pull out his wallet to pay but didn't protest one bit when she put her card into the machine. Greg also asked me not to tell Will that I saw them together. Greg said they had a falling out, and Will denied him an inheritance from the elder Mr. Darcy."

Char grabbed the tin with the uncooked muffins and headed for the ovens. "I don't like it. Gigi's gorgeous, but a man like that is not looking for a girl like her. You need to go to her brother."

"And when she becomes furious with me? We're not her keepers; we're her friends."

"And protecting her from tossers is part of being her friend. You have to admit she's vulnerable to being scammed. She's entirely too trusting. I love her for it, but we've both commented it's going to get her into trouble one day."

"But, Mom, I don't want to see William Darcy!" I whined and stomped my foot for dramatic effect.

My friend laughed. "I get it, but I think you have to. I doubt I'd make it past the door, or I'd do it myself."

"Fine," I said low and drawled. If I didn't care about Gigi so much, I'd have let it go. The girl was just too nice for her own good.

"Can I help you, miss?" asked the doorman when I approached the Midtown building where Will lived.

"Yes, I need to see William Darcy."

"Your name?" He opened the door and held it for me while I entered with him right behind me.

"Elizabeth Bennet."

He spoke to the attendant at the counter just like the last time I'd visited the building while the man placed a phone call. After a moment or two, the one behind the counter hung up and lifted his head. "Miss Bennet, you can go up. Mr. Darcy's on the penthouse floor."

Which I knew, but I still smiled. "Thank you."

The elevator quickly took me to the top floor. When I stepped off, I walked to the door on the right and knocked. This building only had two penthouse units on the top floor. They both had to be huge compared to most of the apartments and homes near here.

"Miss Bennet," said Mrs. Reynolds as she opened the door. "Was William expecting you?"

"No, I'm sorry. I didn't think to call him first."

"Oh, it's no bother." She shifted back as she allowed me to enter. "I did text him, and he's on his way."

I nodded.

"Would you like something to drink? Water or a glass of wine? It *is* after five." She chuckled with the last.

"I don't think I'll be here long, but thank you."

She brought me to the spacious and high-ceilinged living room where most of Gigi's party had been spent. When I turned to face her, she had opened her mouth to speak, but the front door opening interrupted. "There he is. I'll grab his coat and let the two of you talk."

The older lady bustled out. Will's deep voice carried into the living room from the entry, but nothing he said was clear enough to make out. When he entered, his eyebrows were drawn down in the middle.

"Would you like a drink?" He poured himself a Scotch. Why not? Maybe it would take the awkwardness out of this conversation.

"I'll have whatever you're having." He still wore his sleek black suit from the office, which accentuated his broad shoulders and tall frame. When he turned his back to me to pour, my eyes wandered down his strong shoulders to the "v" of his waist. I ripped my gaze from the not-so-terrible view below. What was I doing? Yes, William Darcy was hot, but why was I checking him out? It wasn't like we'd ever be so much as friends!

When he turned, he handed me a glass with two fingers of the amber liquid inside. I took a sip, but it did nothing to make that tight feeling in my stomach relax.

"I apologize for dropping in like this. Gigi came into the shop today, and she was with someone who made me uncomfortable."

He frowned. "Uncomfortable? How do you mean?"

"Well, he was closer to your age than hers, for one. He made an act of reaching for his wallet to pay but didn't argue when she put her card in the machine, which I know isn't much, but it rubbed me the wrong way. Other than to say he set the hair on my neck on end, I can't say that much against him. He did ask me not to tell you he and Gigi had been together—that the two of you had gone to school together but had a falling out."

Will slammed his glass on a nearby table, making me jump. "His name. What was this man's name?"

"Gigi didn't give me a last name, but his first is Greg. He said his father worked for Pemberley Books, and that your father was his godfather." That should be enough, shouldn't it?

"His last name is Wickham, and I have to compliment your Spidey sense because he's the last person I'd want hanging around you or Gi. For that matter, I wouldn't trust him with just about any woman." Will downed the remainder of his drink and bared his teeth when he swallowed. My stomach suddenly churned. What had this Greg done? Will didn't like me, but I couldn't imagine him ever having such a severe reaction to anything said about me.

"Thank you for letting me know," he said. "Now I've got to figure out what to do about it. I don't want my sister hurt, and he'd be happy to drive a wedge between us. This isn't going to be easy."

I swallowed the sip in my mouth and nodded. I had to get out of here. "If you need anything from me or Char, we'll be happy to help. Neither of us wants your sister to get hurt. It's why I'm here."

He nodded. "I appreciate that. Thank you for looking out for her."

"I'm happy to do it." I set down my glass. "Look, I should go. I've told you what I came to tell you, and I'm sure you want me to leave. . ."

Will started as though he'd faded off somewhere else. "I'm sorry I'm not better company. You shocked me is all. I don't know where Wickham got the money to travel here, but—"

"He said he had some modeling jobs in the city. I didn't ask for specifics."

While I spoke, Will straightened a little. "Modeling? Maybe you should take me bit by bit through your conversation." But I didn't want to give a play-by-play! What I needed was to go home.

"It truly wasn't that much. Gigi introduced us and told me he was an old friend." Will snorted. "I noticed he had a similar accent to yours, which is probably because you went to school together. They ordered; Greg got the peaberry coffee you like so much while Gigi got her usual order, a latte and a piece of gluten-free cake. She paid then went to the restroom.

"He then explained how he knew you and his claim of you not giving him his inheritance. Gi returned, and they sat at the table next to the window."

"Where we sat a couple of days ago?" An image of Will licking his lips of his apple pie doughnut popped into my brain, and I shoved that down deep. That was the last thing I needed to think about at the moment!

"Yes," I said. "I went in the back and told Char that he rubbed me the wrong way. One of the times I was putting muffins out, Gigi fed him a piece of cake from her fork. Char went out while refilling another plate of muffins to take a look. She insisted I tell you. I hope I don't alienate Gigi by doing so."

Will shook his head. "I should be able to separate them without bringing you into it."

I exhaled heavily. "I'd appreciate it."

He nodded again. "Of course."

I lifted a hand. "I'll leave you be then. Good night."

Without looking back, I strode from the apartment and didn't slow until my feet landed on the sidewalk outside where I could finally breathe again.

Thank heavens that was done!

# Chapter 10

The bell on the door tinkled as I entered the Buttercream Beanery for the third time in my life. After the door closed behind me, I paused and glanced around before making my way to the counter. It was Sunday, so I hoped this was a good day to come. Gi and some friends had gone up to the Hamptons for the weekend. She'd said it was to study, and they'd all have their instruments. Finals were coming, and they needed to prepare.

Greg Wickham couldn't have gone because I'd ensured my childhood tormentor wouldn't be anywhere near Gigi for the foreseeable future. Thanks to Liz, my little sister was safe.

When I approached the counter, I set my hands down on the surface. "Hi, I'm looking for Elizabeth Bennet. I need to speak to her."

The girl bit her lip. "I'm sorry. She isn't working today."

"I hadn't considered. . .May I leave my name and phone number? I need to talk to her."

"You're William Darcy."

I turned to where a petite Asian woman stood behind me. Her short black hair was cut close to her head, and she wore a pair of wide-legged, ripped jeans and a t-shirt that said, "*I bake because punching people is frowned upon.*" A pair of black Dr. Martens boots peeked from under the hem of her trousers. They were dusted with what could only be flour.

"I am."

She gave a bob of her head. "I'm Charlotte Liu, Lizzy's assistant. Come with me." She waved me to follow.

I glanced around but took a few hesitant steps after her. "Where are you taking me?"

"You said you needed to talk to Lizzy. She's at home, so I was going to show you the easy way from inside the store to the lift that will take you up. Otherwise, you've got to walk the long way around to the side street and have her buzz you in." I stood dumb for a moment. You could access Liz's house through the store?

"Are you coming?" Charlotte turned around and looked at me with raised eyebrows.

"Yes, sorry."

We walked around the corner into the bookstore, and Charlotte took me through a pair of double doors then down a hallway with several storage rooms branching off from it. Shelves lined the walls up to the ceiling where boxes of books were organized and stacked; around another corner was a set of elevator doors. Charlotte led me inside and scanned a lanyard on her neck before pressing a button.

"You need a pass card?" Yes, my voice had taken on a higher pitch, but this was more sophisticated than I'd imagined.

"So the employees can use the elevator to bring books to the upper floors of the store and visit the corporate offices without accessing Lizzy's flat."

The elevator stopped, dinged, and the doors opened. When I stepped into the large marble-floored foyer, I stopped and gawked. In all the talks of buying Novel Books, how had no one told us this was here? Jane had said her uncle had an apartment upstairs, but it had been thought to be one of a dozen small flats and not all that large. That was what original plans showed. Apparently, those were wrong since the floating staircase showed that this was the entire top two floors of this particular building.

"Lizzy!" Charlotte smiled at me and held up a finger.

"Char?" came from a doorway under the curved staircase. Charlotte grinned and beckoned me to follow her into the room.

"What's wrong?" Liz rose from a chair by the window, her eyebrows shifting toward the center when she saw me. Holy shit, my jaw just about hit the floor. She was wearing a muted eggplant crop top hoodie and a pair of casual black leggings that showed off her figure to perfection, her pierced belly button peeking at me over the waistband of the tight trousers.

"Nothing's wrong. Mr. Darcy came into the café looking for you. Since the last time you saw him was because of his sister, I thought it might be important. It's unusual for Gigi to come in on a Sunday, but not unheard of, so I brought him up."

Liz scraped her teeth on her bottom lip, which was distracting—to say the least! "You're right. It's probably better this way, Char. If Gigi saw us talking about it all, she'd never forgive us."

Charlotte jerked her chin toward the door. "I'll let the two of you catch up then."

"You don't have to go," said Liz.

I looked back and forth between them. Liz had said she and Charlotte had discussed the situation. "You don't need to leave on my account. Besides, Gigi is in the Hamptons with her friends. They're having a study weekend before finals."

The petite woman grinned. "Thank you for the offer, but I'm meeting my partner for tea."

As soon as she was gone, Liz clasped her hands in front of her. "Can I offer you a glass of wine? Or water? You don't have to drink, but I was having a glass of pinot."

I trailed behind her to a table where a bottle with a familiar red waxed top sat on a table. Liz typed something on her phone while I picked up the vintage. "I know this one. I keep it in my cellar. It's good." A black and white cat rested on the back of a nearby sofa. He lifted his head and blinked in my direction, obviously undisturbed by a stranger.

"It's a sentimental favorite," said Liz. "My uncle enjoyed it often with meals."

"I keep some of the reserve vintages in my cellar—not that it's a true cellar—"

"It's probably like the one my uncle had put in off the butler's pantry. While not underground, it's climate controlled specifically for wine storage."

After I nodded, I shoved my hands in my pockets, but an older woman bustled in with a wine glass.

"Here you are, dearie. Let me know if you need anything else."

"Thank you, Mrs. Hill."

I couldn't help but allow a small smile. "You have your own Mrs. R." I startled at a nudge to my elbow. The large cat had tightrope walked the back of the sofa so he could beg for pets.

Liz shrugged. "I suppose, except mine is Mrs. Hill, and she bakes as well as I do. She worked for Zio until his death and has been like a grandmother to me.

"Ignore Atticus. He's an attention whore."

I stopped scratching behind the cat's ears and pointed at him. "Atticus?"

"Yes, he's not shy like most cats and will beg for love from anyone. When the chimney company came to inspect the fireplaces, he chewed their equipment and tried to climb up the vent to the woodstove in my bedroom."

"I don't mind him." I continued to stroke his back. "As for Mrs. Reynolds, I was four years old when she came to work for us. Anyway, about why I came. I'm sure you're wondering what happened with Gi."

She handed me a glass of the deep burgundy liquid. "I confess I'm curious, but it's not any of my business."

I swallowed my first sip, savoring the richness of the pinot on my tongue. "I disagree. You and Gi are friends. I'd prefer you know in the unlikely event Greg turns up again. He's like a bad penny as the old saying goes."

She gestured toward a chair near the window, so I abandoned her cat to sit while she took the chair opposite. I glanced out the window. "Is that the courtyard on the side of the café?"

"Yes, although it's bigger than it looks from the café," she said. "That's the part that extends around the back of the building. I love that I have a bit of green in the view from this chair."

"I hadn't realized it was that large."

Her eyebrows drew down. "Once the tables, greenery, and fountain fill the space, it seems smaller."

"I suppose that's probably true." I shook myself. "Forgive me. I was telling you about Wickham. Pemberley Books has several investigators we keep on file for different matters. They've come in handy for theft—employee or customer depending upon the circumstances. I sent them Wickham's information and what you told me. It didn't take long to find him. He'd come to New York for modeling jobs, as he'd told you, but his work here has dried up. He's been offered a lucrative deal in the UK—one that he can't pass up."

"You arranged this?"

I lifted one shoulder. "All of his modeling jobs were coming through a particular agency. I've met the head of the company at numerous functions. He chairs a committee that raises money for art and fashion scholarships based on need. I simply promised him a generous donation should Greg need to leave the States. Wickham was on a flight out this morning."

Her eyes flared as she took a long draw from her glass. "That doesn't mean he can't contact her. He could attempt to maintain some kind of relationship from afar."

A heavy exhale poured out of me. "I confess that I'd hoped you'd let me know if she implies that's happening."

"Why not tell her the truth of what he is?"

"Because that would cause her pain. I'd rather not if I can help it."

Liz set down her glass and rose. "You can't shield her from the world. She's naïve as it is and keeping the truth of this—that he wants nothing more than her inheritance—won't help her mature. She needs to learn from this, so she doesn't trust those who are not worthy of it."

"You sound like Richard."

"Then good for him for standing up to you. I'm sure there aren't many who do, and while I agree with your motives, this was officious. You can't be her guard dog every day of her life. If something happens to you, she'll be left on her own—"

"She'd have Richard."

"Somehow, I think he'd have managed this situation differently. You've spent all of this money with an investigator. Show Gigi the proof of whatever he's done, so if he does turn up again, she's not so trusting."

I shook my head, my insides now writhing. "You've no idea what he's capable of." My voice was lower than I'd intended.

Her finger pointed right at my face. "And that's exactly why she should be told. You're making her more vulnerable to him and any other man like him." Liz's voice was somewhat raised and as she'd spoken, her arm now gesturing to the window as though all of Manhattan was filled with Greg Wickhams.

"I disagree."

She rolled her eyes and threw up her hands. "Of course you do."

I rose and pressed my finger to my chest. "I know how to take care of Gigi! I've been doing it for five years now. Do you know what it's like to go home and tell your fourteen-year-old little sister that she'll never see her mother or father again? As much as I'd wanted to protect her from that, I couldn't, so if not telling her everything of Greg Wickham saves her some heartache and horror, then that's what I'm going to do." The cat had barreled from the room, tail low, when I'd started yelling.

Liz took one step toward me. "As much as we'd love to wrap the people we love in some kind of protective barrier, we can't. It's not reality." Her tone had softened.

"And I suppose your uncle told you everything. He never tried to protect you by keeping something secret!"

"We spoke openly on almost everything! The only thing he never told me was the contents of the trust, but every day, particularly after the opening of the café, he made a point to teach me how his business worked. I just didn't realize what was going on until I was informed I was his heir."

Liz stood much closer than when we'd started arguing. A soft vanilla fragrance tickled my nose and made me lean further in.

"Perhaps that was his way of protecting you."

She gave a slight flinch, and her eyes became glassy. "I-I don't know. I never asked Mrs. Hill if she knew why." A single teardrop landed on her cheek.

My hand lifted and brushed it away. "I'm sorry, Liz. I shouldn't have brought your uncle into it."

Our gazes collided and held, and some invisible tug in my chest made me close that last little bit of space between us and press my lips to hers.

A swift inhale from her accompanied the first touch. A current traveled from my lips and through my entire body. I cupped her top and then bottom lip with mine before she began to kiss me back. My palms slid along the soft waistband of her leggings, grazing the velvet of her sides, to pull her against me.

The richness of the wine lingered on her tongue as I deepened the kiss with a groan. She fit perfectly in my embrace, her lush breasts flush with my chest. One of my hands continued to press into her lower back while the other embedded itself in the silky curls on her head.

I'd never experienced anything like this—this awareness of my entire body. I could drown myself in her and never regret it.

When her hands pushed me away by my chest, I blinked and stared at her. Everything in me screamed to take her back in my arms—to never let her go.

"I need you to leave."

I shook myself. "Did I do something wrong?"

She straightened. "You came to tell me about Gigi and Greg Wickham. Thank you for the information. Now, if you could leave."

From the first moment I'd noticed her at the gala, her eyes had almost been a window into Liz's feelings. But when she straightened, that quality in her gaze shifted. I couldn't get any glimpse of what she was feeling. A sharp pain shot through my chest like something inside it cracked.

"Liz, please talk to me."

She shook her head. "I can't. I need you to go." She closed her eyes and rubbed her forehead.

If she'd shut herself down so completely, I'd never get her to listen, even if I could get her to tell me what was bothering her.

"I'll check in with you later."

When I re-entered the elevator, I studied the selections on the keypad. How was I to get out of here? I didn't know which to press. After hovering over the keys, my finger making a circle as it did so, I hit the bottom-most button. Hopefully, that would take me to the exit.

As the elevator began its descent, I leaned against the wall and adjusted myself in my trousers. How was I still hard?

"You may as well give it up," I said, looking down. "It's not like you would've gotten any anyway."

# Chapter 11

The last week or so between Halloween and Thanksgiving flew by. I spent most of every day in the kitchens, baking cakes and pies to fill the plethora of orders we'd received, which at least helped me get my mind off that kiss! I wasn't going to comment on the two cakes I'd burned or the custard that'd stuck to the bottom of the pot and instead of a bright vanilla flavor had reeked of burned eggs, whole milk, and cream.

Thank all that was holy Char and I had the insight to hire several more hands for the holidays, or we'd have never filled all of the orders. As it was, the kitchens had operated all day with our normal business and some of the excess, and we'd implemented a night shift that came in to prepare some of the special orders that'd been scheduled for the next day. It'd been madness, and I was completely exhausted! I'd need to sleep for a week to gear up for Christmas.

My offer on the building in the East Village had been accepted. My uncle's favorite architectural firm, Gardiner Architecture, was drawing up the plans for the bookstore and the new Buttercream Beanery. While Zio had been one of my uncles, Edward Gardiner was the other. He and his wife Margaret had been around when I was growing up and I still spoke to them often, but they spent most of their days busy with their children as well as the company they'd started not long after they'd both graduated with their architecture degrees. Uncle Ed was nothing like my mother, his sister, which made me grateful. At least I had some family I could rely on now that Zio was gone.

This morning, I'd had an early morning call from Mary. We spoke on most holidays, even if she had to call before our parents were awake. Since I was persona non grata, they'd technically forbidden Mary from any communication with me, but what they didn't know, wouldn't hurt them.

That said, Mary was insisting on staying put for the moment. As much as it made my stomach tighten leaving her in that house, I couldn't exactly remove her by force.

Now, I stood in front of a penthouse door in the posh Hunsford Building. Char's girlfriend, Annie, was hosting Thanksgiving, and I'd agreed to come. The café was closed for the holiday, so I hadn't needed to worry about that for the day. Even so, my eyes were heavy from how busy we'd been as well as the lack of sleep I'd had.

I was going to bitch-slap William Darcy next time I saw him. What right did he have to kiss me and completely screw over my life? Now, whenever I closed my eyes, he was there, those soulful blue eyes closing in just before his lips claimed mine and shattered my ability to concentrate.

I shifted the weight of the cake box I held in my left arm while I lifted my right to knock. When the door opened, Char wore a huge smile and held out her arms.

"Happy Thanksgiving!"

"You can't claim you're English anymore if you're going to get so excited about Thanksgiving."

She took the cake box and ushered me inside. "Hey, any holiday that revolves around food can't be bad. Besides, Annie came out to her mother two days ago."

My eyes widened. "Oh my God, how'd it go?"

"The old biotch told Annie not to come back home, but that's okay. She has an inheritance from her father and this apartment was part of it, so she's fine. I'm also moving in, so you can rent out my apartment if you want. Now that we're in the open, there's no reason to hold off."

"Oh," I said with a start. "This *is* a bit more convenient to the new location."

Annie's apartment was in the East Village and within walking distance.

I nodded. "We'll talk about it on Monday." The café was open tomorrow and would be busy with everyone out Black Friday shopping. We'd have our own specials that day, but we'd go in early in the morning to prepare. Saturday and Sunday we'd both taken off. If we'd learned anything, there was always a lull after the holiday. People came in for coffee and sometimes sweets, but rarely had special orders.

As soon as I entered the kitchen, Annie grabbed a glass from the cabinet and poured me a huge serving of red wine. "I'm glad you could make it, Lizzy."

"Are you sure you don't mind everyone drinking?" I asked. Annie had Rheumatoid arthritis and couldn't drink due to her medications.

She gave a dismissive wave of her hand. "Please, enjoy yourself. Even if I can't drink, I'm not going to keep others from doing so."

As I picked up my glass, I leaned on the counter next to her. "How are you doing?"

She glanced at Char. "Char told you."

I opened my mouth to respond, but she shook her head. "No, it's okay. Everyone coming knows, and I told them about my mother just in case they wanted to steer clear of her bad side. I wouldn't blame them if they did."

"What was the response?"

"They're all still coming," said Annie with a choked voice and shiny eyes.

Char nudged my upper arm with her shoulder. "I never mentioned it, but Annie's mom is Catherine deBourgh."

My eyes bulged. "I've heard of your mother, of course, but I had no idea the two of you were related." I'd never seen Annie at any of the same events as Catherine deBourgh, but from what I understood, Annie had been diagnosed with Rheumatoid arthritis a few years ago, and from what Char had told me, it'd taken some time to figure out her medication regime. She may have also not cared to be a part of that scene. Char had never mentioned her partner's last name. Since Annie wasn't out at the time, I'd never asked either.

Annie lifted a shoulder. "I was always closer to my dad. I'd talked to him and more or less came out to him before he died. He left me in no doubt that he loved me no matter what. I was fortunate to have inherited everything that was his. My mother had her own business interests, and I don't need anything from those, and my father ensured I'd never need to rely on my mother. I won't ever have to work if I don't want to, and I can afford the best medical care at home should I require it."

The buzzer for the front door of the building rang, and Char hurried out.

"Char's been great," said Annie as she poured herself a glass of water. "If I didn't have her, I doubt I'd have been able to go through with telling my mother. I'm not that brave."

I grabbed her hand and squeezed. "I disagree. You face every day and whatever comes with your chin up. I admire that about you."

Annie swallowed a sip of her water and smiled. "Thank you. By the way, Char's told me some of what's occurred between you and William Darcy."

"Yeah, what about it?"

Annie dipped her chin a bit. "You do know—"

A moment later, Char entered with her eyebrows lifted. Before I could ask what that meant, Will Darcy, his cousin Richard, and Gigi followed her into the kitchen." What Annie had been about to say hit me like a brick. She was not only related to Cruella de Bourgh, but also Will. Had Char known?

"We're going to need to move this party soon, or there'll be too many to fit in here," said Richard.

"Lizzy!" Gigi rushed over to give me a hug. "I'm so excited you're here. I didn't know you knew Annie."

"I've known Annie for a while. Char is my best friend and assistant at the café. Annie comes in from time to time, and we've had dinner at my house twice and a couple of times here as well. She was just about to tell me how she's related to you." I gave Char a death glare. She had to have known. How dare she not tell me sooner!

"Speaking of the café," said Annie, "What did you bring? Char said you'd insisted on baking even though she'd told you not to."

"A pecan caramel cake." I looked to Gigi. "Char told me to make it gluten-free." More proof that Char knew of Annie's cousins before today.

"Hi," said Will.

My cheeks burned like they were pressed to a stovetop. God, how I prayed my face wasn't as scarlet red as I suspected. I'd replayed that kiss way too many times to count, and my traitorous imagination had even added to it. Will's shirt and pants might have been discarded somewhere along the way before he sprawled me out on the desk in the library. . .but I'd never tell him any of that!

Richard stepped forward and kissed my cheek. "Lizzy, I didn't know you'd be here. What a relief! I thought I'd be stuck with a bunch of sticks in the mud for the day."

He winked as Gigi backhanded his bicep. "William's the one who's worn a sour expression for the past week or so. The rest of us aren't exactly chopped liver, you know."

Richard wrapped an arm around Gigi's head and gave her a noogie. "I wasn't including you, squirt."

Gigi shoved him away and rushed out with a huff, probably to the bathroom off the hall to check her hair. Richard laughed.

"Don't be a dick," said Annie. "That old nickname might resurface."

I glanced between them. "What nickname?" Thank heavens the attention was no longer on me! Char was watching me with an appraising look I'd seen before, but as long as no one else noticed, I was good. I hoped, anyway!

"Annie used to call Richard 'Dickie' when he behaved like an ass," said Will.

"Hey, Gigi needs a big brother figure," said Richard. "You're more like her father than her brother."

I crossed my arms over my chest with the glass still in one hand. "By necessity, I'm sure. For all intents and purposes, he's had to fill both roles, hasn't he?" Everyone turned. Annie's eyebrows were lifted, and Richard wore an insufferable crooked grin that made me shrivel in place. Shit! "It's just an observation." If only I hadn't been so emphatic in Will's defense. I mean where had that come from? The last time I'd seen Will, I'd berated his officiousness, and now, I was standing up for him? Make up your mind, Lizzy!

Char chuckled. "A valid point, I'm sure."

Crap, crap, crap! I took a large drink from my wine and swallowed hard. Char could read me better than anyone—other than Zio—and I'd just given myself away.

"Who wants wine?" Annie called out.

"We don't have to drink," said Richard. "What's the fun if you can't join us?"

"As I told Lizzy, I'm good. I want everyone to enjoy today. I'm celebrating. It's not every day that I stand up to Cruella de Bourgh—"

I almost choked on my next sip.

"And I fully intend to revel in it." Annie poured glasses of wine for everyone, including Gigi who'd just entered, then held up her water. "To living free," she said. We all touched our glasses to hers before taking sips.

I set down mine on the counter and clasped my hands. "How can I help?"

Annie poured me more wine. "Relax. Char put the turkey in the oven early this morning, all the sides are baking, and what she didn't bake beforehand is prepped and ready to go in the ovens after. I may not fit through the door after this meal she has planned."

"It may be Thanksgiving," said Char, "but we're, more or less, having a traditional English Christmas dinner."

Will straightened a bit. "Sounds brilliant to me."

"She's even made the Christmas pudding," said Annie. "Along with pumpkin pie, apple pie, and homemade ice cream.

Gigi, the desserts are gluten-free, as is the stuffing and dinner rolls."

"Thank you for considering me," said Gigi.

I glanced around. "Are we expecting anyone else?"

"A few friends will come and go," said Char. "Most had plans with their families today, so they can't spend the entire afternoon, but wanted to come by for a glass of wine or dessert."

Annie laughed. "Of course, they want to come for dessert."

Richard rubbed his hands together. "I'm looking forward to it after Gi's birthday cake last month. If your baking, Char, is anything like Lizzy's, we're going to be in big trouble. You might need to roll us all out of here at the end of the night."

"Let's move into the living room," said Annie. "We'll be more comfortable and out of Char's way while she cooks."

Before I could escape, Char grabbed my sweater. "I do need Lizzy for one thing. The rest of you go ahead."

I winced. "Do we have to?"

Char shoved me into the pantry, followed me in, and shut the door behind us.

"It's dark."

With a growl, she flipped the light switch. "What the ever-loving fuck was that?"

I took another gulp of my wine. "I don't know what you mean."

"Bullshit."

The last of the wine flowed down my throat with ease. "That day you brought Will up to my library?"

"Uh huh?"

I shifted on my feet. "Well, he may have kissed me."

Her eyes nearly popped from their sockets. "May have?"

I groaned. "Okay, he did kiss me."

Char crossed her arms over her chest. "What happened to 'he's an asshole,' 'he's a tosser,' he's a—"

"You said he's a tosser."

She pointed at me. "Like you never thought it! I also tried to tell you he liked you, but nooooo, that wasn't possible, was it?"

"I don't want to do this right now. It's bad enough I'll be forced to spend the day in the same room with him. How long have you known he's Annie's cousin?"

She shrugged. "A couple of weeks or so, but that's not important. What happened when he kissed you?"

I lifted my hands. "How am I supposed to know? One moment we're arguing over his officiousness, and the next, I'm about to cry and he's kissing me. You should've told me he'd be here." My lady parts tingle at just the mention of that kiss. Great googly moogly, my body had never come alive like it did when he locked lips with mine. My thighs erupted into flames, and the memory was enough to inspire how many fantasies? Stop it, Lizzy!

I strode out of the pantry and uncorked the bottle to pour another glass of wine. This wouldn't help me cool off, but maybe it'd help me unwind a bit. Besides, I had an entire day of Will Darcy's company to anticipate. Oh, goody!

# Chapter 12

# WILL

Dinner was amazing, and I had to admit that Liz's cake was the best dessert of the bunch—I may have also had small bits of everything to check the veracity of that statement—but Liz was not faring as well as her cake. How much wine had she had so far? She'd had a glass in her hand when I arrived, and I didn't know how long she'd been here before that.

When I'd entered the kitchen, she'd looked amazing in her snug jeans and baggy grey sweater. I'd have never considered tucking in a jumper, but she'd only pushed a small piece into her belted waistband and it accentuated her trim waist without looking odd. Those heeled boots were also a distraction! I could easily envision them digging into my backside while I—No! I wasn't going to think about that. I needed to stop obsessing over Elizabeth Bennet. We were too different, and with the history of me wanting to acquire Novel Books for Pemberley Books, we'd never work out. Our kiss was proof positive that we weren't meant to be.

As much as I kept repeating that to myself, a part of me refused to listen, and I was still as infatuated now as I was that night at the gala—worse, actually.

Liz sat across from me holding a freshly filled glass. For what it was worth, Annie had refilled it a few times over the course of the afternoon. Between that and the wine with dinner and the glass of Moscato Annie had poured to go with the dessert, Liz had gone very quiet, and I hadn't missed the weave she'd made between the dining room and the living room. I'd been to the back of the group, and she'd walked in front of me—not the worst place for me to be, of course, but that one foot sliding in front of the other wasn't missed. I'd had an arm poised to help if she teetered too far off course.

She placed her glass on the end table with both hands. If no one else had any idea she was sloshed, I'd be willing to bet she knew and any others would question it after that move.

"I'll be right back," she said to Char.

She stood and made her way around the couch but hit her hip on the sofa table. The glass baubles and candles clattered, and she froze. Once nothing had fallen, she gave a snort and covered her nose. "Sorry," she said softly to Annie.

My gaze met Char's. She didn't appear as amused as her partner, who giggled. Instead, Lizzy's friend rose and followed her from the room, and after about ten minutes of foot tapping, I excused myself. When I rounded the corner, their low voices were easily discernable.

"Maybe you should lie down," whispered Char. "I'll get you a large glass of water, and once you're a bit more sober, you can always come back out."

"No, I'll just go home." Liz's words were slurred—extremely slurred. "I don't want to fall asleep and leave Atticus alone all night."

"Mrs. Hill can take care of him. You know that."

"Char, I'd prefer to be at home."

"I can take her home."

"You would?" Liz sagged against the wall.

Char turned a look on me that, without words, threatened death and dismemberment if I disobeyed. "She needs someone to watch over her. If Mrs. Hill can't manage—"

I lifted a hand as though swearing. "I've got it. I promise that I'll make sure she gets water and goes to bed. Someone will keep an eye on her after, even if I'm up all night."

Her friend watched me for a moment before nodding. "I'll grab her coat."

"Char—" Liz's head rolled along the wall until she could look me in the eye. "You better not try any fun. . .fun. . .funny bidness."

I drew a little closer to her. "I'd never take advantage of you. I prefer anyone I'm intimate with to be able to consent. You're too far gone for that."

"How much did she drink?" I asked as Char returned.

"She had about two and a half glasses before she left the kitchen. Part of that's my fault. I interrogated her about something that upset her."

"No, Char. I love you." Liz draped herself over her best friend's shoulders.

Char chuckled and hugged her back before pushing her back to the wall. "I think if you consider the drinks with the meal, she's hitting eight or nine glasses. Even though most of it was spread out some, it's a lot. She's usually a one glass drinker."

"She hasn't had any water either. She didn't touch the glass that was on the table."

"Hey! I'm right here!" Liz waved her hand between us. "Don't talk about me like I'm not."

"I'm sorry," said Char.

"You're pretty good at faking mostly sober. If I hadn't known how much you'd drank, I wouldn't have realized."

Those large brown eyes captured mine. "You say the sweetest things."

This time it was Char who snorted. "Okay, you're done. Let's get you into this coat. William will take you home, and I don't doubt Mrs. Hill will make you drink a gallon of water before you fall asleep."

"I love her too," said Liz.

I texted Jared, my driver. "Then let's go see her. You can tell her yourself."

Liz shoved herself from the wall, teetering precariously on her own feet. "Okay." She nodded, then grabbed her head by the temples. "The room is spinning."

Char shoved the coat into my hands. "I'm going to grab you a bucket. Just in case."

I got Liz's coat on her and helped her to the door where Char met us with a black mop bucket. "Let Richard know what's going on. I'll send the car back for them."

After Char agreed, I led Liz into the hallway, but before we could go further, she whirled back and hugged her friend. "I'm sorry. I didn't mean to be upset with you earlier, and I'm sorry I got pissed."

"Pissed?"

Char rubbed Liz's back. "By the time we finished our certificates, she was using a lot of English slang and vocabulary. She said it was easier while she lived in London. When she gets drunk, she uses it more. I'm not sure why."

Liz pulled herself away. "Where's the lift?" She shoved her hair back from her face. "Oh! There it is!"

"Please take care of her," said Char. "I'd take her myself if it wasn't Annie's—"

"I'll text Annie when I get her home. I promise Liz will be fine."

Char pointed with a snicker. "You better catch up then."

When I looked, Liz was walking down the hallway while sliding against the wall with her shoulder. When she reached the elevator, she lunged across, planted her hand above the panel, and pressed the button repeatedly.

"Crap!" I ran down and pulled her to stand straight, keeping her steady with an arm around her back.

Thankfully, she hadn't managed to push the button, so I hit the arrow down. We only waited a minute or so when the doors opened. I helped her onto the elevator, and since she could lean against the wall, the ride down was easier than getting her there. As soon as we were outside, Jared had pulled the car to the curb and opened the door so I could get her into the backseat.

"Liz, what's the address for the side street?"

"Huh?" Her eyes fluttered, and she pressed the heel of her hand to her forehead.

"Liz, don't fall asleep yet. I need the address where the elevator entrance is to your apartment."

"Oh." She mumbled the number and street. Thank God we'd been able to understand what she'd said.

"I'll plug it into the GPS," said Jared.

Liz let her head fall back on the seat with a groan. "I know better than to drink this much."

"Everyone's done it at one time or another. Don't beat yourself up." Goodness knows I'd been in a similar state more than once.

"Stop being so nice to me. You're normally a tosser. Don't ruin your rep."

I laughed. "Don't ruin my rep? Are you an 80's rapper?" I was a tosser? Yes, once I realized who she was, I was an ass at the gala, but I'd redeemed myself, hadn't I?

She elbowed me hard in the ribs. "Shut up." Liz covered her eyes with her hand. "Tomorrow morning's going to suck balls."

"You have to work the day after Thanksgiving?" Didn't she get any kind of a day off? The café and Novel Books did well enough that she didn't have to work at all if she didn't want to.

Her head lifted with an incredulous expression on her face. "Duh! It's the busiest shopping day of the year. You, of all people, should know that."

"I do." She ran a bakery and café. Wasn't that different?

She huffed. "For one thing, Novel Books will be packed with people Christmas shopping which will bring people into the bakery. We also mix up batches of ready-made pie crusts for pot pies. You'd be amazed how many people don't want to make their own crusts. Over the past few years, word's gotten out that they're better than the usual store-bought ones, so our crusts sell like crazy. Not to mention those who come in for coffee or lunch during a break from hitting the sales. We also sell a lot of doughnuts and pastries for those not wanting to cook breakfast over the next few days."

"I had no idea."

She huffed and dropped her hands that had been moving wildly while she spoke. "Don't you have coffee shops in any of your stores? You don't pay attention to their earnings?"

"We have contracts with coffee chains for those. They pay us rent for the space in the store, though they do provide promotional materials to our marketing team to include with our advertising. Nothing we have rivals Buttercream Beanery, though."

Liz was quiet, which made me peer over. Her eyes were closed, and she began sliding away from me, so I wrapped an arm around her and drew her to rest her cheek on my shoulder. She sighed and nuzzled closer.

When the car came to a stop fifteen minutes later, my driver made his way around and opened the door. "Sir, we're here."

"Liz, we need to get you upstairs."

She opened her eyes and groaned. "Can't I just stay here? It's warm and comfy." She snuggled closer. Jared chuckled but turned and faced away when I tried to glare at him.

I managed to scoot her to the edge of the seat and, by looping her arm over my shoulder, I lifted her to her feet. She teetered and dropped back against the side of the car, so I hauled her over my shoulder and carried her to the entrance. Jared opened the outer door and followed us in. I nodded toward the intercom panel on the wall, so he pushed the button.

"Can I help you?" An older woman's voice came after a moment or two.

"Yes, I'm William Darcy. I have Elizabeth Bennet with me. She drank too much and needs to be put to bed." It was as delicate as I could put it. What was I supposed to say?

"Oh, my. Yes, please bring her up."

"That was surprisingly easy."

Jared pointed to a camera in one corner of the ceiling. "She had all the proof she needed."

"Why don't you go home? I'll grab an Uber or a cab. It's late."

My driver perked up. "You're sure?"

The ding behind me indicated the elevator had arrived. "Positive."

Liz didn't stir as we rode the elevator up, and when we stepped off, Mrs. Hill waited in the foyer. When she hurried over, she brushed the hair out of Liz's face and shook her head while tutting.

"I can't ever remember her getting this drunk. What on earth happened?"

"I'm not sure. Char thinks she upset her around the time I arrived. I do know Liz was drinking wine pretty heavily the entire time we were there. If you'll let me know where her room is, I'll take her up for you. I'm sure you don't want her on my shoulder for the entire night." I also didn't want to take a chance she'd puke down my back.

"Forgive me," said Mrs. Hill as she bustled towards the stairs lining the wall. "This way." She led me up then down a hall before entering a room and stepping aside.

The same black and white tuxedo cat from a week ago snoozed on the comforter. At the disruption, he lifted his head and blinked.

I lowered Liz to a sitting position on the bed. "Do you have a bucket or a rubbish bin in case she gets sick?" With the effort of getting Liz into the building, I'd forgotten Char's in the car.

"I'll be back." Mrs. Hill hurried out.

Just to see if Liz would stay seated, I removed my hands from her shoulders but kept them poised if she began to lurch in any direction. Somehow, she swayed but didn't fall, so I unzipped Liz's boots and pulled them off. After I set them neatly on the floor, I supported her while I laid her down.

Her sweater had ridden up some, revealing a tank top underneath. She'd be more comfortable without the thick sweater while she slept, so I removed the heavy top. I wouldn't have done so if she'd not had on the tank, but I hated being hot while I slept.

She stirred a little and looked down. "These jeans need to come off," she said in a mumble. "Won't. . .be able to sleep. . ."

Her fingers fumbled with the button, and she let her hands drop to the bed. "Help me."

My entire body was stiff as a rail while I unbuttoned the waist and released the zipper. "There, now you do the rest while I turn around."

"Of all the times to be a gentleman," she said a little stronger this time. The rustling of sheets filled the room, and I stood stock-still waiting. My foot tapped while I trained my eyes on the doorway. Liz was taking off her jeans behind me. She'd be in a tank top and panties. My hands clenched into fists.

When everything went quiet, my foot came to a quick halt. "Liz?"

Nothing.

Was I supposed to look? Should I wait for Mrs. Hill? Why couldn't Liz have remained conscious for one more minute? I threw up my hands and let them fall. Screw it!

I peered over my shoulder, prepared to whip my head back if needed. Liz was curled into a ball on her side and had pulled the sheet over her. I exhaled heavily. Thank God! Once I covered her with the quilt, her cat came over and sniffed her face then curled up in the curve of her arm, his head resting on her wrist.

"I have the bucket." Mrs. Hill came to an abrupt stop beside me. "You took her clothes off?"

"She was wearing the tank top under her sweater. After I removed it, she woke up long enough to remove her jeans. I swear I turned my back and didn't look. She'd pulled the sheet over herself before I turned around."

"Oh," said Mrs. Hill.

"Anyway, I promised Char that I'd not leave Liz alone in case she got sick during the night. As long as you don't mind, I'll spend the night in that chair."

She patted me on the arm. "You're such a considerate young man, and I'm afraid I'm useless after eleven-thirty these days. I'd fall asleep far too quickly for that job. Why don't I bring you a cup of tea or coffee to help keep you awake?"

"Tea would be nice, thank you. We'll also need some water. Liz will need to drink if she wakes during the night."

"Yes, I'll bring that too."

I stepped after her. "Do you need any help?" It seemed like a lot to trudge up the stairs.

She paused at the door. "Don't worry about me. Mr. Philips had an elevator installed when he began having difficulty with the stairs. I don't use it often, but it'll be a great help tonight."

As soon as Mrs. Hill hurried out for a second time, I settled into the chair near the windows and pulled out my phone. I'd need a charger at some point, but I could worry about it later. It was going to be a long night!

# Chapter 13

# WILL

I shifted and turned. Why was I so uncomfortable? My forehead leaned against something soft, and I began to drift away when a groan made me shoot straight up and blink at the now bright room. "I'm awake." My eyes squinted some as I scanned my surroundings. The sheers on the windows blocked hardly any of the outside light whatsoever so no one needed to turn on a lamp to see.

Liz was lying flat on her back with her hands over her face. "I'm never drinking again."

I rose and grabbed the glass of water I'd had on the ready since she woke at two in the morning when she'd dragged herself out of bed and stumbled to the bathroom. All I'd been able to do was make sure she didn't fall flat on her face, then wait until she finished. I'd ensured she drank a glass of water before I tucked her back in bed. She'd given me a puzzled look, and I was more than convinced she'd kick me out of the house, but after a shake of her head, like she was clearing it, she drifted back to sleep.

"Sit up and drink this water," I said softly.

"If I move, I'm going to puke."

"We'll go slow. Eventually, you're going to have to get up. You can't stay like that forever."

"Why not?" I grinned at her petulant tone. She was cute when she was grumpy. "My bed is comfortable, and the pillows are like clouds. Atticus will cuddle with me. Why should I do anything else?" The aforementioned cat approached and plopped down above her head, his rumbling purr louder than I'd ever imagined possible for a feline. He sniffed her forehead then dragged his paw over his face. He must not have liked how she smelled.

"Don't you have a bakery to run?"

"Shit!" She sat straight up, swayed, and grabbed her head. Meanwhile, Atticus fled the room as though struck by lightning.

Within seconds of being upright, Liz's complexion turned green, and I grabbed the bucket, shoving it under her face. While she retched into the red plastic, I did my best to hold her hair out of the mess. I didn't look—I couldn't. That would be all I'd need to make me sick too. Poor Mrs. Hill wouldn't know what hit her.

"Oh, dear," said Mrs. Hill as she hurried in. "Let me grab the bin from the bathroom."

During a short reprieve, we swapped out the bucket for the trash can, and Mrs. Hill took the nastiness into the bathroom.

Liz shook her head while still sat hunched over the clean receptacle. "This is mortifying." She blinked and frowned up at me. "I had a dream you tucked me in last night, but I guess it wasn't a dream. I have a vague memory of leaving Annie's with you but nothing after. Why are you here?"

"Char made me promise not to leave you alone. She was worried about you." Not that I'd have left her alone to sleep it off anyway.

With a groan, Liz rested her head on the rim. "When Char was twenty, she had a friend who got drunk and asphyxiated because he was left alone to sleep off a night of heavy drinking. She's a bit fanatical about making sure she doesn't lose anyone else that way."

"You can't blame her." He and his friends in college would swap out during the night if one of them was passed out. Too often people didn't take severe intoxication seriously, yet they'd heard more than one rumor of similar happenings during those years.

"No, I don't blame her. I do understand."

I handed her the water. "Try to drink this."

She swished and spit into the bin before swallowing down the remainder. "What time is it?"

I glanced at the clock. "Eight-fourteen."

Liz shoved the trash can into my hands and pushed at the mattress to stand. "I have to get downstairs. Char will kill me for not showing up this morning."

My palm pressed to her shoulder forced her to stay where she was. "I'm sure she expected it after your condition last night. I can always go check on things if you need me to."

With one arm, she cradled the pail while she grabbed a lanyard from the side table to hold out. "Would you? Mrs. Hill will help me. Please make sure everything is okay. If they need me, I'll come down as soon as I can."

I took the card and tucked in my shirt as I headed down the hall. Retracing my steps through the maze of backrooms in Novel Books was a challenge, but after a manager enquired as to why I was in the stockrooms, I showed her the lanyard along with my explanation, leaving out why Liz was sick of course. The employee made a quick phone call then escorted me to the exit nearest the entrance to the café, but not without a sideways glance at my rumpled shirt.

"I'll let everyone know so you can return upstairs without being stopped," she said. "If you need someone to help you find your way back to the elevator, please don't hesitate to ask."

"Thank you."

The swarm of customers in Novel Books made me gape for a few minutes. While I owned bookstores—an entire chain of them—it'd been years since I set foot in one on the day after Thanksgiving. Had Black Friday always been this busy? My insides wanted to curl into a ball and huddle in a corner at the sheer number of people packing the lines to the registers.

I steeled myself. Liz had asked for my help, and I wouldn't let her down. As I wove through the crowd to the Beanery, I did all I could not to bump into every Tom, Dick, and Harry who'd intentionally left their house in this insanity.

Upon reaching the doorway to the café, I halted to gape some more. Yes, the bookstore was flooded with customers but considering its much smaller size, so was the bakery. Liz hadn't been exaggerating. The long line of patrons who stood waiting to reach the main counter extended out of the front door, every register operated by an employee ready to serve. A table with what I could only describe as a small display freezer/refrigerator was set up in one corner. A portable chalkboard reading, "The Beanery's Bestest pie dough," was erected by a table with another register. The line there stretched to the door to the courtyard and crossed the main line. Only a couple of tables were occupied inside the store, but the outdoor tables, where heaters had been set up to ward off the chill of the morning, were packed.

Employees stocked boxes and rushed here and there behind the counter when I made it to the side entrance. The girl who'd taken my order when I'd been here before was behind the counter. She shook her head. "Employees only!"

"Mia, right?"

"Yeah, but that doesn't get you back here." Her head had shaken while she spoke, but she'd never stopped moving and working.

"Lizzy's sick this morning and sent me down to see how things were going. Can I help somehow?" I held up the lanyard.

Mia leaned closer to get a good look at the card. "Char is in the kitchens. You'll need to ask her. Come on through." She lifted the counter and closed it when I squeezed behind those working and slipped into the back.

"Is Lizzy okay?" Char practically jumped on me with her question when I stepped through.

"She's puking her guts up, but Mrs. Hill is taking care of her. I promised to check on things down here to keep her from coming down herself."

"Thank you for that," said Char. Like Mia in the front, she'd never stopped moving while she spoke.

"Can I help you in some way? Make up for her absence?" I'd never so much as measured a cup of flour, but maybe there was something they needed that wouldn't require me burning down their kitchen.

For the first time, Char paused. "Go to the back. In Lizzy's office is a shelf of shirts. Once you've put one on, grab an apron. If you don't mind, you can stock the displays in the front."

"I'm not exactly artistic."

"They're going too fast to worry about that. The biggest issue we've had is the person who usually stocks for us on busy days is Lizzy or Jonathan over there, and he's filling in making pie dough since Lizzy isn't here."

The shirts were easy to find, and luckily, they had multiple colors, so I could choose which I preferred. Once I had on a lighter slate blue like what was in the café, I grabbed an apron off the wall and hurried to the front.

Char pointed at the sink. "Wash your hands, put on gloves, then take that tray of pumpkin cheesecake brioche doughnuts to the front. Swap the trays out and if there's any still on the old tray, put them to the back of the new one. Okay?"

So the tray wasn't knocked from my hands, I lifted it over my head when I exited the kitchen. A perk of being over six feet was the tray was out of everyone's way up there.

The display cases had their contents labeled on the outside, so it didn't take long to find the right door. I slid it open. The old tray was empty, so I removed it and slid the new one into place.

"Thank God!" said Mia. "I've had two orders for a dozen of those. I've been waiting for five minutes for them to come out. If there's more, don't hesitate to bring them. If we can get some of the people waiting out of here, the front won't be so crowded."

"What else do you need?"

"Bagels of any variety, maple scones, and anything you see that's low."

"Got it," I said.

I relayed the information when I got to the back. The bagels were ready to go, much to the relief of those in the front. For the next eight hours, I didn't stop running. Once the breakfast rush had lessened, we prepped for lunch, which lasted until two. When I wasn't needed to stock the displays anymore, I chipped in on wiping down tables.

When they were able to let the first shift leave for the day, Char hugged me. "I can't thank you enough for this. We were struggling until you showed up."

"My feet have never ached so badly in my life," I said with a laugh.

She looked down and laughed. "Well, Italian leather shoes aren't exactly made for standing for long periods. If you ever help us again, you'll need to wear some with better support and cushion." She pointed down to her clunky Dr. Martens. "We all have our favorite go-to so our feet don't hurt.

I changed back into my shirt in Liz's office and threw the apron and shirt in the hamper filled with the other aprons. Liz's lanyard was around my neck, as safe a place as any while I'd helped out, and I made my way back through the stockrooms to the elevator. When I stepped off, Mrs. Hill was coming down the stairs.

"How's she doing?"

"I gave her some acetaminophen after you left, and more water. She fell asleep holding a clean bucket I'd found. I kept an eye on her until she woke about a half-hour ago. She's showered and changed, but she's quiet. I'm not sure what's going on in that head of hers, but I'll warn you now, if she feels she let Charlotte or the bakery down, she'll be way too hard on herself."

"Thanks for the heads up." Do you mind if I go up? I left my phone in the bedroom when I went to the bakery."

She patted my forearm. "I noticed that. I plugged it in on Lizzy's bedside table while you were gone."

"Thank you," I said as I continued toward the stairs.

The door was open when I reached Liz's bedroom, but I still knocked. When she called for me to enter, I stepped inside. Her voice had been muted some and the room was empty, so she must've been in the bathroom.

I hadn't had an opportunity to see the room much last night or this morning. The space was large with paneled walls that were painted a muted blue—a lot like the color in the café—with a grey upholstered headboard, a pale grey comforter so light it was almost white, and a pale blue knitted throw over the foot of the mattress. The wood floors had an area rug that ran under the bed and contained the different colors from the room. Most of her dressers and side tables were whitewashed wood and glass. The effect was a light and airy space that fit Liz well.

When she entered, she still had dark circles under her eyes, but even so, I couldn't imagine anyone more lovely. "How are you feeling?"

"A little better. I should thank you for getting me home. You didn't have to stay, but I do appreciate that you did. What happened when you left? You never came back after going to check on the bakery."

"You were right about the crowd. When I got down there, the bookstore as well as the café were slammed. Charlotte asked if you were okay—"

"And you didn't come tell me. Char needed me. How dare you make that decision for me?"

Even with Mrs. Hill's warning, I balked at her hard tone. "Char was glad I'd kept you from going in to work. What good would you have done while dry heaving every five or so minutes in the closest trash can? Mrs. Hill said you slept, which was probably the best thing you could've done.

"They were cleaning up when I left five minutes ago. The day was massively busy and when you do the figures for the day, I'm sure you'll be pleased. I don't know how you wouldn't be."

I scratched the back of my neck. "Look; I'd like to take you out to dinner."

"Now?"

I balked. "No, not necessarily today. Before you say no, I know we're very different, and you're upset that I'd wanted to buy out your uncle's bookstore—that I was waiting to see if the business would falter after his death. I mean, it didn't, but I also didn't know that you knew anything about running a bookstore when I crafted that plan. You run a bakery, after all." I kind of chuckled while she stood, her mouth slightly open. "That said, I can't say I'm a fan of your family—I met them a few months ago at a party Charles Bingley gave. Your sister Jane makes me nervous. I'm afraid she'll eat me or anyone else alive if given the chance. That company your father runs seems barely solvent, and your mother's obsession with Jane marrying for wealth is obvious. I warned Charles away from dating Jane, but he didn't listen." I shrugged. The one time Charles had shown any sort of backbone, and it was to make Jane his girlfriend. Maybe that meant something. He wasn't exactly an angel either.

I shook myself. "Anyway, what do you think? Would you go out with me?" Why did I suddenly feel like I was eighteen again and stumbling madly over my own tongue?

She stiffened. "What was it you said at the gala? It wasn't like I was beautiful?"

Flinching, I started to speak but she took a step closer.

"I believe that was exactly what you said. I also came to you in the hopes of protecting Gigi, and your solution did nothing to show her where she was vulnerable—to help her become more self-sufficient. You ensured Wickham left, but she remains susceptible to the next shit-for-brains that approaches her."

She crossed her arms over her chest. "As for my family, there's a reason I don't have anything to do with any of them—except Mary, although I'm sure you didn't meet her. My parents prefer to pretend she doesn't exist, but you wouldn't know that since you don't know much about me. You've just stared at me whenever we're in the same room. For some reason, I thought you disapproved of me or were gawking at whatever you found unattractive."

"You aren't unattractive," I managed to blurt.

"You're the one who said I wasn't beautiful. Those were your words. Then there was last night! When I woke up this morning, I couldn't understand why you'd bring me home. When I went to the bathroom in the middle of the night and you handed me that glass of water, I really did think it was a dream. No way would the William Darcy I've known still be here, much less be giving me water.

"But you were still here in the morning and willing to check on the café for me. I'd planned to go down if Char needed me, but you never returned. Of course, I'd fallen asleep so I'd no idea until it was too late. Then you return and tell me they were overwhelmed, and you didn't tell me! You disappeared for eight hours. What'd you do? Laugh that they were in the weeds then went to check on your own profits for the day?"

A sharp slice tore through my insides. According to Liz, I was heartless. I could defend myself, but what was the point? She'd already made up her mind. Anything I said right now would fall on deaf ears.

"Since you aren't arguing, I can assume I'm correct," she said. "Get out! I don't know how someone as sweet as Gigi was partially raised by you."

I didn't need to hear anymore. I strode over to the side table and retrieved my phone and jacket before walking out of the room.

When I stepped into the hall, Char was leaning against the wall. By her tightly pressed lips, she'd at least heard part of what was said, if not all. "Why didn't you tell—?" Her voice was soft.

"Because she won't listen." I kept my own equally low. "Don't worry about it."

I had to get out of here. With a hand lifted, I waved at Char. She shook her head, but I didn't stay. Everything in me was about to collapse, and I needed to be at home—alone—when that happened.

# Chapter 14

I dropped onto the bed and covered my face with my hands. What in the hell was Will thinking? After the gala and everything since, what would make him think I liked him? I doubt he truly even liked me for that matter. His expression when he stared was always so severe. Either he was extremely constipated, or he was confused, and I was inclined toward the former.

"Elizabeth Bennet! What was that?"

My hands dropped. I should've known Char would check in on me. "Will asked me out. Why would he do that?"

Char tossed her coat on the bed then propped her hands on her hips. "Probably because he likes you. And you ripped him a new one—a gaping wound from what I heard. That wasn't well done, Lizzy. You're always so aware and concerned about the feelings of others, then you go and treat him as if he doesn't have one shred of emotion in his heart. I'm ashamed of you."

I shot to my feet, and my head throbbed with the sudden change in position. "You're ashamed of me? We've discussed the situation with Gigi and how he could've handled it better, especially with her naïveté. How does what he did help?"

She sighed. "His methods did get the man away from her. If Mary was in that situation, how would you have handled it? Maybe you need to consider that."

"Okay, fine then! Let's talk about the gala, when he said I wasn't beautiful."

"As I've said before, others have been critical of your looks and figure, and you've always laughed," said Char. "Maybe you need to consider why his comments get under your skin and fester."

Fester? No, any woman would've been insulted. I held up a finger. "He was supposed to let me know if you needed help this morning. The kitchen phone wasn't broken last I checked. He could've called up, but no, he didn't even return until a few minutes ago." I propped my hands on my hips. What excuse could she give for that?

Char's eyebrows lifted. "Are you fucking kidding me? That was part of this?"

"He was probably walking around the bookstore spying."

"Oh, my God. Do you hear yourself?" Char gave an incredulous bark and put her hands on her head while she shook it. "I can't believe this. Do you want to know what that man did all day?"

"There's nothing—"

"Yes. Yes, there is. You didn't let him defend himself—you berated him so badly, I'm certain he didn't see the point in trying. So, I'm going to plead his case for him. I know you don't want to hear it, but tough shit!"

"Char—" It wasn't like Char could say one thing that would make this better, that would redeem Will Darcy.

She held out a hand, palm toward me. "You *will* stop and listen for once. That man who you just stomped all over was at the bakery *all day*, for at least 8 *hours*, working his *ass* off! He didn't have time to phone!"

I opened my mouth to argue back, but her words hit me—really hit me. I bent forward a little. "I beg your pardon?"

"He showed up in the kitchens this morning, said you were sick, and asked if there was anything he could do to help. I told him where to get a shirt and an apron. Then, that man who you just treated like crap on a stick re-stocked the displays, wiped down tables and counters, and loaded the dishwasher. He busted his ass all day, and what did he get in return? He came upstairs, and you told him what a tosser he is. How he can't possibly like you, how he buggered the situation with Gigi, how he stares at you like he's looking to find fault.

"That man was a lifesaver today. Mia was scrambling to fill orders. She'd already come into the kitchens to see if we had items that were depleted in the displays so customers weren't waiting. Even *she* sang his praises after he left, and you know she doesn't give compliments easily. If he were to walk in tomorrow, she'd hook him up with whatever she could give him whether he's a millionaire or not."

The balloon of indignation that had filled my chest since Will stood before me collapsed. Char had delivered a series of sharp jabs and released every last bit of air. My legs refused to hold me up, so I sank to the bed. Why hadn't Will said anything?

"Probably because you were so severe on him, he didn't have a chance. Would you even have believed him if he had? If he'd stood before you and told you that he'd done the grunt work at the bakery, you'd have laughed at the idea. You wouldn't have given anything he said any credit. You know that's exactly how it'd go, too. From the moment you learnt who he was at the gala and he'd said what he did, you were determined to think him the devil. With the exception of trusting him with Gigi's situation, he possessed no redeeming qualities whatsoever."

Had I said the last part aloud? It didn't matter, I deserved everything Char just dished out and more. I squeezed my eyes closed then reopened them. "You're right." What else could I say?

Char was about to say whatever, but she paused, her mouth gaping. "I'm sorry, but did you just say that I'm right?"

"Shut your gob, Char."

She crossed her arms over her chest. "No, I'm enjoying this too much. You don't behave this stubbornly often, but when you do, you're never willing to admit that you're wrong. Let me enjoy it for a moment." She smiled and feigned basking in the sun.

"You're ridiculous." I rubbed my forehead.

"No, I'm your best friend, and because I am, I'll never agree with you when you're wrong, and I'm going to do my damnedest to make you see it. I'm not saying William Darcy is perfect, but he's not the villain you've painted him to be—that you believe him to be. His actions with Gigi are a brother doing his best to protect his sister. I agree that if Greg Wickham is that bad, Gigi should know what he is. Unfortunately, we don't have that information. Maybe, after some time, William will tell her. It's all we can hope. I'm sure you can understand wanting to protect her. You've done your best to help Mary over the years, haven't you?"

"That's a different situation, but yes. She turns eighteen in two weeks. I think I'm going to have a roommate after that."

"She can always move into your old flat."

"When are you moving in with Annie?"

"I'm slowly bringing things over, but I'm already living there. I'll let you know when I get the place cleared."

"You know I'm not going to rush you out. That apartment is yours for as long as you need it."

"And you know I appreciate it. I have to admit that rent free in New York City is a major plus. I'll never be able to repay you."

"I don't need the money, Char. I'd rather you have a good place to live, and I admit that I liked having you close by. We could hang out as often and as long as we liked and not have to worry about one of us getting home. What am I going to do with you moving out?"

She laughed. "Well, Annie's is not that far. We'll have you over, and you can invite us here. We're not just friends, Lizzy, we're family. I'm sure Mary will fit right in with the inmates of the asylum when she comes. We're all a bit mental but we're a friendly bunch."

I rubbed my head and closed my eyes. My temples were starting to throb again. I'd been drunk on wine before and never gotten sick like I was this morning.

"Do you have a bad head?" She sat beside me.

"I can't get over that all I drank was wine and I feel like this." Had I somehow dropped a Jager Bomb without knowing it?

Char gave a snort-laugh. "You also drank about two and a half bottles."

My head popped up, and I pressed my palm to my forehead. "Two bottles? There's no way."

"By my count, you had at least eight very large glasses of wine. Annie didn't hold back when you arrived, but she also thought you'd sip it. Neither of us took into account that you might start drinking it as if it was water and you'd been stranded in the Sahara for two days. By the time I followed you to the bathroom, you were hiding it well, but you were sloshed. I didn't want to leave Annie the first time she'd hosted a major holiday, and William readily offered to take you home."

"And you begged him to stay in case I got sick during the night."

Her eyebrows drew together a bit. "He responded like it was a forgone conclusion—like he wouldn't have expected to do otherwise. If I had to guess, he would've stayed whether I asked him to or not."

"God, I feel like a—"

"Beeotch, wanker, daft prick—"

"Okay," I said with a weak laugh. "Point taken."

"You need to apologize to him."

I shook my head. "I'm not sure how."

"Don't you have his contact information? I thought you said he gave you his phone number after you went to him about Gigi."

I blew out a breath. "I'd forgotten about that. I'll see if I can find it."

"Did you will it to burst into flames or something?"

My head rested on her shoulder. "I put his card in my pocket. Whether or not it's there or Mrs. Hill took it out when it was laundered is another story."

Char sucked air through her teeth. "You never put the number in your phone?"

"No."

"Maybe we can find a reason to get it from Gigi this week? Like to thank him again for all of his help."

I straightened and scrubbed my face. "I think I want to snuggle under the covers and watch a rom-com with Atticus—

forget today happened for a little while. Will we need to go down and clean up the café and bakery in the morning?"

She shook her head. "No, between William's help and everyone chipping in when the crowds died down, we're set to go. When I left, the displays had enough for any late-comers and the evening crew was on for anyone who came for coffees. We were up over last year by about five thousand, which is huge for one day. It's no wonder we had trouble keeping up.

"I wrote down some notes in your office for the day after Christmas. It's not so dissimilar after all."

I nodded. She was right. The day after Christmas was a variation on a similar theme. People shopping to get deals and those who come in looking for a sweet treat, snack, or filler for their leftovers. Selling our pie crusts was the idea of one of our customers three years ago. She'd commented how she wished we'd sell our pie dough. Now, we always kept some available in the refrigerators and it's on the menu in the front, but it'd become an extremely popular item before and after the holidays. However, the demand for a savory crust was more afterward when everyone was looking for new ways to eat leftover turkey.

"What am I going to do when you move to the new location? I'm going to be lost."

She nudged me with her shoulder. "No, you won't. Mia deserves a promotion and a raise. You'll be able to afford that with my salary coming out of the budget for the new bakery. You'll promote Lucy as well. She's been shadowing me for long enough. When she arrives before me, she doesn't hesitate to get to work and has taken a load off of my back as she's become more confident in her abilities. I don't think you'll notice much of a difference."

"Except I can't gossip with her."

Char laughed. "We don't gossip. We share stories and talk about stupid things—Instagram reels, whatever I've seen on YouTube.

"Now, you'll get to know Lucy better by listening to her ideas on monthly specials and what she can bring to the bakery. I think she's going to be amazing. You'll need to open a location in Queens or Brooklyn or maybe a smaller store on the Upper East Side in a few years for her to run."

I waved my hands in front of me. "One at a time, please! I don't know how Will does it. How many stores does he have?"

"He has an entire high-rise building of employees helping him out."

I sighed. "I've already considered that the apartments over the children's section may have to be converted at some point into more office space. Eventually, we're going to need more management on a corporate level. Two months ago, I offered Gracie a position as social media/marketing executive, and she needs an office. She's been rocking the internet for a while now, and she's one class from graduating with her degree in May. I don't want to lose her. Will's cousin was asking me yesterday who did our social media."

"What'd you tell him?"

With a chuckle, I smiled at her. "That whatever torture and interrogation techniques he was thinking of wouldn't work. That it was a secret I'd take to my grave. He just grinned and told me he'd say the same thing and complimented her savvy with the campaigns she runs."

"Wow," said Char. "Doesn't he run marketing for Pemberley?"

"Exactly. I'm glad I offered her the position before she decided to go job hunting. At the end of six months, we'll evaluate her salary and make any adjustments she needs."

"You're doing a great job, Lizzy. Zio's looking down and beaming at how well you've done."

I blinked back the burn of tears. "I hope so. I can't fail him."

Char put an arm around my shoulder. "Hey, even if you lost everything in some freak circumstance, Zio would never be disappointed. He loved you too much. He'd also not want you to eat, sleep, and breathe either of the businesses."

"Okay, Mom," I said. Char often brought up my lack of a love life. Was it my fault no one appealed to me? Okay, no one but Will had appealed to me. Most of the men I met ingratiated themselves to me when they learned I owned a successful business. I didn't need an overgrown child making a mancave in Zio's living room and playing video games all day long.

"Do you realize that everyone calls William Darcy 'William' except for you. Even Gigi calls him that, but when you're relaxed and not in public, you call him 'Will.' Haven't you wondered why?"

I scoffed and shook my head. "That's only because he introduced himself to me that way at the gala."

"Is it?" asked Char.

"Of course. What other reason could there be?"

Char gave me one of those TV-mom looks. "I think you need to think about that one some more too."

# Chapter 15

*One week after Thanksgiving*

"Lizzy?"

I blinked.

"Lizzy?" It was said louder this time, making me startle.

"Sorry?"

"Where were you?" asked Gracie, who was laughing. "I started discussing my ideas for a Christmas promo, and you completely zoned out."

I shook my head. "I'm sorry. I'm interested. I am, but you do know that I trust you, don't you?"

The younger woman sat up a bit straighter. "You do?"

With a laugh, I sat up at my desk. Gracie had come to the house to update me on what she was working on. She liked to do it, even though I'd never told her she had to. "You've run a bunch of campaigns and made posts to update our customers and bring them into the store for three years now. I believe you started your sophomore year at NYU. Richard Fitzwilliam, the head of marketing at Pemberley Books would steal you out from under me if I was willing to tell him how to get in touch, which I'm not. He raved on Thanksgiving about your ideas."

"He did?" Gracie's cheeks turned pink.

I pointed at her. "Don't get any ideas!"

She held up her hands, palms out. "Hey, I'm not interested in Pemberley Books. This has been a family to me since I came to the city. I love it here. Nothing they could offer would induce me to leave."

"I'm glad to hear that," I said. "Now, about that office. Come with me." I waved her to follow me to the elevator. We took it down a floor where I led her off and through a locked door to the left. "When we built the offices on this floor, we didn't use the entire space. I've been trying to figure out where to put you when I was told this by my uncle's former assistant, Mr. Stone. Turns out we have the skeletons of the remaining apartments on this floor that we'd never renovated.

"The door was installed to keep people from entering." The hallway wasn't long but creepy since it needed work and the window at the end gave an eerie glow to the worn wooden floor.

"I asked that they finish the corridor. The remaining apartments will be gutted, and more offices and a new larger conference room will be put in. Our management team has never been big, but with the addition of the online store last year, we've filled the existing offices we already had. We'll also have a few changes on the other side to maximize our space."

When I opened the door on the first apartment to the right, I let Gracie walk in ahead of me. "I've given instructions that this entire apartment be renovated with a large gathering space in the living room here for you to meet with management or anyone we might hire to join your team. The fireplaces will be inspected and repaired if needed, the bathroom will be updated. I thought it might be helpful since you sometimes change to film different content. The kitchen will be taken out, but you'll have a cabinet installed for a coffee station and a mini-fridge. If you have meetings or an author you're entertaining before a promotion, I'd like you to have an office that stuns. What do you think?"

She gave an incredulous bark. "Lizzy, it's more than I need."

I grinned at her. "Then, I'd say it's perfect."

Gracie had begun greeting our guest authors for their events, and while she typically brought them to the conference room until they were announced, I wanted her to have a more comfortable space for her visitors. We were smaller than the big retailers, but we'd have style and a personal touch they lacked.

Besides, Gracie had always been modest. I'd no doubt she'd use the space, or I wouldn't have planned it that way. She brought in too much business for her to get a tiny corner office with no amenities or view. When she'd asked to do the social media, we'd needed someone, and she swore she'd build our following. She'd more than delivered. We'd given her raises over the years, but this recognition was long overdue as far as I was concerned.

"Hello?"

I frowned and backed out of the doorway. "Richard?"

"Ah, there you are." He stepped from the vestibule of sorts into the hallway and scanned his surroundings. "Wow, this building is huge on the inside." He looked at Gracie then back at me.

"It's still okay if I work in the conference room for now, isn't it?" asked Gracie.

"Of course. Gardiner Architecture will be calling you to discuss the plans and the design. The space has to fit what you need, and you should have a say in that."

She glanced between Richard and me.

With a chuckle, he extended his hand. "Hi, Gracie, I recognize you from Novel Books' social media, of course. I'm Richard Fitzwilliam, head of marketing at Pemberley Books. I'm envious Lizzy discovered you before I could. You do amazing work."

Gracie accepted his handshake. "Thank you." She looked to me. "I'll just be getting back to work."

"Thanks, Gracie," I said, shifting to let her by.

Richard glanced around. "She doesn't have her own office yet?"

"She was hired not long after she moved to the city for college. When she'd asked the store management about her taking over the social media, they were hesitant. I didn't see what it could hurt so I convinced my uncle. We'd all chipped in as best we could for both businesses, but none of us had the time to devote to it full-time. She's managed both Novel Books and the Beanery's accounts and has done a brilliant job."

"I agree."

"If you so much as make her an offer. . ."

He held up his hands. "Relax! That's not why I'm here. I'd need to fire or find somewhere else for someone on my team, anyway. I have no grounds to do that."

"Then why are you here?" I didn't mean to be abrupt, but him showing up here, of all places, had my hackles raised.

With a sigh, he ran his fingers through his hair. "Do you mind if we go somewhere to talk? I don't want to be overheard."

I gestured for him to follow. We entered the elevator, and I scanned my card. "Nothing's wrong with Gigi, is there?"

He shook his head. "No, she's good. I saw her in the café when I came in. I went there first looking for you."

"How did you find me?" It was odd that he just showed up in our offices without an escort.

"One of the bookstore employees brought me up. When you said my name, he returned to the front counter."

When we stepped off the elevator to my apartment, Richard stopped on the marble floor and gawked. "I didn't even know this was up here. How big is this place?"

I shrugged. "I don't know. My uncle had it all knocked out and renovated for him. It's still strange that it's mine now."

"I'm sorry," said Richard. "You speak of him like you were close."

"He was more my father than my own ever tried to be." I led Richard into the library. "Would you like some water? I also have sodas or whatever you'd like."

Richard was still looking around, his head noticeably scanning from ceiling to floor. He paused at the tree near the window. "How many Christmas trees do you have?"

"The one in the foyer has been a tradition for as long as I can remember. Mrs. Hill insisted my uncle needed a family tree in here since this is where he spent most of his time." I kind of liked having one in here. If I ever had a family, I could see putting another in the living room too, but at the moment, just the two.

"Did you want that drink?"

He startled. "Oh, sorry. Coffee would be great."

I pulled out my phone to text Mrs. Hill. "Anything specific? Latte? Your cousin likes peaberry."

Richard shook his head. "I'm not a fan of peaberry. If I can't stand a spoon in it, it's not coffee."

"Espresso it is then," I said with a laugh.

"That'll work."

I gestured for him to sit. "So, what is it you want to discuss?"

"Darcy's been acting odd for the last week. It started when he returned to the penthouse on Black Friday. Char had mentioned he took you home on Thanksgiving and that he'd agreed to stay and keep an eye on you for the night. He'd texted Gigi that morning to let her know he wouldn't be home until later, but when he did return, he looked like he'd been drug home by a car."

"Someone hit him?" I squeaked.

"No, he just looked haggard. He went into his study, and we didn't see him again that evening. Mrs. R. mentioned he'd finished the bottle of Scotch he keeps in there. She believed it was half-full, so we're sure he was drunk when he went to bed."

I winced. That was a lot of alcohol for one man, even if he was over six feet.

"Gigi and I are worried about him. It's just so unlike him. Do you know anything that could've happened?"

Mrs. Hill hurried in and set down Richard's espresso on the side table. "Here you are."

"Thank you," he said.

My palms sweated as I rubbed one hand up and down the leg of my jeans. How was I to explain this? "William did bring me home. He slept in a chair in my room from what Mrs. Hill told me. That morning, I was sick, so he checked on the bakery for me. He was down there all day, helping Char with filling displays and wiping down counters and tables."

Richard's head jolted forward and a bit to the side. "I'm sorry, but did you just say that my cousin engaged in manual labor?" He didn't wait for the answer before he gave a low chuckle. "I would've paid a lot of money to witness that."

"Char said William saved them. We were busier this year than we've ever been, and while we had staffed heavily, we needed a couple more people to keep supplies available and to clean up. Gracie was running flash sales on social media all day.

It brought a lot of people into the café for lunch as well as for some baked goods."

Richard shook his head. "He's never worked in a coffee shop or bakery before. I've never known him not to put his all into something, but it still would've been amusing to see my cousin refilling pastry displays."

I inhaled deeply and released it. "When he returned, I was upset he never texted me or returned to tell me what was happening. He was afraid I'd go down and try to help; so was Char for that matter. We were discussing what happened at the café when all of a sudden, he asked me out."

Richard hit the arm of the sofa with the bottom of his closed fist. "I knew he had a thing for you! Gi even noticed his expression while he watched you. She was grossed out by it to tell the truth."

My chin jerked back. "Why would she be grossed out?"

Richard tilted his head. "Would you want to see desire on your brother's face?"

I jolted from my chair. "Char said that was how he looked at me too, but I never saw it. How did everyone realize that but me?"

"Maybe you didn't want to see it," said Richard.

"First Char and now you're lecturing me on it."

He put up both hands, palms out. "Hey, I'm not lecturing. The first time I met you was at Gi's party, but since Darce invited you that night, I'd say the two of you'd met before."

"We met at the gala for the Starry Night Foundation. It was the first one I'd attended without my uncle. I was exiting the ladies' room when he ran into me from behind. My foot slipped off my heel and the strap broke." I laughed. "He was appalled that I took them off, threw them in the trash, and walked around barefoot. My gown was floor length, it's not like anyone knew."

Richard chuckled and shook his head. "I can imagine his expression. He can be a germaphobe. Mrs. R. has commented that his bathroom is never dirty. She still scrubs it a couple of times a week, but he cleans up after himself. He takes his shoes off in the foyer then carries them upstairs. He doesn't like tracking in the dirt from the street. Anyway, I'm surprised there isn't more to the story."

"Oh, I wasn't done. He offered to buy me a drink to make up for the shoes. I'd decided to be a little ornery, so I'd ordered Aberlour neat—a double."

Richard barked out another laugh. "Another thing he doesn't see much. A woman who isn't afraid to challenge him."

"To be fair, I'd no idea who he was. I knew Pemberley Books wanted to purchase Novel Books, but we weren't for sale, so that was that. I didn't see a need to look up the CEO to see who wanted to buy us out. My uncle had offers as well and had never taken them either. He also had a sale proposal from another large store bookseller. He refused them too. In his journals, he said that he'd always intended to leave Novel Books to me. Since I had no intention of giving up my uncle's legacy, who William Darcy was didn't matter.

"That night, at the gala, we were having a friendly enough time together until Will was summoned by your aunt. He promised to return, but before he did, that guy Bingley and my sister Jane approached him."

Richard almost sneered. "Bingley has rubbed me the wrong way for years."

"Yes, well, then he'll probably get along fantastically with Jane. When they started the conversation, my sister informed Will who I was, and he basically said that he hadn't any idea that it was me and it wasn't like I was beautiful."

Richard's eyes almost bulged from their sockets. "Please tell me you're joking."

"Not in the slightest."

"So when he asked you out. . ."

"I didn't know what he'd been doing all day and my impression of him was not the greatest. What occurred at the gala as well as Wickham and other little things continued to fuel my dislike of him. So, when he asked me out, I told him where he could shove his offer for dinner."

Richard exhaled and took a sip of espresso, obviously thinking about what I'd said. "He mentioned you didn't like how he handled the situation with Wickham."

"Gigi is sweet and trusting. Those are lovely qualities to have except she doesn't always see people's motives. A couple of people who came with her group over the past year have seemed more ingratiating than trying to be a true friend. I'll admit that they never last long, but I've also noticed that some of her friends will give the newcomer a hard time. Two of her friends in particular stick out and almost behaved as though they were Gigi's protectors, although I haven't seen them in the past couple of months."

Richard sighed. "Those two were an argument I'd had with my overprotective cousin. They were bodyguards. They went to classes with her—somehow Darce had arranged for Julliard to let them attend—and they ensured they became friends with her."

"They looked her age." They couldn't have been a day over twenty.

"I know. They were selected by the agency because of that. I felt it was wrong to let her believe they were friends when they were being paid to be there. One said that they were transferring to another school, and the other told her she had to leave to help a sick grandmother. So, you aren't off that Darce can overstep.

He also needs someone who isn't afraid to tell him where he's screwed up. What I have to say doesn't always get through his thick skull."

"Are you here to talk me into giving him a chance?" I regretted being so harsh with Will, but I hadn't decided if I regretted turning him down. Yes, I was attracted to him, and when we talked at the gala, he was charming and not the stiff, staring man I'd come to know. Was that man at the gala an aberration or was he the real Will? The problem was I had no way of knowing.

Richard shook his head. "My uncle and aunt were wonderful people. Darce is one of the most loyal people I know."

"You make him sound like a dog."

With a bark of a laugh, Richard shook his head again. "I do, don't I? Look. You have to make up your mind about whether Darce is right for you. I understand if you feel he's not. It's just that I feel like you'd be good for him."

Richard stood with his brow furrowed. "I need to get back to the office. But just so you're aware; Darce did call off any and all research and development projects for the acquisition of Novel Books."

My insides leaped as I rose. "When did he do that?"

"I believe sometime between Gi's birthday and Thanksgiving. I don't know for sure, but Bingley wasn't happy. He lives for the kill, and Darce cut him off at the knees." As we walked back out to the elevator, Richard glanced at me over his shoulder. "Are you planning to attend the Pemberley Yule Ball? We're raising money for reading programs in underprivileged areas."

I drew my eyebrows together. "I don't remember my uncle ever attending that one."

"As I recall," said Richard. "He did when my uncle was alive. The two of them had a mutual respect and dare I say, friendship. Uncle George had made your uncle offers for the store, but your uncle would turn him down with a laugh. I think it was more of a game between them. Darce didn't understand the nature between them when he took over. He treated it more like any other acquisition.

"I do hope you'll come. I'll have my assistant send you an invitation."

I lifted one of my brows. "You mean I don't have to pay for the ticket?"

He chuckled. "You can be a guest of Pemberley Books. We'll just expect a hefty donation at the event."

I grinned. "I've got most of the business's money earmarked for projects at the moment, but I'll check into our budget for charities and see what I can scrounge up."

He smiled back. "You do that."

# Chapter 16

The Christmas season was chugging along at a frantic pace. Novel Books was packed every day with shoppers searching for gifts. We had extra crews coming in after closing to restock and clean. Meanwhile, the Beanery was way up on profits for another year. The holiday cakes I'd planned were selling like hotcakes to those wanting a slice with their coffee, and we'd had orders galore for whole cakes as well. We'd even agreed to furnish desserts for several office parties coming up, so we'd been prepping what we could in advance so we weren't slammed at the last minute.

This afternoon, we'd just finished a huge order for one party that would be picked up at four. My feet were killing me, I had a crick in my back, and I desperately needed a hit of caffeine.

"Mia, could you ask Henry to make me a latte, please?"

"Salted caramel?"

I nodded and headed back to my office to remove my apron. After tossing it in the hamper, I logged off the computer. Mia would be doing the deposit later, and I'd created log-in information for her. She was learning all of the management duties without faltering—not that she hadn't been running what happened behind the counter for the past year or two. Now, she merely had more authority behind her.

When I returned to the front, the steaming cup was put into my hand, and I could've melted at the aroma wafting from the rich brew. The salted caramel syrup was mixed in well and the flavor exploded on my tongue when I took my first sip.

"How could you?"

When I brought the cup down, Gigi was standing in front of me. "Hi, Gigi." Even if I hadn't heard what she'd said, her red eyes and blotchy face showed she'd been crying. "Richard must've told you that I turned your brother down. I'm sorry—"

Gigi scrunched up her face, her chin drawn back. "What are you talking about? I mean going to my brother about Greg."

Oh, shit!

I held up a finger. "Before you say anything else, come with me." I could see this getting ugly, and the floor of the café wasn't the ideal spot for any confrontation.

Thankfully, Gigi didn't fight me as I took her hand and led her into the back. The stockroom manager's office was empty, so I pulled Gigi inside and closed the door. "I suppose it's safe to assume your brother enlightened you concerning Greg."

She threw her hands up. "Oh, he had all sorts of things to say about Greg. William told me about how you came to him after I visited the bakery with Greg. Why would you go to my brother behind my back?"

I set down my coffee and grasped her by the shoulders, but Gigi wasn't having it. She whipped back from me. "Don't treat me like a child."

"I have no intention of doing so. But you have to remember back to that day in the bakery. Would you have listened if I'd told you my suspicions?"

"What do you mean?"

"If I'd pulled you aside and said that Greg gave me the heebie-jeebies, would you have listened? I had a gut feeling with no proof. He was slick—too slick—and you were blind to that fake move of him reaching for his wallet. He had no intention of paying."

She sniffled. "You don't know that."

"Do I know exactly what was running through his mind? No, no one can know that, but I've had people who used me to get to my uncle. When I was in college, people would behave as though they were my friend, then want to meet Zio. It never took long to figure out who was legitimate and who could've cared less for me. It's a skill you need to learn, which is why I was angry with your brother for arranging matters as he did without cluing you in on Greg. Did he tell you that? Let you know what Greg is really like?"

Gigi deflated and a tear tracked down her cheek. "William had police reports. Greg was arrested when he stepped off the plane at Heathrow. Apparently, he drugged and raped several girls in London. He'd also conned some woman—pretended to marry her somehow—and accessed her bank accounts. He took her for close to a million. Between all the charges, he'll go to jail for a long time." She dropped into the chair. "I'm such an idiot. How was I so blind?"

I knelt before her and took her hands. "You trust what people are saying is the absolute truth. In an ideal world, it's a beautiful, endearing quality, but with your wealth and privilege, it's dangerous. I don't want you to lose what makes you *you*, but

I also believe you need to be more careful in whom you bestow your trust.

"I'm sorry for not saying anything to you in the moment, but he never left your side. If I'd followed you to the ladies' room, you would've thought I was being creepy."

She hiccupped a light chuckle through her tears.

"You also mentioned your family history with the man, so I thought your brother would know whether my instincts were correct. Wickham is also a bit old for you, don't you think?"

Gigi rolled her eyes. "Yeah, but he's hot. It was flattering having a male model who was interested in me—well, who I thought was interested in me."

"I bit my cheek. "I'm going to ask you a personal question. You don't have to answer."

She nodded.

"Did you have sex with him?"

"No," she said shaking her head. "He tried, but I wasn't ready."

A huge exhale whooshed from me. "Good. The last thing we needed was to take you to the doctor to check for diseases."

"He probably would've poked holes in the condom. If he wanted my money, how better to tie himself to me than by getting me pregnant." I hated the dejected tone she had as well as the way her body almost caved in on itself.

"Okay, enough of this. I say we go into the café, pick out some sweets, and take them up to my house. We can binge on them and drink coffee or hot chocolate. Whatever you want."

"I suppose," she said as she dragged herself up to stand. "Your cakes are better than the ice cream fest I'd planned at my friends' apartment."

We returned to the bakery, and I took out a cake box. Gigi picked out two types of cake and the cheesecake brioche doughnut while I threw in some macarons and snowman cake pops, making sure we stuck to the gluten-free displays. Gigi was still red around the eyes when we walked to the elevator and took it up to my house.

Those same eyes widened when she gaped at the foyer of the house, the biggest of the Christmas trees nestled in the curve of the staircase.

"This is amazing. Don't get me wrong. I love our penthouse, but it's so modern. Will moved out of our parents' house when I was younger and bought where he lives now. Even after they died, he never moved back."

"Maybe the memories are too much for him." I could understand that feeling. I had it from time to time living here.

"Probably. He told me I could move into Mom and Dad's one day if I wanted, but if I left the penthouse, he'd be all alone."

I set down the box of baked goods on the coffee table in the living room and texted Mrs. Hill, who bustled in a moment later.

"There you are, dearie." She paused at the sight of Gigi. "You look like you could use some cheering up."

"Mrs. Hill, this is Gigi. She's William Darcy's sister."

The older lady clasped her hands together. "Now that you mention it, I can see the resemblance. You both have the same eyes."

"So, we're pigging out on cake and whatever Gigi wants."

Mrs. Hill nodded. "Would you like some hot chocolate, or maybe a cup of tea? I can make coffee drinks too, but they're not nearly as good as those from the café."

The corner of Gigi's mouth turned upwards. "Hot chocolate sounds perfect. I'll make myself sick within an hour or so."

I patted her back. "We'll pace ourselves. Do you want to watch something?" I handed her the remote. "I have a cabinet full of DVDs on that wall, and I have more than one streaming service. Just pick out whatever you want to watch."

"You don't have an opinion?" she asked.

"If you pick out a movie or show I object to, I'll let you know." I shrugged. "In the mood you're in, it's not like you're going to go watching horror movies. I like most rom-coms and comedies."

Gigi plopped down onto the sofa and pulled the cake box closer. I reached and pulled the coffee table toward us.

Mrs. Hill returned with napkins, forks, and spoons. "We have ice cream too if you'd like some."

I opened the boxes, and Mrs. Hill's eyes widened. "Never mind. I believe you're all set."

While she hurried back into the kitchen, I passed Gigi her utensils and I dug into the Southern Pecan Caramel Cake. The moistness of the cake drenched in caramel accompanied by the caramel buttercream and pecans all but melted into my mouth. I'd always adored cakes, and I made enough different varieties that I never seemed to get bored eating them.

"I haven't tried that one yet," said Gigi. She moaned when she took a bite. "I don't know how you make cakes like this. I wish I knew how."

"It's not that hard. Why don't you come over one day, and I'll teach you."

"Really? Now that we're on break, I'd love to do that."

"Why not between Christmas and New Years? That way things will be a little slower at the café. I'm going to be digging myself out of buttercream by Christmas Eve."

"Yes, but those pies in the display, with the cut-out ornaments on the crust, were beautiful. You and Char put so much into all you do, and it shows."

"Because we love it. If we didn't, we'd constantly complain—not that we don't ever complain. Some days are long and exhausting, and some customers don't want to be pleased. But put flour and a bowl in front of me and let me create, and I'm content."

"That's why I'm studying music. It's my happy place."

I picked up the remote and set it next to her. "What did you want to watch?"

"Oh!" She flipped through until she picked *The Princess Bride*, which happened to be one of my favorites. Before she hit play, she let her hand rest on the table. "Lizzy, what did you mean about turning down my brother."

"I don't know what you're talking about." Suddenly, I became extremely interested in the cake and shoved a huge bite in my mouth.

"Did he ask you out?"

Damn! Why couldn't I look her in the eye? I did my best to chew and not give myself away.

"He did! But why would you say no? He may not always handle matters in the best way, but his heart is in the right place. He's a great brother."

I picked up my now cold coffee and took a sip to help me get down the enormous bite I'd taken. "He may be, but we haven't always gotten along."

"But it'd be awesome to have you as a sister."

Her enthusiasm brought a smile to my lips. "I agree, but why don't you let me and your brother sort out our own messes? It's more than likely that neither of us belongs with the other."

She lifted the remote. "Okay, but I disagree on that."

"You're allowed to disagree. As long as you don't start matchmaking."

She hit play. "I'm not making any promises. After all, 'true love is the greatest thing, in the world—except for a nice MLT—mutton, lettuce and tomato sandwich, where the mutton is nice and lean and the tomato is ripe. They're so perky.'[1]"

I grinned at her bad impression of Miracle Max from the movie and poked her in the ribs, making her shift to the side. Gi would be okay. She had enough people in her corner—including me—to make sure of it.

After way too much cake, cake pops, macarons, and doughnuts, we succumbed to a sugar coma—Gigi more so than me. She fell asleep before the second movie we turned on was over, a grey throw tossed over her legs.

Mrs. Hill crept in when the movie ended. "The poor thing was worn out from crying. I hope she'll be okay."

"I think so. She's got her brother and a couple of cousins to take care of her. I believe they're all close. One of the cousins is Char's Annie."

"I like her."

"You do." I gathered the utensils and handed them to her while Mrs. Hill gathered the boxes and napkins. "Her brother can be overprotective, which was why she was upset."

"That's hard," said Mrs. Hill. "He's probably doing what he thinks is best without realizing that he's making decisions for her or treading on her toes." A ding from the foyer made us both straighten.

Mrs. Hill glanced at her watch. "It's nine o'clock. Who could that be?" She rushed off while I brought the trash into the kitchen and threw it away. As I was putting the utensils in the

---

[1] The Princess Bride. Twentieth Century Fox. 1987.

dishwasher, Mrs. Hill walked in and placed her hand over mine on the counter. "That would be the brother. I'd wager he's looking for her."

"With the state she was in, I'd guess he was worried and assumed she came here. I'll take care of it."

"Don't be too hard on him, dearie. Your uncle could be officious when it suited him as well. Don't forget that he never told you about his will or the trust set aside for you."

"That was different." Wasn't it? Sure, it was a shock when the truth of the matter was revealed, but Zio wouldn't have done it without good cause.

"Your uncle was the best of men, but no man is perfect. They all have their foibles. Some of their faults are more endearing than others, but you must admit women are the same."

I feigned affront by putting my hand on my chest. "You're saying I have faults? I thought I was 'practically perfect in every way.'[2]"

Mrs. Hill giggled. "Okay, Mary Poppins, go greet your guest."

I entered the foyer right as the elevator doors opened, and Will Darcy stepped out. His hair was adorably tousled, although otherwise, his appearance was almost haggard. His eyes had a wild quality about them.

"Is Gi here? Usually, she goes to see Richard or Annie when she's upset, but they haven't seen her. You're the only other person I could think of."

I stepped forward and put my hands on his shoulders. "Will, breathe. She's here. She's sleeping off two slices of cake, a cake pop, a doughnut, and hot chocolate in the living room."

---

[2] Mary Poppins. 1964. Disney.

His entire body deflated. "Thank God!"

# Chapter 17

"Will, breathe. She's here. She's sleeping off a sugar coma in the living room."

I could've collapsed onto the floor. Gigi was safe. I'd searched everywhere I could think of that she might go, but in the end, she'd come to Liz, and Liz had ensured Gigi had been safe.

"Thank God! I know she has friends, but she was angry and crying when she left the penthouse. My first thought was to text Richard and let him know what'd happened, but I decided to give her space. You know; treat her like an adult. When Gi didn't come back after an hour, I called him, then Annie. I—"

"Gigi showed up in the shop. She was furious with me for not telling her my suspicions about Greg."

"She felt we conspired," I said.

Liz shrugged one shoulder. "I'd say she felt more betrayed. Gigi trusted me, and I went to you. For all intents and purposes, I snitched on her to her father."

I exhaled heavily. "I suppose that's a more accurate picture of it."

She waved me toward the library. "Come on in. I'll pour you a drink."

"Can I see Gi first?" I just needed to know she was safe.

After a nod, Liz brought me into a darkened room. I could barely make out the large television mounted on the wall. She tugged the sleeve of my shirt, pulling me around an end table so I didn't knock over the lamp, then pointed. There, snuggled up with a blanket, was Gigi. She was snoring slightly but otherwise, sound asleep.

"Will?" said Liz in a soft voice. "How about that drink?"

I nodded and followed her into the library. While she poured Scotch into a glass, my attention was snagged by some plans on a table.

"What is this? Are you expanding?"

She handed me a glass. "My uncle purchased a building in the East Village years ago. The neighboring building went up for sale and has a great corner storefront. It was a restaurant in the past. We're renovating both buildings and putting in a smaller version of Novel Books as well as another Buttercream Beanery—also on a bit of a smaller scale. Char will run that location." Although she held a glass in her hand as well, her free hand had gone into her jeans pocket, and she was stiff.

"I'm glad you're expanding. I think it's a good time for the bakery especially."

One of her eyebrows rose. "You're being serious?"

I couldn't help but smile a little at the higher tone she'd used. "Why are you surprised? Since I first saw your bakery not so long ago, I've wondered why you didn't open another location. The East Village is a smart place for a second location of Novel Books as well. There's no larger scale bookstore in that part of town yet."

She leaned against the back of the sofa. "Well, we're renovating two floors on the building Zio purchased for the bookstore. The café will have the dining room area and outdoor seating downstairs and the main kitchen on the second floor and the kitchens for gluten-free and allergens on the third, a lot like the one here. Thankfully, there was already an elevator. It makes it so much easier for larger cakes and big orders."

I perused the plans and nodded. "These look great. I'm happy for you." I honestly was.

Both of her eyebrows shot up this time. "You are?"

I nodded with a small chuckle. "I am. After Gi's party, whenever the subject of Novel Books came up at work, I had no interest in pursuing it. You loved your uncle and hope to continue what he started—to make it more than it was. I think he'd be extremely proud of you. As Richard once told me, Pemberley Books doesn't have to occupy every part of the world."

"Are you sure?" A light glinted in her eye. "I'm sure there's some remote part of Greenland you haven't occupied yet—maybe Antarctica. . .Tanzania?"

"Thank you for taking care of Gigi."

Liz set her glass on a table. "Gigi is an adult. She can take care of herself. I just let her talk about what was bothering her, then offered to let her drown her misery in cake, macarons, and doughnuts. Mrs. Hill contributed the hot chocolate."

I set my drink next to hers. "Well, thank you anyway." I shoved down any reservations I had and leaned in to press a kiss to Liz's cheek. As soon as my lips pressed against the softness of her skin, I lingered, my heart beating so hard it filled my ears and drowned out every other sound. Hints of vanilla and sugar tickled my nose. Was that her usual scent or had she not showered after work?

As I made to pull back, our eyes caught, and an invisible thread drew me back in to touch my lips to hers. When she caressed mine in return, the fine thread holding me back snapped. One hand slipped around her waist while the other dove into the messy bun on the back of her head. When my tongue dipped in to taste hers, the Scotch on her tongue combined with the sweets made for an addictive flavor I'd drown in if given the opportunity.

Her fingers wrapped around to the nape of my neck where she threaded them into my hair. A moment later, her soft breasts were crushed against my chest, and my body responded in the most basic way, my trousers becoming painfully restrictive in the front. As much as I'd hate myself for it later, I wrenched myself a step back.

Liz's chest heaved with each breath, her messy bun was even messier and threatening to fall out completely, and her lips were blushed from tangling with my own. She was stunning. I desired her more than I'd ever wanted any woman in my life, but I needed her to want me just as much.

"Lizzy!" I took another step back before Mrs. Hill walked into the room. "Gigi woke up enough for me to take her upstairs and put her in your old bedroom. I gave her a pair of your leggings and a t-shirt to sleep in. I hope that's okay."

"It's perfect, Mrs. Hill. Thank you," said Liz.

The older woman glanced between us then lifted her eyebrows at Liz. "Do you need anything else?"

"No, I can manage. Go watch *The Bachelor*. I know you're dying to know who doesn't get a rose tonight."

"Definitely! That Celia is a conniving one; let me tell you. I've been waiting for Derek to see right through her, but I think he just wants to get into her skirts first."

I almost choked on my own spit.

"Good night, dearie. You too, Mr. Darcy."

"Good night," said Liz while I gave a nod.

Mrs. Hill departed and both of us stood there for at least a minute or two before I glanced through the doorway. "I think she's gone. She watches *The Bachelor*?"

"I'd say she has more of an unhealthy addiction." She stepped forward to stand within a couple of inches of me, and my body tensed to keep from taking her into my arms. "What happened before she entered?"

I frowned. "What part do you mean? If you mean the kiss, I'd think that was obvious."

She shook her head with a curve to her lips and that arched eyebrow that made it nearly impossible not to claim her mouth once again. "No, I didn't expect you to pull away."

"You made it very clear that you didn't or don't like me, so as much as I do want you, I need to make sure you've reconsidered and are interested in more than tonight—that you're certain you won't regret if we continued." She dragged her teeth along her bottom lip—she was so enticing when she did that. How was I to resist when she made it so damned difficult?

"I don't hate you. When we met at the gala, I enjoyed speaking to you until you insulted me to your friend and Jane. I've been compared to Jane my entire life by my mother and others. My older sister has always been considered more beautiful. She could do no wrong in my parents' eyes. So, while you may not have compared us, insulting me stung just as much as it had every single time someone told me I didn't measure up."

My fingers trailed down her velvet cheek, and my palm cupped her jaw. "Those people were blind and never took the time to truly look at you. You're so much more than your sister. You're more intelligent. Moreover, your kindness increases your beauty while her cattiness makes her one of the most unappealing women I've ever met." I closed some of the distance between us while my fingers wrapped around the back of her neck.

"From the moment I bumped into you, I was drawn to you and wanted nothing more than to spend the entire night in your company. Would you believe I cursed my aunt when she demanded I bow to her summons? Do you know she introduced me to some woman she insisted I had to take to dinner? I told the woman it was nice to meet her then told my aunt I had to return to the person I'd been speaking to before we were so rudely interrupted.

"For what I said at the gala, I can only claim shock at learning who you are, which is no excuse. I shouldn't have said it at all."

She pressed her hand on my chest, branding my flesh despite the barrier of my shirt. "And I've been awful to you since. I hardly spoke to you at Gigi's birthday party."

"Which I deserved." I didn't have any issue freely admitting my behavior had earned her cold shoulder.

"I gave you grief for doing what you thought right for your sister. I didn't agree with how you handled the matter, but I failed to acknowledge that you were doing what you thought was best."

I squeezed my eyes closed then reopened them. "No, you were correct. Richard has been the only person who has ever told me where I've been mistaken. Too often, I get told I'm right or I'm told what people think I want to hear. It took a while to understand that one of the traits I so admire in you is your honesty. You'll tell me exactly what you think."

"Do you know what I think right now?" That blasted eyebrow was arched again.

"Do you know what it does to me when you do that with your eyebrow?"

A wonderful laugh bubbled from her throat. "Seriously?"

I couldn't resist another second, and I kissed her in a way that left no doubt of what her coy expression did to me. When I pressed my hand against her ass and drew her flush to my body, my erection pushing into her hip reinforced the effect of that arched eyebrow.

She pulled me backward until we tumbled onto the grey plush sofa. I deepened the kiss while my palm slid down her thigh to lift her leg so I was cradled just so in between her thighs. She still tasted incredible, the flavor of the Scotch lingering on her tongue. I couldn't get enough.

My fingers found their way under the hem of her t-shirt and caressed along her side. She shivered and gasped into my mouth at the contact. My cock twitched at the sound while my palms itched to touch her everywhere—to savor every inch of her until she screamed my name.

Her hands found my butt and held tight while pulling me closer until I was grinding into her warm center. I groaned and wrenched my lips from hers.

"Liz, we've barely done anything and you're killing me. If we're going to stop, we need to do it now. I can't take much more."

Our gazes met and held before she planted both of her palms into my chest and pressed. I lifted from her quickly. Yes, I would be in pain until my erection subsided, but when we finally crossed that line, I wanted it on terms we both accepted—not because one of us wanted it and the other was unsure.

She stood, her chest rising and falling as she tried to catch her breath. She held out her hand, and I set mine in her palm.

"Come," she said softly.

"Come?"

When she nodded, I didn't need to be told again. I sprang from the sofa as she pulled me toward a corner of the library.

"Where are we going?"

"My uncle had an elevator installed. I thought we'd take that instead of the stairs."

"The stairs would be healthier."

Her laugh was husky and turned me on even more. "Yes, but you can't continue to kiss me and touch me while we climb the stairs."

After she opened the door, she backed inside, beckoning me with a curve of her finger. "Are you coming?"

"Not yet," I said as I followed. "But if you continue, I will be before we even get naked."

She whipped off her t-shirt, her sheer bra doing nothing to hide what was underneath.

"That's not helping." Good Lord, my palms itched to mold them in my hands and my tongue craved their flavor. What was it about Elizabeth Bennet that made me crazy? I'd never been this way with any of the women in my past; not that there'd been a lot of them. I'd always been careful of who I slept with.

"If you can't make it, it's not like we can't explore each other while you recover and try again."

Holy shit! She was going to kill me!

# Chapter 18

I'd never been the most confident about my body or even sex, but here I was teasing Will Darcy like I knew exactly what I was doing. Even so, my insides shook, and my fingers trembled just as badly. It'd been years—and I mean *years*—since I'd had sex. I didn't do one-nighters, and I'd never been into sex without feelings attached. If you'd asked me earlier tonight if I'd be here now, I would've laughed, but now, I wanted Will more than I'd ever wanted anyone else—ever.

Will's eyes flared for a second after my taunt before he stalked toward me like he was going to devour me whole. Hopefully, he wouldn't be disappointed in my basic cotton panties when we reached that point. I didn't wear silk or lace bottoms on most days. I hardly wore anything that sexy at all to tell the truth.

Right before he reached me, he removed his henley and dropped it on the floor. We both hissed when his muscled chest and chiseled stomach met my bare flesh, and I rose onto my toes to kiss him again. He was so different than any of the other boys I'd ever kissed, and I mean boys since they obviously hadn't known how to do it properly. Will's lips were soft, and while he used his tongue, he wasn't trying to gag me with it. Each caress sent a current straight between my legs. I was already aching for him, and we'd barely begun.

While our mouths continued their duel, his hand slid up to my ribs, his thumb trailing the underside of my breast. I needed air! When I tore away from him, he nibbled and suckled down my neck while I struggled to breathe. I was going to faint into an ugly heap on the floor.

The elevator dinged, and I shifted from the wall. He groaned at being dislodged so I could open the door and peer down the hallway. The coast was clear!

My hand grabbed his, and I pulled him to the first set of doors, my bedroom doors, and led him inside. I pushed the panel closed behind me and dropped my arms, letting my bra hit the hardwood floors.

Will's eyes darkened as they dropped to my breasts. "They're more gorgeous than I imagined."

His heated stare gave me a confidence I'd never possessed in my life. Nothing crossed my mind about what I was doing or how I went from almost loathing Will Darcy to wanting him to shag me senseless. Instead, I took his hand and pressed it against my breast, watching his rapt expression as he squeezed and massaged. He flicked his finger over my nipple, and I gasped while I rubbed my thighs together. He was afraid of lasting long enough, but I wasn't doing much better. At this rate, I was going to orgasm before he ever touched me below the waist. Would that be embarrassing? I had no way of knowing.

When he bent to take the tip in his mouth, he picked me up and wrapped my legs around his hips. My fingers entwined through his locks and held his head in place. As much as I wanted more, the flame this was igniting was too delicious to ignore. He took a heavy draw that sent an even stronger jolt to my core, and I groaned.

"Will, please."

He laid me down in the middle of the bed and grabbed the waistband of my leggings, drawing them and my underwear off in one go. I guess I didn't need to worry about how unappealing my panties were. He'd never even looked at them.

As he crawled back over me, his palm caressed a trail of fire up my leg, over my hip, and back to my breasts. He took the other nipple and began to repeat what he'd done to the first. I writhed to get closer to him, to have his erection pressed between my legs. That ache was screaming for him to do something, but he was too busy with my breasts to notice that I was almost climbing at him to get closer.

I startled when he grazed his fingers along the seam between my legs. "Oh, yes, please!"

"God, you're so wet," he said low and gravelly against my cheek.

His lips traced their way across my clavicle while he continued to lavish attention upon my breasts, but his fingers didn't stop. They slid further and further until they caressed over my clit then down to tease lower and back. When his fingers returned to that sensitive button of flesh, he lazily traced circles over it.

My hips lifted in the hopes of increasing that friction while he bit and licked and kissed his way down my stomach. He traced around my bellybutton with his tongue then placed an open-mouthed kiss to the inside of my thigh.

I lifted onto my elbows. My ex had tried to go down on me once, and it'd been disappointing, to say the least. So, with Will being so talented at everything else, I craved his mouth on me like I craved a rich chocolate cake. I would've never turned down either!

I could've sworn my hips lifted to meet him, and when he first suckled, and I fell back into the mattress with a keening groan. One finger slipped inside and pressed into this magic place that increased the mind-numbing pleasure from his lips and tongue. I was going to die. Here and now, I would perish from this and never have one single regret. In fact, if I'd known Will was so good at this, I might have jumped him earlier despite my previous feelings toward the man. I could've gotten over the one-night stand thing for this, right?

My fingers curled into his hair to keep him from stopping. I had no idea if he planned to, but I was going to find satisfaction this way. I'd been denied for too long.

The flame that he'd ignited spread and blazed until it was consuming me whole. My toes curled into the sheets, and my grip tightened on his hair until waves of the most unbearable pleasure shot through me and I cried out. Even though I'd climaxed, he continued on, drawing out every last spasm, until I began to pull away.

"It's too much. I can't take it."

His warmth disappeared, and I opened my eyes to him removing his belt and trousers with frantic hands. I forced my limp body up and as soon as he'd pushed his pants to his knees, I'd taken him in my hand.

"Ugh, Liz," he said. "I can't think when you do that."

"Then I'm returning the favor." I lightly bit his shoulder while I tugged him over me and guided him so he was at my entrance.

He kissed me deeply, and while I could taste myself on him, I didn't care. I wanted him inside of me, filling me with his impressive size like no one else could.

At the first thrust, he stopped kissing me with a guttural noise while I winced at the slight sting. "You're so tight."

"It's been a long time."

"Am I hurting you?"

"No, don't stop." Sure, it was a white lie, but once he was fully inside of me, the awkward part would be over. I was certain of it.

My palms found his ass, and I pulled him deeper with each thrust until I'd taken every last inch. When he began a slow rhythm of drawing in and out, I wrapped my legs around him. I needed him as deep as he could go, and I wasn't going to settle for less.

He guided my hips and shifted to another angle that brought an unintelligible sound to my lips. As he lifted slightly off of me, one hand braced him over my shoulder while the fingers of the other dug into my hip while he continued to caress that place that would have me shattering sooner rather than later.

"I'm so close." I couldn't tell if that was a groan or a moan.

His gaze met mine and held. "Don't close your eyes."

How was I supposed to do that? So far, I'd lost all control when he made me orgasm. Was this time going to be different? Regardless, I nodded.

That familiar heat began to rage, starting between my legs and spreading as it had before. That ache had blossomed and hadn't ever abated. I'd never climaxed during sex before, and Will was going to have me coming again in seconds. It seemed like it anyway!

His thrusts became harder and faster, and as I tightened around him, I froze, my legs clenching him to me. He wasn't going anywhere. I couldn't say how I'd kept my eyes open, but somehow, I'd witnessed him fighting to keep his own eyelids from shuttering as I'd started to peak. Then, he reddened before his eyes fluttered. When he bellowed, it was so loud, I was thankful his sister was on the other side of the house.

After he collapsed on top of me, my body continued to tingle. Will was shaking. My eyes suddenly began to sting, and a warm tear slid down my temple. Why was I crying?

He kissed my shoulder, my neck just under my ear, but when he propped himself on his elbow, his eyes widened. "Did I hurt you? What's wrong?"

I shook my head and began to cry harder.

He tried to pull off of me, but I tightened my legs around him. I didn't want him to go.

"Liz, you're scaring me."

"I feel so stupid." The high pitch of my voice was ridiculous. "I'm not sure why I'm crying."

His chin dipped a little. "I didn't hurt you?"

My palms cradled his cheeks. "No, I've never experienced anything like that. I suppose my ex was inept." I gave a pathetic laugh. "I don't regret this, nor do I want you to go."

He made an odd face and shifted a little. "Shit! I forgot a condom."

I wiped at my cheeks with the back of my hand. "I'm sure you never expected this. For what it's worth, I'm on the pill. I never stopped taking it after my ex and I broke up. It made my periods more manageable, so I preferred to stay on it. As you could probably tell, it's been a long time for me, but I've had my yearly checkups several times since."

He gaped at me for a moment. "Years?"

I covered my face with my hands. "I haven't dated since the Cordon Bleu. Casual sex isn't quite my style, and I'm not willing to be so intimate with just anyone."

He pulled my hands from my eyes. "I'm not upset. It just means I have fewer men to want to maim if I ever meet them."

A super attractive snort-laugh was my response. "Sorry." I covered my nose for a moment.

"I'd rather see you laughing than crying."

I shook my head. "I'm not sad—I think it was just a relief of sorts. I found sex a bit dull, and I've often wondered if it was me."

"I'd say it was him," said Will with a cocky grin.

"Yes, well, you don't have to let it puff up your ego too much."

He gave me a sweet and tender kiss. "I haven't been with someone in almost a year. It's going to sound bad, but I've never wanted a relationship with emotional ties until I met you. The last was an exclusive friends-with-benefits sort of arrangement, and it ended ten months ago. As a precaution, I had a checkup and was tested after it was over. I'm all clean."

My hand stroked from his chest up his neck to his cheek. "Thanks for being honest."

"I don't want this to be a one-night or one-time thing."

"Maybe you should try taking me out." Had I truly just said that? I suppose if we were at this point, I'd decided I wanted to date Will Darcy—not that I could say when that happened.

"Are you going to the Pemberley Yule Ball?" He seemed so timid all of a sudden.

I laughed and tilted my head. "I may have procured a ticket to your exclusive event."

He rolled his eyes. "Would you be my date?"

"Yes, but only if I can attend barefoot under my dress."

His warm laugh made my insides tremble. "You can wear a burlap sack, and I'd still only be able to look at you."

I feigned a gasp. "Such flattery, sir."

He tickled my side, and I burst into laughter. "That's for teasing me."

I gasped when he rolled us so I was on top.

"I'll need to leave early to change and get to work, but can I stay? I'm not ready to let you go yet."

His unsure tone and expression tore at my heart. "I'd like you to stay." I longed to know what it felt like to sleep in his arms. This was all crazy. I'd just hated him how long ago?

I shifted a little. "Will, are you still hard?"

He grinned widely. "I'm not sure how, but yes." His hand clenched my butt cheek. "Do you want to. . .again?"

With a matching grin, I sat up a little and bit his shoulder then bestowed a peck to his nipple.

"Liz, wait. Do you think we can finish taking off my trousers this time? Removing my socks would be preferable as well. I kept slipping while trying to get leverage."

I rose to my knees and backed off the bed. After removing his socks, I pulled his khakis from his legs and dropped them on the floor. "If you want a condom, I do have a small box in the bedside table. Even though I haven't needed them, I replace the box every year just in case."

He sat up and pulled me into his lap. "If your birth control failed and you got pregnant, would you be upset?"

"I want children, and I'm at a place where I could manage. I have Mrs. Hill, and somehow, I doubt you'd leave me to raise a child on my own, although I'd be good doing it if I had to. It's not like I need money from you. I have my own. What about you?"

"First off, I'd want to be a part of my child's life. Second, I want children, but I hadn't found anyone I wanted to have them with until now—not that I want to have one *right now*. I'd like to date for a while, maybe ask you to marry me first."

My entire face bloomed. "Slow down. Whatever this is just started tonight."

He laughed. "No rush. I guess what I'm saying is that if you did happen to get pregnant, I wouldn't be upset about it."

"Well, now that we've had that completely unsexy conversation." I started to get up, but he pulled me back into his embrace.

"As for what this is, I hope it's the first evening of a lot of time we'll spend together. I want to take you out, but I'm just as content to stay in and watch a movie or whatever." He nuzzled under my ear making goosebumps pebble down the back of my neck.

"I'll have to test you on that sometime."

He grazed his teeth along my earlobe. My breath hitched in my chest. "You'll find that I'm a homebody. I'd prefer to stay in than to go to any gala, although I like to have a nice dinner out one or two nights a week."

"That doesn't sound too bad. I suppose." His hands had joined his lips in the pursuit of dissolving me into a puddle.

"As long as you're there."

As of that moment, I wanted nothing more than for him to shut up and kiss me.

# Chapter 19

I jolted awake and looked around. It was still dark, but I usually woke before daybreak to make it down to the bakery before everyone else. My phone alarm was set as a backup, but I rarely needed it.

I snaked an arm from the warm cocoon of the covers to grab my phone. Three-thirty. I groaned and tried to slip from under Will's embrace, but he tightened his grip, murmuring and nuzzling my neck. And woah, was that his morning wood pressing into my butt?

After the second go-around last night, we'd spooned and fallen asleep. Will had been utterly ridiculous and insisted on holding onto my breast, which he was still doing. The man was definitely into boobs! I hadn't thought mine were that spectacular, but by the starstruck way he gawked at them, they seemed to be his ideal.

"Will?" I patted and rubbed his arm, but he didn't stir. "Will?"

With a groan, he tightened his hold on me. "What time is it?"

"Probably five minutes later than I needed to get up."

He squeezed and began to caress my breast. "That doesn't answer my question."

"About three-thirty-five."

"That's insane. Can't we sleep another hour and a half?"

I rolled to face him. "You can if you like, but I need to take a shower before I go into the bakery. I don't want to reek of sex. Char would never let me live it down."

His expression perked. "Shower?"

With a shake of my head, I started laughing. His hopeful expression gave away exactly what was in his mind. "Oh, no. I'll never get to work." Before he could pull me back into his arms, I darted from the bed and into the bathroom. I kept a nightlight in there so I didn't have to turn on the lights. My opinion was that there was nothing worse than bright lights first thing in the morning.

I turned on the water to warm up, relieved myself, and by the time I stepped into the spacious shower and let the hot water wash over me, Will had come in, his tall silhouette moving around the room. A moment later, the shower door opened, and I turned.

"What are you doing?"

"I need a shower too." That curve to his lips gave him a mischievous look that made my body come alive. Stand down, girl!

My arms went out in front of me. "You have to behave." I'd always thought Will Darcy was stiff and entirely too serious, yet he was relaxed and even silly last night when we'd talked or as we'd made love.

He stepped up and tugged me into his arms. "Where's the soap?"

"That bar is body wash and those are shampoo and conditioner."

I picked up the conditioner bar, but he took it from me and began rubbing it through my hair.

"How do I do this?" He turned me around and continued.

"After I rub enough into my hair, I'll comb my fingers through it to remove the tangles. A brush does nothing but make my hair frizz." I closed my eyes as he worked the conditioner through my curls and removed the knots.

"Why do you use bars?"

"Since I discovered most plastic labeled recyclable isn't recycled, I began trying alternatives. I feel guilty throwing away plastic. It's unavoidable on many things, but if I can find a workable alternative, then I replace it. I prefer the shampoo and conditioner bars to my old products."

"I did notice you use stoneware cups in the café for people eating in—as well as dishes."

"We do. The local farms that I use to supply any fruit or vegetables we need also take back their packaging to reuse. We have storage behind the kitchen where they're kept."

Before I could pick up the soap, he had it in his palm and was lathering my back. His strong hands stroking along my sides and shoulders weren't helping my resolve to get to work. When he ran the bar over my breasts, I leaned back against him.

"This isn't fair."

"I'm not sorry. I love these." He held them in his palms. "They're not too big or too small, the shape is perfect, and the blush pink of your nipple is now my favorite shade."

"You're ridiculous—and obviously a boob man."

"I like your ass too. If it's feeling neglected, I can massage it as well."

I laughed and turned in his arms. "You're ridiculous! I *have* to get to work. Can you talk to him?" I pointed between us where his erection was prodding at my thigh. "And tell him he's going to need to wait."

Will kissed under my ear. "Ignore him. He'll go away."

"I think he's too persistent for that."

I rose on my tiptoes and pressed my lips to Will's as I pushed him to lean against the wall. When I dropped to my knees, his eyes flared. I'd never done this before, but hopefully, he wouldn't notice!

Char was turning off the mixer when I walked into the kitchen. She looked up with a crooked smile. "Since when do you oversleep?"

"I'm sorry." I usually told Char everything, but it didn't feel right this time. For some reason, I wanted to keep those stolen moments with Will to myself—hoard them for now.

She removed the metal bowl from the stand mixer and began pouring batter into the muffin tins. "Well, I started these for you. The first batches of blueberry, pumpkin, and banana muffins are in the ovens. These are gingerbread. If you can take over, I need to get going on those quiches I'd planned for this morning. Thank heavens I prepped the crusts yesterday."

Before she could move, Char's eyes narrowed. "Why are you wearing a turtleneck?"

"Because it's cold today. You know it's supposed to snow this morning." I resisted every urge to bite my lip. Char knew all my tells, and that'd give me away in a heartbeat.

She stared at me for a moment while I tried not to fidget. "I'm not buying it." She stepped closer. "Is your hair wet? You showered before work and not last night?" Char glanced around then peered around me.

"What are you doing?"

After a lightning quick step to my side, she reached up and yanked the side of my turtleneck down. She'd moved so fast, that I couldn't duck away. She released the fabric with a gasp. "You had sex!" Her finger pointed right at that spot under my ear. "It doesn't cover it completely; you know. The foundation has also rubbed off on the black cotton. You should've worn a peach or a beige."

I rolled my eyes as I strode to the sink and washed my hands. My best friend was enjoying this far too much. Thankfully, everyone else was working in the back of the kitchen, so no one was close by to witness what was sure to be an inquisition. Char, meanwhile, wore a huge grin and stood with her arms crossed over her chest while she watched me.

"You're staring."

"And you're not sharing."

"Nope, I'm not."

I threw on an apron and picked up the bowl to finish scooping the batter into the muffin tins. "Don't you have quiches to make?"

The oven beeped, and Mia walked in, took the tin out and brought it to the back to put on the cooling racks. As soon as she wasn't within an easy hearing distance, Char shifted up to my shoulder.

"At least tell me who. This isn't fair. We always tell each other everything."

I lifted my eyebrow. "Like you told me about Annie?"

"I told you her name."

"The rest was too personal." That'd been similar to what Char had said. I paused for a moment while that sank in. My insides flipped, and I had to take in a deep breath.

"Don't freak out," said Char.

When Char and Annie started seeing each other, Char didn't tell me all that much. "It was different," she would say. Now they were moving in together. Char had even mentioned marriage in their future now that Annie was out to the world.

"Shit! Lizzy, sit."

A stool hit me in the thighs, and I dropped onto it.

"Lizzy, look at me."

My gaze met Char's. Was I having a freaking panic attack? "How did this sneak up on me? How did *he* sneak up on me?"

She watched me for a second, then inhaled sharply. "It was William Darcy, wasn't it? I told you he liked you, but you were so adamant that you couldn't stand him. I should've known you were in denial." She started to laugh.

"What's so funny?"

An annoying shrug was her first response. "Oh, maybe that the saying 'there's a fine line between love and hate' isn't so off. I did think your response to him odd. Every little thing—him staring as well as his insult at the gala—they all grated at you. I was certain he had a crush on you. I think I also said you wouldn't have been so worked up if you didn't find him attractive."

"No one likes a know-it-all, Char."

She tittered like an old woman. "Lizzy and Darcy sitting in a tree, k-i-s-s-i-n-g—"

"You might want to stop, unless you want to lose a tongue."

"Please tell me that he gave you at least one orgasm." At least she asked in a hushed tone!

One side of my lip tugged upwards while my cheeks burned. Char cackled in glee.

"Way to go William! By that expression, I'd say he rocked your orgasm virgin world."

"Someone's going to hear you." I stage-whispered.

"Don't mind me," said Mia. "But congratulations on the orgasm—or orgasms."

I buried my face in my arms. "Oh, my God."

"Come on," said Char. "You need to finish those muffins and get started on the scones. We've got cranberry and traditional on the menu for today." When I dropped my arms, she pushed the mixing bowl into my hands.

Once Char started cracking eggs into a bowl, she ceased her inquisition except for the smug glances she'd give me from time to time while I worked. After about ten minutes, I put in my earbuds and tuned everything out while I was baking. After the muffins were the scones, then I made more muffins, apple cinnamon turnovers, and more. We each had a system of how to mix one while another was baking or having something rise while we worked on another pastry. Char and I had this down to a science of sorts. I was putting my first cakes of the day in the oven when the opening front-end staff trickled in.

Char, being the amazing friend that she was, made me my own little quiche for breakfast. Other than the time I took to eat between taking the first cakes out to cool and putting the next batch in the oven, I'd had no breaks. During the Christmas season, it wasn't unusual. June was always busy due to weddings, but Christmas had become so much more.

When the music stopped, I took my earbuds out and put them in the case to charge. As I was washing my hands, the kitchen door opened and whooshed closed.

"Well, if it isn't the hickey-maker," said Char with a shit-eating grin.

If my hands hadn't been full of soap, I would've covered my face. How many times had my cheeks burned today? I'd lost count when Char started in on the hickey this morning.

After I dried my hands, I straightened and returned to the front of the kitchen. The clock over the door said two-thirty. "I wasn't expecting you so early."

"I wasn't sure when you were off," he said.

I glanced at my watch. "I've got a couple of hours yet. If you want, I can get you some coffee." Without looking at my best friend, I rushed out to the café.

# WILL

Liz's cheeks had been adorably pink before she ran out to the storefront. When I turned back to Char, she stared at me with her arms folded over her chest.

"I told her a while back that you were interested. She didn't want to. Believe me. Now that she's opened herself up to the possibility of a relationship with you, I want to make something perfectly clear."

I laughed. "Is this where you threaten my life if I hurt her."

Char laughed low in the back of her throat. "I'll take something more valuable to you than your life. Without your bollocks, you'll only wish you were dead." The last she said with the creepiest smile I'd ever seen.

"Has Annie seen this side of you?"

Char snorted. "Of course, she has. Every time her mother is mentioned."

I nodded. Annie needed someone who'd defend her against the fire-breathing dragon that was Cruella DeBourgh. I was inordinately proud of my cousin for standing up to her mother when she came out, but it wasn't within Annie's usual capabilities. Char's protectiveness of my cousin helped reassure me of Annie's choice.

"Your threat is noted, but you won't need to remove my bollocks. I've no intentions of hurting Liz."

"Liz? No one calls her Liz."

I shrugged. "That's how she introduced herself to me when we first met."

Char leaned one hip against the work surface. "And you introduced yourself as Will."

"I did." Liz must've mentioned it at some point.

"It's kind of cute that you have nicknames for each other that no one else uses."

The girl from the front, Mia, came through the door and into the enormous refrigerator to one side of the room. When she came out, she held a container of something in her hands. She paused in front of me. "I heard a rumor you own Pemberley Books."

I nodded. "I do."

"And you're interested in our Lizzy?" Her eyes held a challenge I wasn't going to back down from.

"I am, but I'm not pursuing Novel Books anymore. Acquiring it became less attractive after I met Liz."

Her chin hitched back a little. "I'm not saying Lizzy isn't amazing, but you're willing to give up a major expansion into Manhattan for her?"

One of my shoulders lifted. "Pretty much."

Mia watched me for a moment. "Okay, but if you hurt her—
"

"Char already threatened to remove my balls."

She turned to Char with her eyebrows lifted. "You did?"

"His bollocks, and yes."

"Nice," said Mia. "Anyway, I know a guy." She pointed at me when she said it.

I frowned. "You know a guy who'll do what?"

With a glance over her shoulder at Char, she grinned. "It'd be fun to see if they find the body." After a steady glare, she returned to the front of the store. What the—?

Char laughed. "Don't mind Mia. She's Italian and plays up like she has family in the mafia. Her father has come into the store when he visits. He's the sweetest old man who loves cannoli and our espresso. He let it slip the last time he was here that he's a dairy farmer in Pennsylvania. Completely obliterated Mia's street cred."

The door opened and Liz entered with a French press of pale coffee that I didn't doubt was peaberry. She set it next to me with a cup. "What's going on?"

"Mia threatened to sic her mob family on William," said Char.

Liz rolled her eyes. "I'm so sorry. I'll talk to her."

"No, don't do that. She doesn't want to see you hurt. I can respect that." I could. I'd feel the same way about anyone wanting to date Gigi.

While Liz poured the coffee into the cup, Char went into the back and returned a moment later.

"Since you're here, you can be my guinea pig."

I looked at Liz. "Should I be scared?"

She smiled and shook her head. "No, Char's only given someone food poisoning once or twice."

I leveled a hard look at her, making her laugh.

"I'm teasing you. We have specials we make for each month. I take care of the cakes, cupcakes, and doughnuts, and Char manages the puff pastries and savory bits for the café."

When Char returned, she placed two plates in front of me, each with its own fork. "I'm making a filled croissant for January. This one is Italian sausage and mozzarella, and this one is ham and Gruyère."

I tasted the Italian sausage croissant. "This one's good, but a bit like a calzone without the sauce to dip it in." The second melted in my mouth, the flavors melding perfectly. "This one is the clear winner. I think the choice of filling works with the pastry better too."

"I told you," said Liz.

"Well, I figured a second opinion couldn't hurt."

She moved to take the plates away, but I held onto the ham and Gruyère pastry. "I'm finishing this."

Char held her hands up, palms out to me. "Don't worry. I'll let you keep it."

My heart skipped a beat at Liz's laugh as she washed her hands and pulled cake layers from the refrigerator. "I need to finish this, then prep for tomorrow morning. If you don't want to wait, you don't have to. I can call you when I'm done."

I ate my pastry and drank my coffee while she spread jam on one layer then added the other cake to the top. She appeared completely focused while she spread the frosting. After, she used a piping bag to add some decoration to the top and finished it with some blackberries.

"What kind of cake is that?"

"A Prosecco cake. It's a special cake for New Years, but I usually start making them this week. This will go in the display and people can buy slices of it. It helps drum up orders for New

Years. Although I did give your cousin an early preview. He taste tested it for me."

For the rest of her workday, I sipped coffee while she worked, but I was never bored. The detail and care she put into everything she made fascinated me. Elizabeth Bennet had a creative flair with a business acumen that helped her be successful. It didn't hurt that she was beautiful and had a body I now craved with every part of me.

She was the whole package. I couldn't have resisted if I'd tried.

# Chapter 20

"What do you want to do about dinner?" asked Liz as we stepped from the elevator into her foyer. "It's Mrs. Hill's night off to go play bingo with her friends at St. Stephens, so I usually fend for myself."

"Do you want to go out?"

She scrunched up her nose. "Maybe after the holiday season is over. My feet are killing me."

I took the two large slices of cake she'd brought home from her hands. "Then let's settle somewhere comfortable and order pizza. What kind do you like?"

"I'm not usually picky, but pepperoni and mushroom sounds so good right now."

I followed her into the living room and set down the cake. A few touches to my phone screen and I'd ordered a large pizza that'd be delivered soon.

Liz plopped down into the corner of the sofa, her head lolling back. "I hope the new location helps a little with how busy we are this time of year. One woman told Mia she'd come from Queens to pick up a gluten-free cake. One of the perks of having an online order form I suppose."

I sat closer to the opposite end of the couch and pulled up her feet. After unbuckling her Dr. Martens' Mary Janes, I pulled them off her feet and dropped them onto the floor. At the first dig of my thumbs into the sole of her foot, she moaned. "The reputation of the bakery has spread. It might not be a bad idea for you to consider another location in Brooklyn."

"I need to get the one I've planned up and running and earning a profit before I can even consider another. Using what I have as collateral to expand quickly isn't my favorite idea, especially in the food industry. I don't mind expanding when I have the funds, and if the right buildings come available."

Restaurants were one of the riskier business ventures, but with the current bakery's reputation, I didn't see her failing. I could understand her point of view, though.

"How about no more business talk?" she said, her eyes drooping.

"What do you want to do?"

She hissed as I found a knot and rubbed. "We could watch a movie or play a game, but only when you're finished there. I wouldn't want to deprive you."

I chuckled. "If you had some lotion, this would be better. I'll go get it. You don't even have to get up."

"There should be some in the half-bath just down that hall."

"I found a tube of lemon and white verbena hand crème," I said as I returned.

"That'll work. What do you want to watch?" She turned on the television with the remote and started scrolling through options.

A familiar title popped up, and I rolled my eyes. "My sister is always trying to get me to watch that one. I don't know why it's such a big deal."

Liz propped herself on her elbows. "You've never seen *The Princess Bride*? It's a classic."

I dipped my chin with a chuckle. "You sound just like Gi."

"That's it, then. We're watching it."

With a groan, I popped the lid on the lotion. "How about a good action film?"

"Nope! I insist. You can't refuse because you don't know what you're missing."

As the first of the movie started, I applied the lotion over her soles. While I rubbed both of her feet thoroughly, she giggled a little at the first parts of the movie with the grandfather and grandson.

About a half-hour into the story, a buzz from the foyer startled me.

"That's going to be the pizza." Liz jumped up and ran into the foyer.

I let out an exhale. As much as I didn't want to admit it, I'd been enjoying the movie, laughing at the antics of the characters on the screen, in particular, Vizzini the Sicilian criminal and mastermind who couldn't stop saying, "inconceivable."

When Liz returned with the pizza, she waved me to follow her to the kitchen. I paused the movie and ambled in after her. She placed the box on the island. "I was thinking about a glass of red. What do you want to drink? I think Mrs. Hill keeps beer in here for guests." She leaned down and looked into the wine fridge. "She has several craft varieties."

"I'd rather have wine with you."

She poured us both a glass, grabbed us plates, then we returned to the living room and ate while we finished the movie.

After the end of the film, she turned off the TV. "So what did you think?"

"It wasn't what I expected."

She huffed. "You won't admit that you like it? Seriously?"

I chuckled at her exasperated tone. "Okay, fine. It was good—funny as hell."

She gave a definitive nod. "That's more of what I expected. It's still too early to go to bed so what's your favorite game?"

"Scrabble." Of course, I answered without hesitation. I'd always loved the challenge, and I rarely got to play anymore. Richard and Gigi refused since I beat them each and every time.

Liz's lips curved in a way that made me want to spread her out on the coffee table and make her cry my name. "I'm the world's best at Scrabble."

"Kind of hard to be the world's best when you haven't played me." It was true. Who'd she play in the past? Char?

"Challenge accepted," she said with a grin. "When I thrash you, what will I win?"

"Well, aside from the game, I'll give you as many orgasms as you want. Throw out a number and I'll do it."

Her eyebrows twitched and her nipples were suddenly poking a bit from her t-shirt. She was intrigued—and turned on.

"What about if you win?"

I shrugged one shoulder. "How about I determine the number of orgasms?"

Her brow furrowed. "That sounds like I could win either way."

"That depends; I could refuse to give you any." I couldn't help but let my lips curve.

"Would you really do that?" Her eyes widened.

"You'll have to play me to find out."

"I thought I did that this morning in the shower." Her tongue peeked out at the corner of her lips, and I was instantly hard. I wasn't going to last through a game of Scrabble if we kept up the suggestive conversations.

As soon as Liz had put away the leftover pizza, she grabbed the game and we set up the board. She picked an 'e' and I'd drawn a 't,' so Liz would play first. We selected our tiles, and Liz bit her lip while she stared at the letters in front of her. She would move one here and there until she leaned forward and began putting down her word, one letter at a time.

When she'd placed the last tile with a satisfied smile, I gaped. "No way. How'd you get two letter p's? There's only two in the game."

She gasped. "You watched me pick out of the bag; just like you. Are you saying I cheated?"

Her t-shirt was short-sleeved, and she was right, I'd watched her pull the letters from the red bag. "I wasn't saying that. But, 'nipples'?"

"It's a good word, and I get fifty bonus points for using all my tiles on the first word." She held up a finger. "And don't forget the double word score."

I added up her score for "nipples." She'd gotten seventy-two points on her first turn. I wrote down the score, which made her do a little happy dance, then took stock of my own tiles. I managed 'ankle,' which earned me a double word score. Not as good a play as Liz's but respectable at least.

We continued on but as we played, Liz's words all seemed to fit a theme: nipples, wet, tight, slick, and finally thrust. Was she seducing me by Scrabble?

I leaned in right next to her ear. "I know what you're doing. If you're not careful, I'm going to smear cake all over you and lick it off." Her breathing quickened, and her teeth suddenly grazed my ear lobe. We'd not dug into our dessert yet, and I was beginning to have creative ideas for it.

"Not until I finish kicking your ass, Mr. Darcy. I want those orgasms you wagered. I believe I get any number I specify."

I couldn't resist my next word being 'tease.' When Liz put down her last letter and grinned with her victory, I couldn't bring myself to be upset.

"Now, I believe you owe me four orgasms," she said.

"You could at least make it a challenge." I actually scoffed before I said it.

"Fine, then I want seven!" She rose to her knees and pushed her finger into my chest. "Is that challenge enough for you?"

"What time does Mrs. Hill get home?"

"Not until ten. They go to a wine bar over by the church after Bingo."

I shoved the Scrabble board from the table and hoisted her up, placing her right in the middle. Her work shirt was the first thing to be removed followed by her bra. When I started on her leggings, she frowned.

"Hey, why am I the only one getting naked?"

Without hesitation, I stripped off my tie, shirt, belt, and trousers until I was in nothing but my boxer briefs. "Better?"

Her eyes flitted down my body while her tongue peeked out and licked her bottom lip. God, I loved the appreciation and unadulterated lust in her expression. I removed her leggings and panties and reached for the box of cake and opened it. I removed a piece, and she sat up.

"You were serious?" she said in a high-pitched tone.

"If you'd brought one of those bags with the decorative tips up, I wouldn't have complained." I took the cake and swirled the rich frosting around her nipple. After feeding her what was left on my fingers, I sucked the buttercream off while Liz gasped.

"I'm going to choke if you keep doing that."

What followed was a complete mess. I'd never thought to try anything like this, but I smeared cake over her breasts, down her stomach, and lower so I could kiss and eat it off her delectable body. By the time my fingers dipped between her legs, she was so swollen and ready for me, she shattered in seconds.

"That's one," I said as soon as she'd returned to earth. "The prosecco cake is phenomenal in case you were wondering; the frosting is even better smeared on your breasts."

She snort-laughed in the most adorable way. "You're ridiculous. I believe that leaves six more."

I laid down on top of her and relished the feel of her under me while I kissed her lips. That night we'd met at the gala, I'd wanted nothing more than to kiss her senseless, and instead, I'd made an idiot of myself. A part of me couldn't believe we'd reached the point where she'd forgiven me and we were here together like this.

We had all night, so I didn't want to rush things. By the time I kissed my way down between her legs, her body had reset enough to bring her to her to another high peak instead of being oversensitive and more pain than pleasure.

"That makes two."

I rolled her to her stomach and massaged and kissed her back before I helped her reach number three. Then I brought her onto my lap to grind herself to number four. She sobbed during five, and by six, she'd begun to shake her head.

"You win. I don't think I can manage another."

We were on the floor in front of the gas fireplace, which we'd turned on with the remote when she'd complained she was cold. With ease, I slid home and began to rock over her, gripping the blanket we'd spread so we didn't get the remnants of frosting everywhere.

More than once since we'd started this sexcapade of sorts, I'd almost failed to hold back my own orgasm, so now, my body was demanding satisfaction, but I had one more debt of honor to fulfill so I gritted my teeth and prayed I could make it.

When the tell-tale signs of Liz's next climax began to roll over her, I could've wept. My pace quickened, and within moments, she cried out and I followed her over the ledge into the depths. The orgasm held me under for so long that I almost blacked out before I collapsed on top of her.

"That was bloody fantastic."

She gave a weak laugh. "That was one way to describe it. I think I'm going to need at least a week to recover."

I propped myself on my elbow. "I seriously hope not!" She only chuckled more.

After a few moments, I lifted off and pulled her up into my lap. She wrapped the blanket around us while I grabbed the second slice of cake and fed her a bite.

"We're in desperate need of a shower," she said after swallowing.

"One of my favorite activities with you."

She arched that one eyebrow my way.

"That list isn't just comprised of you naked or sex you know. Watching you work ranks up there as does this. I know we're naked, but having you wrapped in my arms is one of the best things ever. Don't get me wrong, the sex is ahh-maz-ing! But it's not why I started liking you, or why I've started to fall in love with you."

"Will," she said softly.

"It's okay if you can't say it back yet. When you finally do tell me, I want it to be without you feeling any pressure from me. However long you need, I'll wait."

Her eyes were glassy as she leaned in and gave me a soft peck on the lips. "I don't think you'll have to wait long."

Once the cake was eaten, we picked up everything we could find, throwing away the cake box, and making the dash upstairs before Mrs. Hill came home. I had the privilege of lathering up Liz in the shower before she returned the favor. We fell into bed exhausted, and I, for one, slept like the dead.

The next morning, Will slipped on his shirt then rummaged through his clothes on the chair.

"Liz, do you remember picking up my underwear last night?"

"No, I thought you did." I stepped out of the closet and pulled on my work shirt.

"Screw it!" He slipped on his pants commando, which gave me a great view of his backside before he pulled them all the way on. He had a great ass: firm with not a ton of hair. The man definitely worked out. "I'll check around the sofa when I go down."

"Don't make too much noise. Mrs. Hill has a mother-in-law suite that's off the living room."

He gave me a quick but passionate kiss before he rushed downstairs. I pulled back my hair, then followed. I found him next to the coffee table.

"Did you find them?" I whispered as best I could.

"No, and I checked the sofa cushions just in case, and under the coffee table."

A light clicked on, and we both jumped like teenagers being caught by our parents.

"I thought I heard someone in here," said Mrs. Hill, her voice still groggy. She looked at me and Will then shook her head. "Those must've been your underpants I found peeking out from under the sofa last night. I also found several Scrabble tiles under there as well. After, I disinfected the coffee table for good measure. It looked a little. . .sticky."

My cheeks heated to a temperature they'd never reached before. "I was going to do that, Mrs. Hill. I'm sorry."

"No worries, dearie. I was young once too."

If I could've sunken into the floor and died of mortification, I would've. I would need to give Mrs. Hill one heck of a Christmas bonus!

# Chapter 21

# WILL

Now that my driver knew where the entrance was for Liz's home, he drove me directly to the door so I could pick her up for the ball. As soon as he pulled up to the curb, I hopped out and strode inside the vestibule of sorts then rang the buzzer.

"Yes?" came Mrs. Hill's voice a moment later. My face burned. Would Mrs. Hill cause that reaction for the rest of my life?

"Hi, Mrs. Hill, it's William Darcy. I'm here to pick up Elizabeth for the Pemberley Ball."

"Yes, of course. Come on up."

The next door clicked when it unlocked, and I entered, ensuring the door closed behind me. While Liz had mentioned the entry had monitored surveillance cameras and she had security on site for the businesses as well as the apartments that remained in several of the buildings, I still wanted to do my part to ensure she was safe.

The elevator opened as I approached. Mrs. Hill had likely pressed the first-floor button to send it down. The ride up was quick, and when I stepped out into the large foyer, Mrs. Hill waited for me.

"Don't you look handsome," she said with a smile. Meanwhile, I was a little warm under the collar. Ever since the housekeeper had mentioned that she'd cleaned the frosting from the coffee table, I hadn't been able to look the older woman in the eye. Thank the good Lord it wasn't Mrs. Reynolds! I would've probably searched for somewhere else to live, letting her keep the penthouse for herself.

"Thank you."

"I let Lizzy know you'd arrived. She should be down—"

"I'm coming," said Liz who stood at the top of the curved staircase.

My jaw surely dropped so far it hit the floor when I first noticed her. The navy gown she wore boasted of two straps over her creamy shoulders, the silky fabric making a deep "V" between her breasts. A bead and rhinestone trim cupped the underside of her bust before the fabric draped in a soft wave to the floor. Her thick curls were pulled away from her face. As she continued down, the back had a similar line, dipping down almost to her waist, but her shoulder blades were blocked from view by her luscious curls that trailed down her back. The look complemented her well. Her hair was so often worn up for work that I loved seeing it falling around her shoulders. A diamond strand glittered around her neck with a larger teardrop in the hollow at the bottom of her throat while two dangly matching earrings hung from each lobe.

"You're stunning."

She grinned and gave a flirty bat of her eyelashes. "Why thank you. You look pretty good yourself."

"Only pretty good?"

She laughed. "Okay, good enough to eat."

"I believe that's my cue to leave," said Mrs. Hill who handed me a long, navy wool coat. "For the ride over. It's supposed to snow tonight. She'll freeze without something to cover her up."

I nodded. "Thank you, Mrs. Hill." As much as I despised the thought of hiding all that lovely skin, Liz would certainly freeze without something to shield her from the cold.

My hand slipped around Liz's waist when she reached me, pulling her in for a light kiss to her lips. Just like the night at the gala, she wasn't wearing a lot of makeup, but I didn't want to mess up anything she'd worked to do.

"Are you ready?" I asked.

I held open her coat, and she slipped her free hand into a sleeve. "Yes, but for some reason I'm nervous." She traded her clutch to her other hand. "Isn't that ridiculous?"

"I admit I'm a bit nervous too. We've never been anywhere as a couple, so I think it's normal."

She turned so she was impossibly close. "Is that what we are—a couple?"

My heart dropped into my stomach. "That's what I'd thought. Do you feel differently?"

Her palm pressed against my tie, smoothing it. "No, but I didn't want to assume."

I covered her hand with my own. "I don't just sleep with anyone, much less smear frosting all over them and lick it off."

One of those adorable snort laughs escaped before she covered her nose. "Point taken."

I held out my hand, and she extended hers. As I tugged her toward the elevator, my chest, for once, didn't have that almost empty place I'd lived with for the past few years. Liz had somehow filled it. Since I met her at the gala a few months ago, she'd wheedled her way into my heart. I was in love with her, but she wouldn't be ready to hear that. She'd been hesitant enough when I told her I was falling. This was moving fast, and though I didn't have any qualms about us, she might need more time to accept what was happening between us.

"You've gone quiet," said Liz once the doors to the elevator closed.

"I'm just happy, here and now, with you."

She laughed. "In an elevator?"

I kissed her temple. "I think I could be in the worst place imaginable and still be happy because you were there."

"You exaggerate to flatter me, sir."

I lifted her chin so she could see the honesty in my gaze. "No, I'm telling you the absolute truth." Her cheeks turned a beautiful blush, and she entwined her fingers with mine as she turned to face the doors.

When we exited the building, my driver opened the door, so I could help Liz into the car. Once we were both inside, he shut the door and rushed around to hop inside and move the vehicle into traffic.

The ride to the ball wasn't long, and I didn't wait for my driver to get out of the car and extend my hand for Liz. Photographers jumped forward to take our photo, and I did my best to behave normally as they snapped tons of pictures. Our marketing department always had a red carpet of sorts for the charity event, but I'd always despised it.

Liz's eyebrows rose when she stood. "Oh, I hadn't expected this."

"I should've warned you. I'm sorry."

"No," she said, shaking her head. "I'm not upset. I just hope I don't look too bewildered in some of the photos."

Members of Pemberley Books marketing team were stationed along the entrance. As always, they cued us where to pose as we moved up the walk. One of Richard's assistants ushered me over to give a quote to one society page reporter who was waiting for my arrival.

By the time we were inside, I blew out a heavy exhale.

Liz chuckled. "You hated every moment of that, didn't you?"

"With a passion." I faced her. "Let me take your coat. We can check it at the desk there."

The attendants worked quickly, so I was able to lead Liz into the ballroom within minutes. As I'd expected, the room was decked out with Christmas trees and lights. The decorations also included some for Hannukah, the menorahs lit appropriately for tonight's place in the festival of lights.

"It's beautiful," said Liz in a breathy voice.

"The planning committee does an excellent job."

"Lizzy!" Gigi emerged from the crowd and hugged Liz. "I'm thrilled you came! Tonight is always dreadfully boring, so it'll be nice to have some company."

"Gi, Liz came with me tonight." I put my arm around Liz's lower back.

My sister's eyes about bugged out of her head. "Seriously!" She bounced on her toes. "I'm so excited for you, William!" She threw her arms around me. "Now you won't be so lonely when I move out."

Gi and I'd made plans for her to move closer to college, and for her to live with her friends—on the stipulation they live in a building with security. I owned one nearby—not that my penthouse was that far, just on the northern side of midtown. Thankfully, an apartment was available. The building manager needed to overhaul it. The former tenant had been in the flat for decades, and the carpet and decoration was still living in the early eighties.

"You're moving out?" asked Liz.

"Years ago, I purchased a building not far from Julliard—an additional investment so to speak. One of the larger flats opened up a month ago and the one next door comes available in two months. I'm going to renovate both into one, so she has plenty of room for her and her friends."

Liz squeezed my hand. "Sounds like the perfect place." Her gentle smile as well as the gaze she was giving me made my chest want to puff out. She approved. I could tell.

My sister clasped her hands in front of her like a little girl. "Exactly! So now that the two of you are together, I know my brother will be taken care of."

"Gigi, we've only been seeing each other for a few days." Yes, Liz's tempering of my sister's enthusiasm certainly burst my bubble. Few days or not, I was all in. She'd mentioned she wasn't into casual sex or flings; wouldn't that make me more as well?

Gi waved away Liz's comment. "I don't care. I know it'll work out."

"Hi, Lizzy," said Richard as he walked up. He kissed Lizzy's cheek then glanced where my arm was wrapped around her middle. "Don't tell me you let this grump bring you? When he won't dance with you, come find me. I'll twirl you around the floor. My mother didn't make me take lessons for nothing."

"You forget that I had to take those lessons with you, Dickie."

Richard gave that annoying chortle he used when he was hell-bent on pestering me. "But you haven't ever used them. How do you know you won't step on her toes?"

"Maybe Will doesn't need to do something often to be good at it." Liz's one eyebrow was lifted and arched just so. She was talking about more than just dancing, and I could've laid a big, wet sloppy kiss on her right now in appreciation.

Richard's head jolted back a little. "Is that right? I'm glad he doesn't disappoint."

One of my cousin's staff approached and whispered in his ear. "Excuse me a moment."

"Richard's right," said Gigi. "You should dance with Lizzy. You can avoid Aunt Catherine. She's going to have a stroke because Annie brought Char. If I were you, I'd steer clear."

I immediately glanced around the room. "How's Annie?"

"So far, doing a brilliant job of avoiding her mother and pretending Cruella isn't here. She's with Char on the dance floor at the moment."

Liz stepped forward but took my hand to lead me toward the dance floor. Since I knew what she was up to, I drew her back some so I could step to her side. When we approached Annie and Char, I took Liz in my arms and began to dance. With it being a work function for me, I didn't pull Liz as close as I would've preferred, but close enough that it'd be obvious we were together.

As we swayed to the music, I caught a glimpse of my aunt, who, by the puffing of her cheeks, was blustering to her assistant Collins. The little toad was red-faced and speaking quickly, no doubt attempting to placate my aunt while kissing her ass at the same time. It was a skill he used often although not always very successfully.

"Have you seen your aunt?" asked Liz.

"She's furious. She's gesturing toward Annie." I winced when my aunt's arm flew up in my direction. "Now, she's motioning toward us."

"Us?"

"Unfortunately." I rotated us so neither of us could see Aunt Catherine. "Liz, do you know who my aunt is?"

She drew back enough that I could see her face. "Yes, she's Cruella deBourgh. It's come up once or twice."

I gave a bark of a laugh. "I'd forgotten about that. I only asked because I wanted you to be prepared."

"Prepared for what?"

What possibilities were there? A raging inferno? Nuclear meltdown? Nothing was off-limits with my aunt. "For anything—anything at all."

# Chapter 22

The Pemberley Ball appeared to be a raging success. After Will and I danced, he was approached by quite a few of the guests who desired a word with him. With his arm around my waist, he smiled and listened to them, skillfully finding ways to solicit a donation for the charity that Pemberley had chosen to donate this year's proceeds. No one could complain of a stand-offish demeanor; however, I had a different perspective of those interactions.

Will's arm around me was tense as was his entire body, yet others would only see subtle self-assurance. In flashes of a moment, his unease with the attention would peek through. I doubt it was obvious to everyone, but at some point, I'd become more in tune with his tells, and right now, I wanted nothing more than to whisk him to a quiet place and kiss away his discomfort.

I took Will's hand in mine, and we worked our way across the room but before I could drag Will through a door to the side of the room, someone familiar stepped in front of us.

"Elizabeth Bennet? Excuse me, but I haven't seen you since the funeral."

I grinned at my uncle's good friend. "Mr. James, I'm happy to see you!" I accepted the old man's hand, but we didn't shake. He held it and covered it with his spare.

"I must admit I'm surprised to see you at a Pemberley function. I hope you don't intend to sell Novel Books. Your uncle—"

"No, I have no intentions of selling. I've simply become friends with the Darcy family. If you didn't know, my best friend is also involved with Annie deBourgh."

"We are also no longer seeking to purchase Novel Books," said Will, whose hand had tightened around mine. "At one time, we'd considered the acquisition, but Liz is responsible for the success of that store as well as The Buttercream Beanery, her own brainchild. She's also become an important person to my family, and I've no intention of interfering with her uncle's legacy."

Mr. James lifted his eyebrows. "I'm pleased to hear this. Luca was a wonderful man. I know he wanted his Betta to follow in his footsteps. It'd be heartbreaking if his wishes couldn't be fulfilled."

I squeezed Mr. James's hand. "I don't see any reason why anything so unfortunate should take place, but I appreciate your concern."

He nodded. "I should've checked in before now, but I promise I won't go so long in the future. Your uncle asked me once to keep an eye on you if something happened to him, but I've failed him so far. I'll have to come have a cup of coffee and some cake in your café."

"You'll always be welcome." As soon as Mr. James kissed my cheek, I tugged Will through that door I'd noticed.

"Where are we going?"

"I honestly have no idea."

The next door along the hallway opened, and I pushed Will inside. "Liz, this is a supply closet."

"So?"

After I turned on the light, I slipped my hands around his neck and pulled his head down so our lips could tangle. After no more than five minutes, his body relaxed, and he drew back, resting his forehead against mine.

"What was that for?" He was a bit out of breath.

"You seemed to need it. From the moment we stepped out on that dance floor, you've been stiff as a board."

"I hate these things."

"You told me something similar at the gala."

He kissed my forehead. "Your uncle called you 'Betta'?"

"He's the only one who ever has. My parents called me 'Elizabeth' while my friends call me 'Lizzy.' That night I introduced myself as 'Liz,' I wanted to use a name no one else did. I don't know why. It just seemed right."

His knuckles grazed down my cheek. "And I did the same— I felt the same."

After one last peck to my nose, he grimaced. "We should get back. I'd prefer to put you back in the car and go home. My aunt's making me nervous. She keeps glaring at you."

"Yeah, I noticed. I can't imagine her saying something in public, though."

Will chuckled, but not in a good way. "I wish I could be so optimistic. They don't call her Cruella for nothing."

When we returned, I glanced and met the eyes of my sister Jane, who'd now joined the glare-fest. The woman standing and glaring with Jane was familiar. That's right! She was at Gigi's party. She was that awful sister of Charlie Bingley. What was her name?

"Caroline is here. At some inopportune moment, she'll latch on to my arm in her best impression of a lamprey."

"Have you ever dated her?"

He shuddered. "God, no! I feared for my body parts—that she might cut them off and try to use them in her artwork."

I covered my nose as I gave a small snort. "She mentioned at Gigi's birthday party that she makes artwork out of doll parts, but I forgot to look her up afterward. Is she any good?"

Will pulled out his phone and after a few touches, held it out in front of me. I recoiled.

"Is that a rabbit?" The head was covered in doll hands with two prominent teeth made of. . .Were those tongues? Two doll arms reached from the poor creature's head to complete the work. "I think that will give me nightmares tonight."

The chuckle that met my ears was a good one this time. "Just protect me from her, will you?"

"I'll consider it."

He whirled me to the dance floor. "No, no considering. I need you."

"Well, when you put it like that."

During the dance, Jane and Charlie danced nearby. When the song ended, we started for the bar.

"Darcy!"

When we turned, Charlie wore a huge grin while he took Will's hand and pumped it madly. "I thought I saw you as we entered, but you disappeared. Anyway, great turnout tonight, isn't it?"

"Yes," said Will. "I'm pleased. I'm sure we'll raise a substantial sum."

"William! Yoohoo!" Will flinched when Caroline barreled through the guests and, true to Will's prediction, grasped his other arm, her pointy neon orange talons digging into his bicep.

"I was beginning to think we wouldn't see you tonight. You're going to join us for Christmas again this year, aren't you?"

"I'm so sorry, but Will's joining *me* this year, aren't you, honey?" It took everything I had to keep a straight face. Charlie's eyebrows had risen to his hairline, which was receding quickly it seemed. Jane glowered, and Caroline's jaw dropped.

"*You*," said Jane. "Since when are the two of you a thing?" Jane's tone was one I knew well. It held just a hint of a sneer, enough that someone who didn't know her wouldn't hear it, but I always did.

"Since you're not close to either of us, I don't see how it's any of your business." Will's voice was hard. He must've recognized the tone as well.

I leaned across Will a little. "And Caroline, would you be so kind as to remove your talons from *my* man's arm? I prefer it without poke marks."

Caroline snapped her jaw shut and lifted one corner of her mouth. "You should know Will's an old friend. If he had a problem with me touching him, he'd tell me himself."

"Caroline," said Will in a warning tone.

She flinched and removed her hands.

"And my name's William to you. Only Liz calls me 'Will.'"

Charlie's sister shrank back next to her brother and joined her hands in front of her. She bent forward a little and glanced at Jane, who rolled her eyes.

"If you'll excuse us," said Will. "We were just going to get a drink."

I let my hand fall into his and followed him to the bar, his shoulders tighter than they'd been before we'd slipped away. Was he angry about what I said to Caroline? I couldn't imagine him being upset, but Charlie did work for him. I doubted that he wanted to upset the man.

"Will?" I shifted my hand up to his shoulder. Was that shaking?

"Excuse me! Two doubles of Balvenie, please. Neat." With both hands gripping the edge of the bar, he chuckled low and soft. "Caroline's expression when you told her to remove her talons from your man. It was priceless. I've never seen her turn white before."

I relaxed as I smiled. "Well, I had to show my appreciation to you for chastising Jane. No one ever speaks to her that way."

"It's about time someone did."

"You know; I'd say Caroline is turning rather green right now." The woman was staring at us as I spoke. I slipped my hand down his back as I leaned into his side, my breast crushed to his chest.

He was laughing harder when he handed me my drink. "She's watching, isn't she?"

"Yes, she is." I brushed my fingers along the top of his ass cheek for a brief second before setting my palm on his shoulder. "I'm sorry if I went too far since this is a work event for you, but I did glance around first. Dear Caro was the only one looking."

He brushed my curls over my shoulder. "It wasn't that risqué. Besides, if she gets the picture that I'm with you, it'll be worth it. Maybe it'll discourage those that want to try later as well."

"Do you get hit on often?" A part of me didn't want to know.

"Often enough. Most of the assistants who've tried haven't lasted long. I'm quick to make reports and document any advances. My assistant, Gavin, also sits in on all meetings under the guise of taking notes for me. Most would think I can't remember what I'm supposed to do, but he's my safety net."

I shook my head. "I'm glad I don't have that problem. Most of the employees, other than management, are college students. I think enough fear of being fired exists for them not to try."

After a sip of my Scotch, I glanced at the dance floor. "Who is that Gigi is dancing with?"

Will shot around and narrowed his eyes. "Grayson Chamberlayne. His parents own Chambers Publishing."

I was familiar with the company. They made reference books and academic textbooks. Since we'd started selling books online, we'd begun carrying some college-level books to help compete with Pemberley and other collegiate book sites.

My date was quiet and glared until Gigi and Grayson stepped over to where Richard stood and began to talk.

"She can take care of herself, you know?"

"Hm," he said low.

I set my empty glass on the bar. "I'm going to the ladies'. Will you be okay while I'm gone?" I didn't want him to embarrass his sister when I couldn't stop him.

"Do you want me to escort you?"

I grinned at his concern. "I can manage. Thanks."

The facilities were easy to find, and once I'd washed my hands, I reapplied my lip gloss before stepping back into the hall.

"You aren't good enough for him."

I turned to face the owner of the voice behind me. None other than Mrs. deBourgh sat in a plush chair against the wall, her walking stick propped straight up with her hand on top.

"That's for him to decide, not you."

The older woman stood and stepped toward me, her walking stick being thrown forward with each step of that leg. "No, it's for his family as well, and I am the closest relation he has."

My eyebrows shot up. "Not that I'm aware of. I believe he would count Gigi and Richard as closer—Annie as well, of course."

The woman slammed her walking stick on the marble floor. The wood vibrated so vigorously, it should've shattered with the strength of the impact. "Do not mention my ungrateful child's name! She is dead to me."

"That's a shame. She's a lovely woman, and Char is my best friend. They're a great couple."

"This has nothing to do with Anne and everything to do with you believing you can date my nephew. He deserves more than a harlot who would use him for his money."

I opened my mouth to respond.

"I saw you run your fingers over his. . .over his. . ." She waved a hand in front of her. "Oh, you know what you did! It was the most shameful display I've ever seen."

With a laugh, I crossed my arms over my chest. "Will certainly didn't object, and that's his decision to make—not yours. As for money, I may not have the Pemberley coffers at my disposal, but I don't need whatever he has. I have my own home and my own money. I don't want or need Will's."

"Will? His name is William—Fitzwilliam to be exact. He's named after his mother's great family. It was natural that she marry a Darcy, who was from a good family. Don't think I don't know about yours, Miss Bennet. Your father's business is bankrupt, your mother is using her credit cards faster than her husband can bring home his paychecks, and your sister is clinging to my nephew's friend in the hopes of marrying well. I expect your father will be arrested for embezzlement at some point in the near future. He can't help himself to his customer's funds, whether he knows it or not."

I kept my body straight and ensured no surprise whatsoever crossed my face. Even when I still lived at home, my father always argued with my mother about her spending habits. She wanted to decorate the house and dress like they possessed unlimited funds, which they didn't. Nothing Mrs. deBourgh was saying was a surprise. In my opinion, it had been a long time coming.

"I have nothing to do with my parents. My uncle was, for all intents and purposes, my father, and he was the best man I've ever known. What my father and mother do doesn't concern me or have anything to do with me."

"It will tarnish the good name of my nephew!"

"Because he's dating the estranged daughter of someone suspected of a crime? Somehow, I doubt Will will care." I hoped he wouldn't.

"Regardless, I'll carry my point! He'll not continue seeing someone like you. I have the perfect young lady—"

"Good luck with that. For your scheme to work, he has to be interested, and I can guarantee he won't be."

"Because you've bewitched him!"

A bark of a laugh escaped before I could stop it. "What is this? The 18$^{th}$ century? You need to worry about your own concerns and let others live their lives."

My cell phone rang, and I pulled it from my clutch. "If you'll excuse me, I have to take this."

At the sight of the number on the screen, I pressed to accept the call and brought it to my ear. "Mary, what's wrong?"

"I finally told them. . ."

"How dare you!" My phone was pulled from my ear, taking several strands of my hair with it. "I did not excuse you, and how dare you turn your back on me!"

I didn't release my phone, even though my scalp where the hair was yanked out from the root stung like hell. "What the fuck are you doing?" I wrenched my arm back from the old bat, who was stronger than she looked.

"Hello? Mary?" I glared at the old woman. "You hung up on her!"

"What's going on?" I rubbed my head while Will strode up. "I could hear the commotion from the end of the hall."

"This harlot thinks she can have you no matter what!" When Mrs. deBourgh lifted her arm to point at me, the hair she'd pulled out hung from her rings.

"Is that your hair?" Will asked pointing.

I nodded. "I had a phone call from my sister Mary. I told your aunt I had to take the call, and she grabbed the phone when I tried to answer it."

My phone vibrated in my hand. When I looked down, a new text had come in. "*Lizzy, I'm at the café. Mia let me stay when it closed. Mom and Dad kicked me out.*"

"I have to go," I said.

"Liz, wait!" Will took me by the upper arms. "I swear what my aunt says means nothing."

I winced at the shrieking of his aunt behind me. "We'll talk, but my sister is at the café waiting for me. She needs my help. I'm sorry, but I can't stay. Please understand."

His shoulders drooped but he kissed my forehead and stepped back. "You know I understand. Take care of your sister, but I *will* call you.

"Take my car so you don't have to wait for a taxi or a car service. My driver will come back for me once you're home."

"Thank you!" I kissed him quickly on the lips, and without looking at Cruella, I hurried for the door.

# Chapter 23

The moment Liz rushed off, my aunt marched up to me, a giant scowl marring her features. "What do you think you're doing with that little whore?"

I stepped up to my aunt and glared. "Not one more word."

"But—"

My teeth ground together while I pulled out my phone. Funny, I didn't even have to say anything, but my aunt's jaw clapped shut with a snap. After I texted my driver, asking him to take Liz wherever she needed to go, I slipped the device back into my pocket. "What in the name of all that's holy did you think you were doing?"

Aunt Catherine pointed in the direction Liz had gone. "That woman—"

"Is the most amazing woman I've ever met. She has an MBA as well as went to the Cordon Bleu. She came up with the concept for her bakery, which has become a raging success. Not only that, but she inherited her uncle's bookstore on the Upper West Side, which has flourished under her leadership.

Moreover, she displays more heart and caring than most people in this world. Gigi adores her as does Annie—"

"Your sister's name is Georgiana, and my daughter's name is Anne, after *your* mother."

"And she prefers Annie and has for as long as I can remember. Liz was the one who made me see that I was disrespecting Gi by not abiding by her wishes."

My aunt sniffed. "What a load of rubbish. As parents, it's our job to name our children and to know what's best for them. Since your own dear mother isn't here to guide you, that job falls to me. I've selected the perfect young lady—"

"Aunt Catherine, no! The last thing I want is you picking my dates, much less who I'll marry. My mother made it clear that I was to choose the woman who made me happy, and that's what I'm going to do!"

My aunt sucked in a breath through her teeth, making an odd whistling sound. "You most certainly will not! You have a responsibility to ensure the Darcy name retains its prestige and its connection to the wealthiest families in the world."

I recoiled. "What do you think this is, Georgian England? I will marry for no other reason than to ensure my happiness, and if you continue on this tirade, you'll no longer be welcome in my homes. And just so you know, Gigi and Richard won't take this sort of interference in their lives either. If you don't begin treating us like the adults we are, you'll end up bitter and alone, because no one will want to be around you."

"William," she said in a breathless tone.

"Yes, I'm being serious. You've already alienated your own daughter, who's with someone who makes her happier than I've ever seen her. She'd waited for so long to come out to you, and she'd been so terrified that when she finally found that strength she'd been needing, the end result was that she's experienced a freedom she's never known. It's never too late to be a part of her life."

"I will not accept how she's living, nor will I accept you with that woman you're dating. You *will* abide by my wishes, or you'll be dead to me too."

"Then goodbye, Aunt." Much as Liz had, I turned my back on Aunt Catherine and strode back into the ball. As I entered, Richard was walking toward me.

"Security heard yelling. When I checked it out, it was you and Aunt Catherine. What the heck happened?"

I ran my fingers through my hair. "From what I can tell, our aunt ambushed Liz when she came out of the ladies' room. Just considering what she likely said horrifies me. At some point, Liz had an urgent phone call from her younger sister and somehow, Aunt Catherine hung up the call."

Richard's eyes widened. "You're kidding."

"No, unfortunately, I'm not. She took some of Liz's hair with it too. Liz needed to leave, so I told her to take my car."

"And you had it out with Cruella."

I chuckled and shook my head. "Do you know how difficult it is not to call her that to her face?"

My cousin perked up. "Can I do it?"

"Be nice. I do need you to have security show her out. Aunt Catherine will tell everyone here how she's been mistreated, and I want to keep tonight about the charity."

After he nodded, Richard made to pass, but put a hand on my shoulder. "What are you going to do about Lizzy?"

"I have to finish out this event, then I'll call her when I'm leaving. If I can go over and talk, I will, but I need to respect that her priority this evening is her sister. I just want to make sure we're okay."

His eyebrows drew down a little in the middle. "Do you have reason to believe it isn't?"

I sighed. "She did kiss me quickly before she left, but if you were in her place and accosted by Aunt Catherine, wouldn't you have second thoughts about being in a relationship with me?"

Richard laughed. "I don't need second thoughts—or thirds for that matter. I'd never consider a relationship with you." He scrunched his nose. "You're too needy." After a stupid grin, Richard walked away, grabbed two of the men on the security detail, and waved them to follow.

As I scanned the room, Gigi was dancing again—this time with our uncle, Richard's father. She was safe at the moment.

Since I was stuck here for the duration, I may as well make this the most successful Pemberley Ball in history. One of our most dedicated donors stood across the ballroom, so I made my way around the dance floor and approached.

"Good evening, Mrs. Jenkinson. How are you tonight?"

## LIZ

When the car was a block away from home, I sat forward. "I need you to pull up to the café, please."

"Yes, ma'am."

A moment later, the driver pulled up to the curb and hurried to open my door. After he helped me out of the car, I lifted my skirts and climbed the steps. Even though I wanted to move faster, I didn't want to fall on my face in the heels I was wearing.

Before I reached the door, Mia opened it. "Good timing, Boss." As soon as I entered, she locked the door behind me. "I'll go turn out the lights and lock up. We just finished in the kitchen ten minutes ago."

"Thanks, Mia." I nodded, but my sister's presence in the middle of the café held my attention.

Mary sat at one of the tables. Dark circles lined the undersides of her eyes, which were red and a bit puffy. She held a cup in her hands and a plate with the remnants of something sat in the middle of the table. She had two enormous suitcases nearby.

"I thought you wanted to stay longer. What happened?"

My sister shook her head. "My early decision came in from NYU. Mom went snooping on my laptop and found the email, which she then showed to Dad."

"What program did you apply for?" I was certain I knew, but I needed her to say it.

"Fashion design."

A snort came out before I could stop it. I covered my nose. "I'm so sorry. I can just imagine our father's reaction to that little nugget."

"I've never seen him turn that shade of purple before," said Mary.

"I heard a rumor he's been embezzling from the business. Whether or not the source is reliable, I don't know—"

Mary winced. "I've overheard things. It's why I stayed so long. From what he's said on the phone, he wanted you to join the business to cover everything up. He thought Zio would pay out if you were involved."

"But I'd never do that. Dad had to know that."

"I don't think you had to do anything at all," said Mary. "If he rigged everything so it looked like you were guilty, Zio would've done anything to keep you out of it. Dad's known that for a long time. How many summers did he want you to work at the office?"

"And I always worked for Zio."

Mary nodded. "Exactly. You made it impossible for him for a long time. From what I've understood, he started when you were at business school. He'd convinced himself you'd come work for the firm."

"Which was why he was so angry when I wanted to stay in Manhattan." My stomach clenched even tighter. Why was my father like this?

"Right, but he couldn't burn his bridges with you. He needed you to ultimately come work for him. He's always intended for one of us to come work for him, hasn't he?"

"I think he planned for me until I refused, and his ambitions ended up shifting to you."

"Because he's planned for one of us to be his get-out-of-jail free card if he gets caught."

I rested my head in my hands. "We shouldn't talk about this anymore down here. Come on."

I stood and grabbed one of her suitcases and led her through the storage rooms of Novel Books until we reached the elevator. Once we were in the house, I led Mary into the elevator in the library. It was a heck of a lot easier to get those two heavy suitcases up that way than the staircase in the foyer.

As the doors closed, my mind immediately went to the last time I was in here. I leaned my head back against the wall and fought tears. "Mary, do you know if Dad put our names on any of that paperwork already? If he's gone this far, what's to stop him from falsifying records?"

"Last week, Jane came to the house, and she and Dad shut themselves in his study. Since Mom never pays any attention to where I am, I managed to sneak into the back stairwell and listen at the return air vent." That vent shared ductwork with the return air in my father's study. "I couldn't hear everything. At times, Jane spoke too low, but our names were mentioned. Jane said something about forging a signature."

I winced. "I'll need to check with my attorney and see if she's had access to my most recent signature. It's changed since we were in high school."

Mary shrugged one shoulder. "They've never seen mine. I've always printed anything they see. I've heard Dad speak of way too much to trust him or Jane, and our mother has never made any secret of the fact that I wasn't wanted. I'd be stupid to trust any of them."

Poor Mary had been a lot like Gigi in that she was a later-in-life baby for my parents. Except that where Gigi was adored and wanted, Mary was tolerated by my father and resented by my mother because Mary wasn't the boy my parents had hoped she'd be.

I brought Mary to the room Gigi stayed in when she visited. It was on the other side of the upstairs, so she'd have all the privacy she wanted. "You can stay here with me for as long as you want. I'm going to call my attorney in the morning. We need to meet with him, and if this is as bad as I'm worried it is, we'll need to contact the authorities. Neither of us going to jail for Dad's bullshit and Mom's selfishness if I can help it.

"Once that's handled, if you want to live with me, you can, or you can live in one of the apartments in the buildings around me rent free while you go to school. You'll never have to go back to our parents ever again. I can promise you that. You can do whatever you want with your life free of them. You'll never need to even see them again if you don't want to."

Mary lunged into my arms. "Thank you! You always said I could come to you, but with all of this, I wasn't sure what would happen."

My heart split and bled. "All that would ever happen is that I'd help you. You're my little sister and we've always been close, no matter what. I love you, and that'll never change. We'll get through this and be stronger than ever. Got it?"

"I can't argue, even if I wanted to."

"Nope." I shook my head. "You're stuck with me."

"Lizzy?"

When I turned, Mrs. Hill was in the doorway. "I thought you were in bed."

"I was watching a movie when the buzzer went off. Mr. Darcy's downstairs. You left your clutch in his car, and I think he wanted to speak to you."

I squeezed the bridge of my nose. "Thanks, Mrs. Hill. Mary will be staying with us for now."

Mrs. Hill gave a grandmotherly smile. "I think we both knew she'd find her way here sooner or later. If you need anything at all, dearie, just tell me and I'll make sure it's done. Do you want some help unpacking your things?"

Mary glanced at the two suitcases. "Maybe tomorrow. I think I'm just going to shower and change into some pajamas right now. I'm exhausted."

I could only imagine how tired she was. The falling out I'd had with our parents was hard as hell, but Mary had more backbone than I had at her age. She'd gotten away from it all long before I was willing to sever the connection.

"I took off tomorrow because of the ball tonight."

"I'm sorry for taking you away from it," said Mary.

"No, you needed me. Will, my date, has a younger sister, so he understood. But in the morning, I'll let you know the plan for the day. With the possible severity of this, I'm sure Mr. Goulding will have us come in first thing."

"Lizzy," said Mrs. Hill. "Why don't you let me help Mary get settled while you talk to Mr. Darcy?"

I nodded. "Yes, of course. You're right." I hugged Mary one more time. "You can come to my room and ask me anything if you need to. It's the last one on the other side of the staircase."

When I made it to the foyer, Will was pacing, my clutch in his hand.

"You look good holding a purse of silver and blue rhinestones."

He chuckled and held it out. "I want to apologize about my aunt. She told me some of what she said. It was unforgivable. I've told her she has to accept you as someone important to me, or I won't have anything to do with her."

Without warning, my eyes stung and tears began pouring down my cheeks. I didn't want to do this—my heart was screaming in protest—but what choice did I have? "I appreciate you doing that, but your aunt made some claims about my dad that I need to sort out."

"What does that mean?" He stepped closer which made it that much harder to spit out what I had to tell him.

"Will, I don't know exactly what's going on yet, but I won't have it harm you. You have to go. If this all blows over, then I'll get in touch."

He frowned and took my cheeks in his palms. "What do you mean *if* this all blows over? What's happening?"

"I don't want to say anything until I know for sure. It may be nothing, but it may be everything too. I don't want you harmed by your association with me."

"Association? We're more than that, aren't we?"

I couldn't ignore the pleading in his eyes. God, my chest hurt worse than I could imagine. "Will, you need to let me go for now."

"But I don't want to." His voice trembled, and my chest cracked open.

As much as it killed me to do it, I pulled his hands away from my face. "But I need you to."

"Liz, let me help you," he said, his voice tearing my shredding heart into smaller pieces.

"I can't. I need to do this on my own. If you have any feelings at all for me, you'll respect my wishes." I barely got the words out. It was all I could do not to choke on them.

Will squeezed his eyes closed, turned, and walked into the elevator while my legs threatened to buckle underneath me. As the doors closed, he didn't turn around or face me.

I gripped my stomach and choked back a sob. My entire heart just traveled down an elevator, and in those final moments, I'd realized just how much I loved Will Darcy. What was I going to do?

# Chapter 24

I'd woken up early—heck, I'd hardly slept if I was telling the truth. Despite it being five in the morning, I called my uncle's assistant Mr. Stone, who'd become my right hand after my uncle's death, and gave him the bare bones of the situation. Before eight, Mr. Goulding was sitting around a table in the library with me, Mary, and Mr. Stone. Thankfully, it didn't matter whether it was Sunday or not. Both men were loyal to my uncle and willing to treat me as they did him.

Over coffee, Mary and I told Mr. Goulding what we had reason to believe while he took notes. Once we'd finished, he sat back and twirled his pen in his fingers while he stared at the notepad. "I think we need to be the ones who bring in law enforcement. If we let this sit, then you'll look guilty of whatever your father intends—if not directly, then by association since you now have some clue of his crimes."

I nodded. "I had a lot of time to think this over last night, and I agree. All of my financials as well as those of Novel Books and Buttercream Beanery will be available for investigation. I've nothing to hide." Mary grabbed my hand, squeezing it with a death grip. I winced. The bones would break soon if she didn't let up.

"I'll contact our accountants and let them know what's coming," said Stone.

I let out a breath. "Thank you."

Mr. Goulding glanced around at each of us. "Why don't you get some breakfast while I call the FBI?"

"The FBI?" said Mary in a squeak.

He leaned forward and rested his arms on the table. "You mentioned a large sum of money earlier. Cases where a substantial sum is involved typically fall under their jurisdiction. If it doesn't, I'm sure they'll put us in touch with whomever we require to resolve this matter. We may not be able to meet with them until tomorrow, but I'd rather get the ball rolling now."

As soon as the attorney stepped into the foyer, I covered my face with my hands, dropped my head back, and groaned. "I can't eat. I'm sure it'll come right back up."

"You managed coffee," said Mr. Stone.

"And it's sitting in my throat."

He dipped his chin, looking at me over his glasses. "You need to relax. You've done nothing wrong. I know that, and the management of Novel Books knows that, as does everyone at the café."

"That doesn't mean my father hasn't succeeded in making me appear a criminal."

I stood up and paced for what seemed like an hour before Mr. Goulding finally returned. He held his cell phone in his hand. "I was put through to the agent in charge of investigating Longbourn Investments. An anonymous tip a few weeks ago made them look into transactions your father's been making.

They'd rather keep whatever is going on with the case quiet for now, so they're coming here with a couple of agents to talk to you."

"I'll have Mrs. Hill make a pot of coffee. Would it be tacky to get a box of pastries from the bakery? I don't want it to look like I'm bribing them."

Mr. Goulding smiled as he set his phone down. "I don't think you have anything to worry about. You're inviting them here to give evidence. If it takes all morning, I'm sure they'll be thankful that you considered feeding them at all. I doubt everyone thinks to do it."

Stone stood. "If we have three agents coming and there are four of us, then what do you want me to bring?"

I crossed my arms over my chest, hugging myself. "A half dozen bagels and a selection of doughnuts, cinnamon rolls, and a few of Char's individual quiches. Have Mia ring it up. I'll get you a card." I occasionally gave out coffee or baked goods for promotional purposes or as complimentary while people ordered cakes and so on, but this was different.

As I hurried up the stairs, my phone buzzed in my pocket. When I pulled it out, I paused to see what was on the screen.

*"I missed waking up with you in my arms. Even though I understand why you believe this to be necessary, it doesn't mean that I don't hate it. I love you. There. I said it. I debated all night whether I should tell you by text, but there it is. Please call me when you have a chance. I want to say it so you can hear it and believe that no matter what happens, I'm here for you."*

I squeezed my eyes closed and covered my face. I wouldn't cry! I wouldn't cry! I hated this! Why did my parents always try to fuck up everything? Whenever I picked out my school schedule in high school, they'd call in and have it changed. College was the first time I had any autonomy, yet I still remembered those times when I was little and my parents still seemed "normal." Mary never had that time with them, which is why I'm sure it was easier for her to tell them to shove their plans up their asses.

"Lizzy." A hand landed on my shoulder.

I was crying when I dropped my hands and looked at Mary. "Can you get my card? It's in my purse on my dresser, and please let Mrs. Hill know about the coffee. I want to lie down for a bit."

"I'm worried about you."

"I'll be fine. I'm just tired, and the timing of this sucks."

Mary held my hand while we walked to my bedroom. After she grabbed my card, she ran it downstairs while I curled into a fetal position on the bed. I just needed a quick cry, and I'd be ready to face whatever was coming next.

"Lizzy?"

I dragged my eyes open to Mrs. Hill standing over me, then shot straight up in bed, sending Atticus bolting from his perch on my hip. "Shit! What time is it?"

"It's ten o'clock, dearie. Mr. Goulding told me to let you sleep a while when the agents showed up at the door. From what little I've gleaned while bringing in coffee and cleaning up, they've presented what evidence they have to him and Mary has talked about what she knows. Since most of what you know is from Mary, they let you sleep while they didn't need you."

After I stood, I went to the bathroom and checked my appearance in the mirror while I washed my hands. It was obvious I'd been crying, which must've been why it felt like my eyes had sand in them. They were red-rimmed with dark circles underneath. God, I'd just woken up and I was tired! How was that possible?

I splashed water on my face and returned to Mrs. Hill waiting on me. "You should've come and gotten me when they arrived."

"What good would that've done? They didn't need you. It was better to let you sleep."

As much as I had the urge to argue, Mrs. Hill was being the mother I'd always needed, so I didn't bother. She'd never concede that I was right anyway.

When I entered the library, two men and a woman, all in dark suits, sat at the table with Mr. Goulding, Mr. Stone, and Mary.

"Good morning. I apologize for not being downstairs when you arrived."

The female agent stood. "Please don't worry about it. I'm Special Agent Forster, the lead agent on the Longbourn Financial case. These are Special Agents Pratt and Carter." Both men nodded.

"It's nice to meet you all," I said. It sounded odd, but what else was I supposed to say?

Mr. Goulding stood and slid a legal pad across the table. "Before we say anything, Lizzy, I want you to sign this piece of paper."

I frowned, stepped forward, picked up the pen, and signed as I had on all legal documents since I'd inherited Zio's estate, "Elizabeth Rose Bennet."

Special Agent Forster pointed at the paper. "May I take a closer look?"

I passed the pad over, and she held what appeared to be a document to it. "There are similarities, but I agree; the others are not Miss Bennet's signature."

After a scan of the people at the table, I set down the pen. "I don't understand."

Mr. Goulding nodded. "I apologize, Miss Bennet, but I wanted you to sign that without seeing or hearing anything we'd discussed before you entered the room."

Special Agent Forster fanned some papers in front of her that looked like bad photocopies of documents. "Your sister Mary provided us with audio recordings and pictures she took while still living in your parents' home. The documents in your father's possession are signed with your name, but they're not your signature. There are obvious variations."

I immediately whirled around to Mary. "You recorded Dad and took pictures in his office? Why didn't you tell me?"

"Because I didn't want you freaking out."

"Dad would've killed you if he found you there." He'd slapped me once for being in his study. I was looking for a stapler for a school project. I'd had to stay home the day after because of the red handprint still on my cheek.

Mary shrugged. "I wasn't stupid about it. I waited until he left for work and Mom went to the salon, then I crept into the office. Somehow, he'd missed that the safe hadn't clicked shut, so I was able to find more than I'd planned. I was late for school, but it was worth it."

I flinched. "I completely forgot about school. We'll have to update your records."

"Friday was our last day before the holiday. That can all be done after the break. It's not like we need to rush."

"And I can drive her if you're worried about her safety," said Mr. Stone.

My legs relaxed and I sagged into the chair behind me. "Is there a way to know when this nightmare will be over?"

Special Agent Forster sat as did the other two agents. "We'll keep you informed through your attorney as we know anything. Unfortunately, it's up to the prosecutor, who will ultimately decide who and what charges to pursue. We just present our evidence."

The agents asked me a series of questions that I answered without any hesitation. Mr. Goulding chimed in when he was required, but the morning was uneventful—if you didn't take into consideration I was answering questions from the FBI.

Eventually, Special Agent Forster stood. "I believe we have what we need for now. As I said earlier, we'll be in contact with Mr. Goulding if we require anything further. Thank you for the bagels and pastries. All three of us had just walked into the office when your attorney called. None of us had much time for coffee or to grab a bite before we left."

The other two agents nodded in agreement.

I frowned. "I didn't realize agents worked on Sundays."

One of the other agents lifted a shoulder. "Only when it's necessary."

Only when it's necessary? Did that mean my father's case had a high priority or was I reading more into it than was truly there?

"Did you need Miss Bennet's financial records?" asked Mr. Stone. "I can give you a flash drive with the accounts of both businesses as well as her personal accounts."

Special Agent Forster nodded. "Yes, and we appreciate your willingness to provide those."

I stood long enough to shake the hands of the agents before Mr. Stone escorted them to the accounting offices. The moment they left the room, I sank back into the chair and scrubbed my face with my hands.

"Lizzy?"

When I turned my head to face Mary, I rubbed my forehead. "I'm stressed is all. I'll be okay. Do you need anything? If you forgot your brush or facial cleanser or whatever, Mrs. Hill can send out for some. Just let her know what it is. I'd go to the store with you, but I'm not in the mood."

Mary stood and kissed me on the top of the head. "I'm good. Don't worry about me."

Mr. Goulding patted my shoulder. "Your uncle would be proud of you. He griped to me often about your parents when we were preparing his estate. He wouldn't want you to take the fall for what they've done."

As soon as he left, I sat in Zio's favorite chair in the library and watched the snow fall on the city as the light changed from morning to afternoon.

"You need to eat," said Mrs. Hill.

I startled. Had I been asleep? If I was, it was one of those waking dozes where you never realize you were sleeping. If that makes any sense at all.

"I'm not hungry."

She tsked and shook her head as she left. I stood and poured myself a glass of whiskey. Yes, I was likely going to regret this in the morning, but I didn't care right at this moment.

With my glass in hand, I grabbed a blanket and sat back in Zio's chair.

"Liz?"

I blinked when Will stepped forward and knelt before me. "You aren't supposed to be here."

"I took a taxi and wore a baseball cap and sunglasses. I never dress this casual; no one would recognize me."

He stood, put on the hat and glasses, and held out his arms. "What do you think?"

His baggy jeans hung low on his hips, and he wore a white t-shirt with a plaid flannel over it. He kind of looked like a skater punk. "It isn't your usual look."

"I left out the backdoor to my building and caught the taxi two blocks down. I paid with cash." He squatted back down and slipped his hands under the blanket to rub my thighs. "I missed you and wanted to see you."

I pulled off his hat and tossed it over the chair. "I missed you too."

As the first tear hit my cheek, he took the glass from my hand and set it on the table. "You're exhausted. Let's get you to bed."

His hands slipped under me, and he lifted me into his strong arms. I was dreaming, but it didn't matter. What I wanted more than anything was Will with me—holding me. If this was the only way I could have it, I'd stay in Zio's chair all night long.

# Chapter 25

## WILL

I held Liz to me and savored the feel of her in my arms. Yes, she'd told me not to come, but I couldn't stop thinking about her—I couldn't stay away. She'd been understandably upset after the ball, so upset I'd hardly been able to do anything all day. I'd been distracted and grumpy and not fit for any sort of company.

Gigi had asked me over and over if I was okay. When Richard and I'd gone to the Chelsea Piers driving range, I'd sent a horrible chip shot right at my cousin's head. That was when we'd called it a day, loaded our clubs into the car, and gone to a quiet bar for a drink. As much as Richard had tried to make me unload what was going on, I'd avoided telling him. I was a horrible liar. He asked me more than once about Liz. I'd changed the subject every time.

When I arrived at the apartment entrance and rang the buzzer, Mrs. Hill had let me in. *"She needs you right now,"* was all she'd said before pointing me in the direction of the library. Liz had been dozing in a chair near the windows of the library, a blanket over her lap, and a tumbler in her hand that was about to spill whatever was left in the bottom. Atticus was perched on the arm of the chair, likely peeved he couldn't take the place of the drink in her lap.

She hadn't awakened but instead, had burrowed into me as I carried her into the elevator, which was the quickest way upstairs, and let's face it, the easiest.

Now, I lay here with her in my embrace, my hands not straying as they'd love to do. My erection begged for relief, but Liz had more important problems to solve, and sex wasn't the answer, no matter what my dick wanted.

Liz groaned and rolled in my arms, nuzzled her nose into my chest like a kitten before blinking and looking up at me.

I tightened my arms around her. "Good morning." I almost held my breath at her response to my being with her in bed.

"I'd thought you were a dream."

My lips pressed to her hair while I inhaled that familiar scent of her. "A good dream or a bad dream?"

She sighed. "A forbidden one, if you must know. Please don't think that I want you to go, but you need to stay away from me for a while."

"Tell me what's going on."

She covered her face with her hands and shook her head. When she removed them, her eyes were shiny, as though she'd break down and cry at the drop of a pin. "My father has been embezzling from Longbourn, from his clients, for some time now. Your aunt mentioned it at the ball."

My chin hitched back. "I don't care about what your father has done. You've mentioned him before. You don't have any kind of relationship with him, do you?"

"No, I don't, but he's somehow implicated me as the one who stole the money. From what I understand, Jane helped him with it."

As insane as it sounded, her expression told me without question that she spoke the absolute truth.

"That's crazy," I said. "Have you ever worked for his company?"

"I haven't even set foot in the building since I was sixteen. I called my attorney yesterday, and he contacted the FBI. I had agents in the library yesterday going over pictures and audio my sister Mary took in the house before my parents kicked her out. Her eighteenth birthday was a couple of weeks ago, and she was staying longer to try to help me."

"That was incredibly brave of her."

She pressed her palm to my chest. "It was. I'm grateful to her for doing it, even if I wish she'd gotten out earlier. They're miserable to live with."

"And you're sure Jane is in on it?" I couldn't ignore that she was involved with one of *my* corporate attorneys."

"Mary has them talking about it on video. There's a return air in the back stairwell of the house that connects to the one in my father's study. She recorded them talking about their plans on her phone. I had to provide the FBI with a copy of my signature as well as flash drives of my finances and those of Novel Books and the café's.

"In the meantime, if this goes public, anyone I'm linked to could be brought up in the news. This could ruin Novel Books and the café, and I don't want you and Pemberley Books raked over the coals with me." What a frigging mess! "You need to do what's best for Gigi, yourself, and your own company. Once this is over, we can consider us and what comes next, but I don't want your reputation to suffer. I'm begging you; please don't make this harder than it already is."

"Liz, I love you. Don't you understand? I can help you."

"I'm doing this for you. Don't *you* understand? Everything I've worked so hard to build could be taken away." She wiped tears from her cheek. "What if I'm forced to sell everything off to pay back whatever my father has done? My reputation would be in the toilet."

"We don't know that yet. Plus, if you're in trouble, let me help you. If it comes down to it, I can buy Novel Books and the café separate from Pemberley Books—with my own money. I'd ensure you retain full control of everything. We'd sign legal forms. I'd own it, but it'd still be your baby. Then, when everything is back to normal, we can talk about you regaining full ownership."

"I can't ask you to do that."

"You're not asking." I held her gaze. She had to understand that I'd do anything for her.

Her hands cradled my face. "Since Mary told me what she knows, I've realized that I love you so much."

My breath hitched in my chest.

"And I'd do anything to protect you from this. As much as I want to say 'fuck it all' and keep you with me, that's the most selfish thing I could do right now."

I took her hands in mine. "Then let me help you! Let me go to the attorneys with you tomorrow. Fuck, let my attorneys help yours. We'll make sure to nail your father to the wall for this."

She shook her head. "Let me deal with this. I want you so far away no one could question whether you were a part of it. If I need you to take care of Novel Books and the Beanery for me, I'll let you know. In the meantime, I'm going to do what I can to protect you and Gigi, which means you need to respect my wishes and stay away."

"Liz—"

"This is killing me, Will. If you push me too hard, I'll cave, and I can't cave. I need you to go."

I hated this! My hand slipped around her, and I pulled her in for a long kiss, my lips attempting to convey how much I wanted to stay with her—to be the rock she'd need through this mess.

"I love you," I said when I pulled back.

She kissed her fingers and pressed them to my lips. "I love you too."

As much as my entire body protested, I drew away and threw my legs over the side of the bed. After putting back on my socks and sneakers, I pulled on my t-shirt.

"I never thought I'd see Will Darcy in baggy jeans."

I could barely manage a smile before I kissed her on the forehead. "I'll see you soon."

"I hope so."

My feet had bags of sand pulling them back as I trudged to the foyer and down the elevator. I hailed a taxi when I made it outside. Once I'd given the driver the address, I pulled out my phone and called Richard.

"Hey, Darce. You never call me this early unless you need something, so what's up?"

"I have a problem, and I need your help." Richard knew me well enough not to question when I asked.

"Okay, when I come into the office—"

"No, come to the penthouse. I don't want anyone overhearing."

"Do you want me to call Bingley?"

"No! He has to stay out of this. I have a gut feeling." Charlie was too close to Jane right now, and I couldn't afford him running off at the mouth to her.

Richard was quiet for a moment. I'd been friends with Charlie for a long time, but he'd been different in some ways for a while. What if he wasn't what he seemed anymore?

"I'm already on my way," said my cousin.

"Thanks."

When the taxi pulled up to the curb, I paid the driver in cash and walked into the building. The doorman greeted me, as did security. I smiled and did my best to behave as though this was a normal day.

My foot tapped in a furious rhythm on the tile of the entrance while I waited for the elevator to make its way down to me. A familiar voice greeting the doorman made me turn.

"You didn't take long."

Richard waved to security. It wasn't like they needed to get his name. Most of the building employees down here knew my cousin since they logged him in so often. They just didn't need to ring him up since I was down here.

"I was heading for the subway when you called, so I turned around and came straight here. It's only a few blocks."

The elevator opened, and we stepped inside. As soon as the doors closed, Richard turned and leaned against the wall. "That's the most casual I've seen you in a while—at least outside of the house."

"I went to Liz's last night."

He crossed his arms over his chest. "Why do you say it like that?"

I furrowed my brow. "Like what?"

"Like it was a death knell. Has something happened with the two of you?"

I exhaled and tipped my head back and forth. "Yes and no."

Richard's chin hitched back. "That's cryptic, even for you."

When the doors opened, we entered the penthouse, and I led Richard straight to my office and shut the door. School was out for Christmas break, so Gi wouldn't come down before ten. We had all the privacy we'd need for some time.

"What's going on?" asked Richard.

"So, you probably don't know this, but Liz isn't close with her family."

He laughed. "I could guess by the chilly atmosphere in a room when both she and her sister are in it. What's your point?"

I scrubbed my hands over my face. Good Lord, give me strength! "Liz has another sister named Mary. Mary is a little like Gigi and is younger. She turned eighteen last month, but even though she doesn't get along with her parents and wants a different life than they envision, she stayed until they kicked her out.

"Mary, during that time, was apparently spying on her father. You see, he's been embezzling money from his company for some time now and apparently, has some idea he's about to be raked over the coals for it. Mary discovered this at some point, and stayed because she overheard him and Jane cooking some plan to frame Liz for it."

"What the actual fuck?" Richard ran his hand over his mouth. "And now Liz knows."

"Yes, and she's insisting I stay away until everything's fixed. She doesn't want me getting dragged through the mud with her if the worst happens."

Richard began to pace as he usually did when thinking. "What happens to Novel Books and the bakery if that occurs?"

"I've offered to purchase them with my private funds while signing a contract that ensures she remains in control. She'd also be able to purchase the businesses back from me when she's in a position to do so."

One side of my cousins' mouth quirked up. "So, she's the one, huh?"

I nodded. "Yes, she is. But I need us to brainstorm this. I know she and her attorney have spoken to the FBI. She's handed over everything financial on her end as well as her signature."

"They would've had to forge it to implicate her." He wagged a finger. "But what doesn't make sense to me is why steal a bunch of money just to screw over his daughter?"

I sat on the sofa and rested my forearms on my knees. "Perhaps he's hiding a certain amount in an offshore account while he manipulates his books. He might be showing payouts to Liz somehow to make it appear as though she was involved."

"I know someone who might be able to help," said Richard. "He was in the FBI for a while before he branched out doing security and investigation for big companies and celebrities. His staff are former military and law enforcement. He may be able to figure out what we're missing."

"Call him." I ensured there was no hesitation in my voice. If it was up to me, Liz would lose nothing to this. "I'm going to call my personal attorneys. I want them to reach out to Liz's and offer their services."

Richard held his phone out ready to dial. "I doubt she'll take it."

"Then no one will tell her."

He laughed. "Good luck getting that one past her attorney."

"I can try."

Richard sighed. "Yeah, you can. But it doesn't mean it'll work. Especially if she's bound and determined to keep you out of it."

"As I said before, I can try."

# Chapter 26

The days leading up to Christmas were interminable. I spent my days, from early in the morning until late at night, in the bakery. Our business this year was booming, so I stayed busy even though Char busted my ass about not taking my breaks. Mary, who'd offered to help, joined Char's chorus of entreaties to pause and catch my breath, but I hugged them for their efforts and kept going. I needed to keep busy. I needed to not think about the case, which I'd heard precious little about since Mr. Goulding left three days ago. Today was Christmas Eve. Nothing would happen now.

I also needed to not think about Will. God, I missed him! When I left work, I trudged through the back of the shops to go upstairs, then up to my bathroom where I leaned against the shower wall and let the hot water wash away the day. Most nights, I was so exhausted, I was asleep before my head hit the pillow.

That didn't stop Will, though. Every morning when I woke, I had a new voicemail on my phone. As I dragged myself up to sit on the edge of the bed, I grabbed my phone off the mattress.

As there had been each morning, a notification let me know I had a voicemail. I pressed the play symbol and put it on speakerphone.

*"Good morning, beautiful. I just finished a long day at work and wanted to hear your voice. Yes, I know you aren't going to answer. You're probably asleep after a long day in the bakery, but even the short message on here helps calm my soul. If this is the only way I can hear your voice and speak to you, then this is what I have to do. I can't wait for this to be over. I want to see you, I want to hold you in my arms, and I want to press my lips to yours. Hopefully, you'll be returned to me soon. I love you."*

"You should call him."

I shifted on the bed to face Mary in the doorway. "I can't let him be dragged into what's going on."

She shrugged. "Maybe you should let him decide for himself. He's a big boy, you know.

"I was going to head down. I think I can manage the blueberry muffins on my own this morning." She turned but must've thought better of it since she turned back around. "Thanks for letting me have the job. If I'm not helping, you can always fire me. I won't hold it against you."

Poor Mary. She'd been treated like a pain in the ass for so long, she truly thought of herself in those terms. "You've been doing a fantastic job. I can't wait to taste the muffins. I'm sure they'll be amazing."

She beamed as she disappeared down the hallway. I'd had Zio, and I'd honor him by being exactly what Mary so desperately required, for as long as she needed me.

As I had every day before, I operated on autopilot once I rose from the bed. Get dressed, brush my teeth, pull up my hair, and go to work: new day, same old routine.

By the time I entered the kitchen, Mary was mixing the muffins while Char was pulling out a brioche dough she'd made yesterday before leaving. Her entire morning would be spent making her star-shaped cinnamon pastry. We'd advertised the sinful family-sized sweet roll and had a multitude of orders. We'd also accounted for how many people would want to pick up one at the last minute. She'd made some yesterday and had wrapped them well, not to mention the huge bowls of dough she'd prepped for today. They'd been popular last year. We'd planned ahead for them being just as sought after this year.

With the blueberry muffins in hand, I started on the other varieties, including a white chocolate cranberry I'd been alternating into the rotation this past week. They were so good!

The day dragged on and on while I finished the muffins and moved on to cakes and cupcakes. I'd zoned out while decorating my last chocolate Yule Log when the door to the kitchens slammed open.

"Lizzy! You've got to see this!" Char charged in, grabbed the remote off the shelf, and turned on a television we kept in the corner. We didn't use it often, except when something big was happening, like a disaster or an election, and we wanted to keep tabs on it.

When the screen came to life, Char changed the channel. "Annie called me and told me what's going on. You're not going to believe it."

My jaw dropped at the video of my father, my mother, and Jane being led up the stairs of a big building in handcuffs. They all had their heads down while trying to avoid the constant flashes of the photographers.

"...Henry Bennet is accused of embezzling four point five million dollars, some of which he deposited into a bank account in the Cayman Islands. With the other portion, he wrote out *checks that his family cashed at various businesses around New York while posing as his estranged daughter Elizabeth Bennet, owner of Manhattan bookstore, Novel Books, and The Buttercream Beanery in the Upper West Side. An undisclosed source on the case claimed he did this in an attempt to make the authorities believe his daughter was the person who actually perpetrated the crime. . ."*

As I watched, I set the piping bag on the work surface and stood, then stepped around the corner and drew closer to the TV. No freaking way!

"Lizzy?"

"Am I dreaming?" I pointed to the person on the portico of the courthouse. He stood with Mr. Goulding and several other suit-clad men and women, his expensive suit fitting him like a glove.

Char gasped. "That's William? I wonder what he's doing there."

I gave her a side-eye. "You don't know? You swear?"

She crossed her chest with her finger. "Yes, I promise I don't know what's going on. But doesn't this mean it's over?"

"I don't know. I need to call Mr. Goulding."

"Well? What are you waiting for? I'll finish that, and you go make that phone call."

My best friend shoved me toward my office before she headed to the sink to wash her hands. When I stepped into the small space I used for nothing more than making schedules and submitting payroll to the accountant, I closed the door and hit send on Mr. Goulding's number.

"Miss Bennet! You must've seen the news!"

"I have so many questions." Like what in the name of all that was holy was Will doing there?

"I'm sure you have a litany of questions, but I can't answer them right this moment. We're finishing up everything. Your family will be held until they can be arraigned. It's over. As it turns out, they'd been channeling the funds into an account in your name and writing checks made out to you that were being cashed all over town. They'd gotten their hand on fake IDs with your name. All our people had to do was pull the security footage from the bank as well as the different check cashing locations to find out who was truly claiming the money. You're cleared."

My eyes stung. "Mr. Goulding, what was William Darcy doing there—at the courthouse?"

My attorney went quiet for a moment and some of the background noise faded. "Well, when he called and offered the help of his own attorneys as well as the investigation service he'd hired, I wasn't about to turn him down. It was his investigators that tracked down the offshore account where your father's hidden almost three and a half million. They also followed your parents and Jane. They have evidence galore implicating each and every one of them."

I rested my head in my hand. "Good Lord." I'd have to repay him—every cent.

"Tell me about it! Like I said, we'll meet up after Christmas and I'll give you a summary of the last few days. It's been a whirlwind! Oh! And while I'm thinking about it. Mr. Darcy seemed pretty adamant you not know he had any part in clearing you. Of course, it's his own fault he got caught on the news. My wife will never forgive me but I'm going straight to bed when I get home and not getting up for a week! Happy Holidays, Miss Bennet!"

"Happy Holidays."

The line clicked, and I sat staring at the bulletin board in front of me for God only knew how long before I stood, slipped my phone into my pocket, and walked like a zombie into the kitchens.

"What happened?" asked Mary.

"It's over. My name is cleared. It's all good." I could hardly believe it.

Several of my employees hugged me. Char hugged me. When Mary wrapped her arms around me, I heaved in a shuddering breath. "Mary—"

"You need to go to him, don't you?"

"I do."

"Then don't let us stop you," she said as she stepped back.

I grabbed my bag and made for the door.

"Lizzy," said Mary, making me turn back.

"Yes?"

"I won't expect you home tonight."

Char guffawed while my cheeks burned. My little and typically quiet sister had a sense of humor!

"I can't believe you just said that."

"I definitely like you, Mary Bennet," said Char.

I didn't stick around to listen to their ensuing conversation. I had a man to meet about. . .well, about the fact that I loved him and he loved me. We needed to have a conversation about where we were going from here and it couldn't wait. At least I hoped we were going somewhere. I didn't see much point in staying in the same place, figuratively that is.

The third taxi I hailed stopped, and I hopped into the backseat. As soon as I gave him the address, he merged back into traffic in the direction of Midtown. I turned my phone over in my hand and opened the screen.

When I opened the messaging app and tapped on Will's name, a page of little messages he'd sent me over the past few days popped up.

*"I need to talk to you. I'm on my way to your penthouse."*

Three dots flashed below my message indicating he was responding.

*"I need to finish up something here, but I'll be there as soon as I can."*

It wasn't "hurry" or "I've missed you desperately," but given the circumstances, I guess it's what he could manage. He'd not held back over the last couple of days, so I could get over that my announcement didn't garner a gushy response, especially since he was probably at work.

Security for his building called up, and I was admitted easily. Mrs. Reynolds was waiting for me when I reached the door.

"William texted that you'd be on your way. Come on in." As she led me through the house, she peered over her shoulder. "Would you like some water or tea? I can make coffee."

I shook my head. "No, thank you." I glanced at what I was wearing. "I apologize. I'm a mess. I came straight from work."

"No worries. I'm sure William won't notice a thing."

I stared after her when she smiled and excused herself. We'd never spent the night in his place. How did she know?

The view from the window interested me for a bit, then I wandered the room. He had several pieces of art that were intriguing but didn't hold my attention for long. I peeked through an open door. "This must be his office." I spoke softly as I looked over my shoulder and slipped inside.

The room boasted of tall glass windows like the rest of the apartment but with a bit more than the minimalistic design the rest of the house had. He had shelves of books lining the walls with a sleek desk. A table stood in one corner of the room and was covered in what appeared to be papers. When I approached the window, a picture on the top caught my eye. It was my mother at a counter while a cashier counted out bills.

I turned it over.

The next was of Charlie Bingley entering Longbourn. I shook my head. It just went to prove that Jane was a siren. Her beauty called to men, but whether they'd survive her song was another matter.

"It was Jane's idea to put your name on the local bank account, but Charlie came on board with cashing checks so they could access some of the money as well as ideas to ensure you were the only one implicated."

I startled and backed from the table. "I'm sorry. I shouldn't have been snooping." Here I was in William Darcy's pristine study with my Buttercream Beanery polo on, baggy and ripped jeans, and low-quarter Dr. Martens, all covered in flour.

He stepped further into the room. "Gigi called me and told me I'd made the news. You already knew I helped out with the investigation, didn't you?"

After I nodded, I set my bag on the chair. "Char turned on the news in the kitchen, and I saw you. Mr. Goulding told me about your attorneys and the investigators. You couldn't leave well enough alone, could you?" I let a hint of a smile peek through.

"Of course not. I love you. Besides, you wouldn't last a day in prison."

I barked out a laugh. "I bet you're wrong."

He wrapped an arm around me and tugged me to him. "We won't have a chance to test that out. Thank heavens!"

"You're going to be covered in flour."

He laughed. "The only thing better would be to cover myself in you."

I buried my face into his neck and inhaled deeply. When I looked up and our gazes caught, I smoothed some of the hair back from his face. That was when he claimed my lips and kissed me as though his life depended upon it. When he finally drew back, I bit my lip.

"Your attorney tried to help frame me." I still needed to wrap my head around that part.

Will nodded. "He thought I'd be thrilled. You'd go to jail, and the court would seize everything. I could buy Novel Books and the café if I wanted it. He was stunned when I fired him. He'll be tried as an accomplice. He'll never work in corporate law again, although I should never say never." He kissed my forehead. "I don't want to talk about them anymore. Please tell me we don't have to spend another night apart."

I grinned. "But Will, we hardly know each other." I totally faked my shocked voice.

His fingers tickled my sides while he growled in my ear. "I don't care how long we've been seeing each other. I'm in love with you, and I don't want to be separated from you again. If that means I have to move in with you because of Atticus and your sister, I can live with that."

"What about this place?" One thing was certain: I couldn't live here. It was beautiful, but it didn't feed my soul.

"I initially bought it as an investment. When my parents died, I needed to get out of their home. I loved it, but their ghosts lurked around every corner. Now, I just want to be with you whether it's at your home or whether you want to move into my parents' home one day."

As much as giving over so much to him should terrify me, I had no trembling and no uncomfortable quivering in my belly—other than the usual butterflies Will caused.

I donned what I hoped was a thoughtful expression. "Before you start packing, I require a bit more persuading."

"Persuading?"

"Yes, Will." I shoved his coat off his shoulders. "You'll need to plead your case."

I backed away and pulled my shirt over my head.

He grinned. "I think I can manage that."

# Chapter 27

I stretched my toes toward the foot of the bed while I pulled Liz's very naked and very lush body closer to my side. Even though I didn't open my eyes, I could just imagine how her breasts looked pressed flush to my ribs while her head rested on my chest. She was a goddess—my goddess—and I was in no hurry to get up and disentangle myself from those enticing curves I'd explored until early in the morning.

"Mmm," she moaned. "Go back to sleep."

A chuckle rumbled low in my chest. "It's nine in the morning. We're going to have to get up at some point."

"How do you know what time it is?"

I opened my eyes and grinned as I pulled her on top of me. "I may have glanced at the clock about four minutes ago." My palms reached down and caressed her ass. Gigi would kill me, but the last thing I wanted to do this morning, Christmas morning, was get out of bed and go downstairs to open presents with my little sister. No, I wanted to stay right here in our warm cocoon and ravish Liz until she begged for mercy.

"I don't want to get up," she said.

"I know. I don't either, but I can't leave Gigi alone on Christmas, and you can't leave Mary." The dirty lecher down below wanted to keep Liz here all day long, but I did possess some rational brain cells above my waist that knew it wasn't possible today of all days.

Liz's soft lips began kissing my chest. "That isn't fair." Rational Will was making one last-ditch effort to do the right thing.

She pulled her hair back from her face and flashed a wicked grin. "Whoever said life was fair?" Her words were spoken in low, seductive tones that sent a jolt straight to my morning erection. Maybe we could get away with one more time before we went downstairs.

I lifted up and caught her lips in a kiss that threatened to devour, but she didn't hold back. While I sat on the bed, Liz was straddling me and ground down, making me hiss. I could never get enough of her—enough of this. Sex had always seemed so superficial until now. I'd never realized someone could give over their entire body, mind, and soul in the process.

My lips began to trail down Liz's neck when something clicked. "Oh, my God!"

When Liz squeaked and dove under the comforter, a sharp pain jolted through my dick and balls, and a familiar nausea made me fall sideways onto the bed. I didn't need someone to tell me what happened. Gigi had opened my bedroom door. My little sister had then seen me and Liz in a compromising position, and when Liz scrambled off my lap, she had kicked the hell out of me.

"You're old enough to know how to knock!" I was going to die a slow and exceedingly painful death.

"I've never needed to! When I passed fifteen minutes ago, you were snoring!"

"I don't snore!" Why did she always claim I did?

"Yes, you do," said Liz from the foot of the bed. Her response was followed by peals of laughter. "We'll be down in a bit, Gigi. We need to figure out how to handle today. Mrs. Hill is making a big afternoon dinner for me, Mary, Annie, and Char."

I looked to the door that was now mostly closed, but Gigi's back was to the crack and an arm was up by her head. Was she covering her eyes too?

"Gi, go downstairs. Once I can stand, I'll get dressed, and we'll talk out our plans."

The door clicked, and I dropped my head onto the bed with a groan. This was the worst pain in the world!

It became cold when the comforter was pulled away and Liz emerged from underneath. She frowned when she saw me in a protective fetal position, my hands over my groin. "What happened?"

"You kicked me when you dove under the covers."

She snorted, the little devil!

"How is this amusing?"

Her lips pressed tightly together until her features evened out. "You're right. It isn't at all." She snorted again.

"Fine! Have your laugh. I gingerly rose. "I'm going to get in the shower. Maybe a cold shower will prevent any swelling."

That one infuriating yet sexy eyebrow rose. "You act like swelling is a bad thing."

I paused long enough to glare, but she wasn't intimidated in the slightest. Her teeth scraping across her bottom lip while she attempted to stifle a grin made *that* abundantly obvious.

A few minutes after I had the hot water running, Liz slipped into the shower. "I'm sorry. I shouldn't laugh. The entire situation was just so embarrassing. How am I going to look Gigi in the eye ever again?"

"She's twenty. She knows how to knock. Usually, she does."

Liz smoothed my forehead. "You're so cute when you're grumpy."

"I'm not grumpy."

"Should I call you Scrooge McDarcy or Grinch?" She was enjoying this far too much!

"How about you call me Will?"

Her head shook while she soaped her hands and began washing my chest. "I don't think so; not today anyway." With her bathing me, I wasn't going to argue. Maybe later when she wasn't making me forget how much pain I'd endured less than ten minutes ago.

We didn't linger in the shower, and once I dressed, I begged Gigi for some clean clothes for Liz to borrow. When she joined us downstairs, I handed her a latte Mrs. Reynolds had made for her.

"Will Mrs. Hill have enough food for us to join you and for Richard to join us later if he wants?"

Liz gave a bark. "Are you kidding? She makes enough for twenty people since a few stragglers always stop by. Mia didn't make it home for today. It's a long drive to spend one day, so she spends a few hours with friends and comes over for a while in the evening." I shook myself. "What I'm saying is, yes, you and Gi are more than welcome to come over. We'll be happy to have you."

"Maybe we should open gifts here first," said Gigi.

"Let me see how long it'll take to have a car here." My driver was off today of course. We'd be using a car service that was always open on holidays. The wait was thirty minutes, so I went ahead and submitted the request. We then gathered around the tree.

Gi gave me a couple of books, some nice bars of shave soap I loved, and a couple of ties and socks. As far as I was concerned, her gifts were perfect. I was well aware that I was difficult to buy presents for, and since I detested shopping, Gi was doing me a favor.

Since I'd bought Gi her piano for her birthday a couple of months ago, I had nothing major for her. Some new sheet music, a gift card to her favorite bath products store, and a necklace that made her gasp when she opened it.

"This was mom's."

I nodded. "Opals were her favorite. Dad bought it for her not long after you were born."

"It's beautiful," said Liz.

Gi threw her arms around my neck. "Thank you!" When she pulled back, she turned and lifted her hair. "Help me put it on."

As soon as I had it clasped, I pointed to Gi's gifts. "Why don't you take those up to your room?"

My sister glanced between us, and with a grin, did as I asked. Thank heavens she didn't decide to argue. It wasn't exactly in her nature, but she was learning from Liz all the time. A year ago, she was incredibly shy. Now she had friends and was more willing to tell people what was on her mind.

Liz was side-eyeing me. "She had to put her things away right now? What are you up to?"

I scooted closer to her on the floor and held out a jewelry box in my hand. "This."

She shook her head. "Will—"

"No, hear me out." I opened the box and revealed the ring I'd been debating over. Yes, it was soon, but I wanted to put that ring on her finger more than anything. We didn't have to marry tomorrow. The caveman in me just needed to know it would happen—one day.

I took in a deep breath. "I know it's quick. I do. But being with you is different. There are a bunch of crazy theories out there, like past lives and soulmates and such, but I've been comfortable with you since we met. I admit it weirded me out some at first, but it's true. Deep in my heart, I know you're who I was meant to be with for a lifetime—or maybe more if those theories are right. We don't have to get married tomorrow or even next month, but I want you to be mine in more than just words. I want you to wear my mother's ring. So, Elizabeth Bennet, will you marry me?"

## LIZ

I couldn't stop gaping at Will while he spoke. We'd only known each other for three months! Was this normal? Was I insane for even considering it?

The thing was. . .no hint of fear surged through me at the idea of it: no trembling, no uncomfortable pang coursing through my gut, no tightening either. The only protest seemed to be my brain questioning whether we'd known or liked each other long enough. Did that honestly matter? There were couples who married after twenty-four hours or two weeks, or even two years, but the time they spent getting to know each other didn't necessarily contribute to their happiness, or their longevity as a couple.

"You're too quiet," said Will. He must've run his fingers through his hair while I'd stared at the ring. A few of his curls were sticking out. His hair was never completely tidy. Longish hair with curls rarely was.

"It's not freaking me out, but we hardly know each other." Way to state the obvious!

He scooted closer. "I know you're funny and I love talking to you. You're also business savvy and I find that as well as your body being an enormous turn-on, there's no one I'd rather lick buttercream off of."

I covered my face with my hands but didn't keep them there. "That's incredibly simplistic."

"Do you want children?"

"Well, yes."

He threw his hands up. "Hey, so do I! How many?"

I shrugged one shoulder. "Two maybe three?"

He nodded. "I can live with that."

Oh, my God. "Wait. How many do you want?"

He grinned. "With the way I can't keep my hands off of you, I thought we'd end up with six—at least."

My eyes bulged and had to be huge by the way my vision became a bit distorted. "Six! When you have to carry them and give birth, then we'll talk. In the meantime, I'd rather keep to a smaller number—do our part for overpopulation and climate change."

He chuckled. "And I have no problem with that whatsoever, as long as we can practice as much as we want."

My cheeks burst into flames—as did other parts of me. "Where is this Will coming from? I don't know that I've seen him until recently."

"That's because you make me like this. I'm happy when I'm with you."

I rose to my knees and cradled his cheeks in my palms. "Then, yes, you mad, crazy man. I'll marry you."

He wrapped his arms around me and pulled me into his lap at about the same time a squeal made us both jump.

"I'm so happy! I can't believe this!" Gigi came running through the door and took us both in a big hug. "I want to be a bridesmaid!"

I smiled when I caught Will's gaze. "I suppose we don't need to ask for Gi's approval."

He pressed his lips to mine. "Now, let's get this on your finger."

"Um, Will? That ring is bigger than anything I wear. How many carats is it?" The white gold band had a large white diamond in the middle with two smaller ones flanking it.

"Only three."

"All the stones are three carats?"

"No, just the middle; the other two are one point five."

Only three? Will's perception might be somewhat skewed. "Most people don't have six carats on one finger, Will."

"I know you probably won't wear it to work. I can imagine it'll get in the way. But I wanted you to have it."

Gi finally released us. "She could get one of those silicone rings people wear. They're very trendy. They can also be washed easily." I didn't know if silicone rings were trendy, but I wasn't going to burst Gi's bubble.

"Get what you need," said Will to his sister. "The car should be here soon."

As soon as Gigi was out of the door, Will took the ring out of the worn jewelry box and slipped it onto my finger.

"It fits." I sounded surprised, but I was. What were the odds another woman's ring would fit my finger?

"I believe that's further proof you're meant to be with me."

I kissed him on the lips. I loved his lips. They were soft and when they touched or caressed me in the right places, they were my favorite things on the planet. "You would say that."

He laughed and lifted a shoulder. "I can't help it if it's true." He brushed some of my hair behind my ear. "You should know that I don't care where we live or how many kids we have or whatever little things that most people quibble over. The only thing that's non-negotiable in my life is you."

When he said such sweet things, all I could do was turn in his arms and devour his lips like they were my last meal.

"Eww! What is wrong with the two of you?"

# Epilogue

**WILL**

*Christmas: Three years later*

As it turns out, "best laid plans" and all that was truer than any other statement ever made. We schedule and outline and like to think we're in full control, then life. . .or God. . .or whatever higher power you believe in, laughs at us.

I'd proposed to Liz on Christmas. Yes, I'd hoped to marry her before summer; no, I never thought she'd make me wait for three years; and no, I never thought we'd have our first child before we were married. But *"the best laid plans of mice and men often go awry"*—paraphrased, of course, from Robert Burns—has become a motto of sorts for me these past three years.

Now, here I was in the bedroom—our bedroom of our home—which was once her uncle's home, buttoning my tuxedo and straightening my cufflinks.

"Cold feet?" Richard was grinning like a madman over my shoulder. Why was this so funny to him?

"Of course not. We've been all but married for three years. We have a son together. Why would this make me nervous?"

Almost two years ago with the birth of our son, Liz had almost died from pre-eclampsia. If anything, that had solidified my resolve to put that second ring on her finger—the one that had us officially spending our lives together. "Just because you're commitment-phobic doesn't mean we all are."

He scowled. "Hey, I've been seeing Mia for a year."

"And you've made a point of saying it's 'easy, breezy, and casual' for just as long. After a while, she's going to get tired of that bullshit and expect you to put a ring on it." I also had it on good authority that the café's newest manager wasn't too far off from that option.

My cousin narrowed his eyes. "What do you know?"

"Nothing I can tell you." I gave one last tug to my coat. "How much longer?"

"Five minutes. We should be heading down. Gi said Lizzy wouldn't leave the room until she had confirmation you were in the courtyard."

Yes, it was December in New York City, but Liz got the harebrained scheme to have the wedding in the courtyard of the café of the original bakery. A special-made tent had been rigged up, and heaters would keep the inside from becoming chilled. In the meantime, the large space had a running fountain in the middle and trees strung in fairy lights surrounding the perimeter. It was Liz and Mary's project to make it a winter wonderland. I still hadn't seen it.

"Then let's go." I didn't need to be dragged. This wasn't my demise, but what I wanted more than anything in this world—or the next.

When I reached the foyer, Mrs. Reynolds wore a wide grin while she held my son Luca, who was almost two. We'd found out the Easter after we were engaged that Liz was pregnant. She'd never missed a pill, but a course of antibiotics she'd taken during a particularly bad bout of walking pneumonia had been responsible for our little surprise. Neither of us was upset; we'd just decided to roll with the punches—until Liz's blood pressure began to creep upwards.

The day she'd had a seizure and was rushed to the hospital was the most terrifying of my life. While I joked that I wanted six kids that day as I hopefully held her engagement ring in my hand, I was just fine with one. As long as I had Liz, I could breathe. The entire time I didn't know what was happening to her or our baby was suffocating. I couldn't go through that again.

Luca held out his chubby little arms. "Daddy!" He was adorable in his tiny suit. Liz had found the blue velvet jacket and insisted upon it, even though my tux as well as Richard's were of the garden variety. Neither of us would be caught dead in a blue velvet suitcoat, but it worked for Luca, whose hair was dark and curly—a natural by-product of my and Liz's hair.

"Are you ready to go see Mommy?"

He nodded with a smile. Like me, he wasn't overly talkative, but he was happy, which was all I needed.

When we entered the elevator, Luca leaned forward. "Button!" I stepped up and pointed where he needed to press then backed against the wall.

"Actually," said Richard, breaking the silence, "I've thought that what you have isn't so bad. It may be worth giving it a try."

My gaze shot to him. "Who are you and what've you done with my cousin?"

Richard rolled his eyes. "I'm thirty-nine, Darce. I don't want to spend my entire life alone. It sounded great in theory when I was twenty-two and enjoyed hooking up. Now. . ." He sighed. "It's lost a lot of its appeal."

I managed not to laugh. He wouldn't appreciate "I told you so."

"Oh, don't look so smug. Yes, you told me. If you're going to gloat, go ahead and do it so I don't have to hear it later."

I turned back to my son and straightened his little tie. "I wasn't going to say a word."

As soon as we were off the elevator, Luca began to squirm to get down. He knew the way as well as I did, so I had no worries about allowing him to run ahead.

His tiny legs carried him through the stockrooms and storage until we reached the doors that led to the café. When I opened the door, he rushed through.

"Gi!"

My sister knelt and scooped him up, giving him an exaggerated kiss on the cheek. "You look so handsome. Are you excited about today?"

Luca nodded, even though at his age, it was unlikely he understood how today was different than any other.

"You should go take your places," said Gi. "I'll text Liz and tell her you're ready."

After kissing my son's soft curls, I exited through to the courtyard and gawked. "Wow." The tables were covered with silvery-white tablecloths, and the center of each had a wine bottle filled with fairy lights surrounded by what appeared to be a Christmas wreath. A silvery-blue ribbon wrapped around the bottom of the bottles.

The trees around the perimeter were bedecked in white lights that twinkled in the low light of the covered courtyard. When I rounded the corner, rows of chairs had been set up on one side of the fountain, facing a small dais flanked by two Christmas trees laden with twinkling lights and silver and blue ornaments. A string quartet was set up in the corner, composed of Gigi's friends and fellow students from Julliard. Lights trimmed the ceiling of the tent, and smaller, matching Christmas trees and silver and blue accents filled the space. Heaters were scattered around so as not to be intrusive. We hadn't wanted a huge wedding, but I hadn't been sure about the courtyard. In the end, I'd bowed to Liz's wishes, however, and the result was amazing.

I followed the aisle down the center and around the fountain. The guests who were seated watched while Richard followed me to the altar where an officiant stood, a welcoming smile upon her face.

When we took our places, both of us pivoted so we faced the back of the aisle. The music the string quartet was playing came to an end and another piece began. It wasn't a traditional wedding march, but the melody was familiar.

Wait!

"Is that the music from *The Princess Bride?*" asked Richard.

I grinned. "That's exactly what it is." As much as it now killed me to admit it, Liz had been right. That movie had become a favorite.

After no more than a moment, Liz made her way down the other side of the courtyard to the beginning of the aisle. Gigi released Luca at the end of the aisle, and in a fit of giggles, he ran down the center where I lifted him up and settled him on my hip. My sister followed at a more sedate pace.

Mary came out next. All the bridesmaids were wearing a matching blue, and although their dresses were designed and made by Mary, she'd varied each so they flattered the figures of the woman wearing them. Char was the last, and she hugged me when she got to the altar.

"I'm so happy for you two," she whispered in my ear.

I stared at the fountain just as Liz rounded it and stood at the end where I could finally get a good look at her in her gown. She was the most stunning thing I'd ever seen. The dress was white and off the shoulder and wrapped around her with what appeared to be buttons down the side. A bow on that side also highlighted a split in the satin of the skirt where organza trailed down to the floor. Mary had outdone herself on the design!

Meanwhile, Liz's hair was pulled up, but tendrils escaped and curled around her face and on her neck, her veil sitting to the back and hanging to the floor as well.

I had no doubt I was grinning like a fool, but I didn't care. We'd been waiting for this day for too long, and whatever anyone thought wasn't important to me. Only that woman now walking down the aisle mattered.

When she reached me, I handed Luca to Richard and took my bride's hands in mine. "You are. . .I have no words."

She grinned. "I do." She leaned forward and pressed her cheek to mine. "I'm pregnant."

Was it bad form for the groom to faint on his wedding day?

**Eight Months later**

Liz winced as the doctors worked. She'd had a c-section for the first pregnancy, and her doctor wasn't willing to chance a traditional delivery, so here we were with Liz draped up and waiting to meet our second child.

"You're going to feel pressure, Lizzy," said the doctor.

"No shit," my wife said under her breath. "Why did I think this would be a good idea?" She flinched.

"Because when they put Luca in your arms, you forgot all about this part." I hoped that was why anyway.

"You're right." She breathed deeply in and out. "Will?"

"Yeah."

"I'm never doing this again."

I nodded. "That's your call. I've told you that from the beginning." We'd have two healthy children—or so I hoped! Instead of Liz's blood pressure being sky-high, this time it'd been mine. I'd been terrified I'd lose her from the moment she'd told me at the altar. I couldn't wait for the baby to be here so I'd know, once and for all, that Liz was safe!

A squalling filled the operating room, and when I looked, the doctor was pulling the baby free from Liz's body. "Congratulations! It's a girl!"

Liz's lower lip shook. "We have a Betta."

Elizabeth Anne Darcy, to honor her mother and grandmother, would also honor Liz's Zio. She'd honored him with Luca's name too—not that I'd argue. He'd been her rock until I could fill those shoes.

Betta was evaluated, swaddled, and handed to me. I immediately held her so Liz could wrap an arm around her. "She's beautiful, just like you."

"You're blind."

I shook my head. "Even now, you're the only woman I'll ever want. Whether you're heavily pregnant or whether you're saggy with a postpartum belly, I don't care. You'll still rock my world."

A sniff came from one of the nurses. "That has to be the sweetest thing any husband has ever said. If you don't kiss him, Mrs. Darcy, I might." The entire operating room burst into laughter.

"No, you don't get to kiss him," said Liz, her eyes now twinkling. "Only I'm allowed to do that."

When she pulled me down to press her lips to mine, it may as well have been the first time we kissed. My heart pounded under my ribs and my skin goosebumped. This woman was it—my everything—and now with our children, we were a family. That holiday season I'd met Liz had been something out of a novel. I suppose you could say it was a novel holiday. After all, it's not every day you fall in love with your competitor. I couldn't say it was a mistake. On the contrary, it was the best thing that ever happened to me.

# The End

# Acknowledgements

This has been a crazy year, and it's sometimes been a struggle to keep my head above water. I think it's fitting that I end the year with something that I had some fun writing. I do enjoy it, but I hadn't had this much fun going through Pinterest for inspiration and such in a while. I hope you enjoyed Liz and Will.

That said, I have a wonderful support system in my husband and family. My husband has taken over more of the housework so I can keep up with coaching while having time to write. My little Evie does her part by insisting on a place in my lap while I work on the laptop and stalking the pointer while I'm designing my covers. And my children who each have their own role in keeping me in line.

I also have Carol, my editor and great friend, who helps make my scribblings better, and Marie, who catches the editing mistakes Carol and I miss. I couldn't do this without their help! Over the years, I've made a lot of friends in this genre, and I'm always bolstered by their support.

To my readers, thank you for reading and reviewing. Reviews are important and I can't thank you enough for the time you spend writing them!

# About the Author

L.L. Diamond is more commonly known as Leslie to her friends, Mom to her three kids, and servant to her three cats. A native of Louisiana, she has been a wanderer for the past 20 years, living in Mississippi, California, Texas, New Mexico, Nebraska, England, and Missouri before settling in Maryland.

One day, Leslie may decide what she wants to do when she grows up, but for now, she enjoys writing the stories that live in her head and coaching age group swimming. She has degrees in biology and studio art, certifications to coach swimming in the United States and Britain, and numerous fitness certifications. Leslie is also a member of the Jane Austen Society of North America. Her accomplishments include drawing, watercolor, and playing flute and piano, but much like *Pride and Prejudice's* Elizabeth Bennet, she is always in need of practice!

If you enjoyed this story, get my latest news and a free short story by joining my mailing list! Just click this paragraph for the link.

# Author's works:

## *Regency Works:*
Rain and Retribution
An Unwavering Trust
The Earl's Conquest
Particular Intentions
Particular Attachments
Undoing
Agony and Hope
His Perfect Gift

### *The Montford Cousins:*
*Book 1*: An Endeavour to be Worthy
*Book 2*: A Gentleman of Worth
*Book 3*: A Worthy Woman
*Book 4*: *Worthy of her Love*
*Book 5*: *Worthy in Every Way*

## *Contemporary Romance*
A Matter of Chance
Unwrapping Mr. Darcy
Confined with Mr. Darcy
That Perfect Someone
Catching Lizzy
A Novel Holiday

### *The Wedding Planners Series:*
Book 1: It's Always Been You
Book 2: It's Always Been Us
Book 3: It's Always Been You and Me
Book 4: He's Always Been the One

### Science Fiction/Fantasy Romance
The Peculiarity of Mr. Darcy's Mirror

www.ingramcontent.com/pod-product-compliance
Lightning Source LLC
Chambersburg PA
CBHW070854180626
46817CB00003B/772